Chickpea Lover

Chickpea Lover

(Not a Cookbook)

D-L Nelson

Five Star • Waterville, Maine

Set in 11 pt. Plantin by Myrna S. Raven.

Printed in the United States on permanent paper.

Library of Congress Cataloging-in-Publication Data

Nelson, D-L, 1942–
    Chickpea lover (not a cookbook) / D-L Nelson.
      p. cm.—(Five Star expressions series)
    ISBN 0-7862-4706-1 (hc : alk. paper)
    ISBN 1-4104-0178-2 (sc : alk. paper)
    1. College teachers—Fiction.   2. Sexual harassment in universities and colleges—Fiction.   3. False testimony—Fiction.   4. Separated people—Fiction.   5. Pregnant women—Fiction.   6. Women teachers—Fiction.   7. Boston (Mass.)—Fiction.   8. Extortion—Fiction.   I. Title. II. Series.
    PS3614.E4455 V44 2003
    813'.6—dc21   2002033886

To my best friend, daughter and mom,
Susan Jordan, Llara Nelson and Norma Boudreau,
for their unconditional love

CHAPTER ONE

I'm in love with a chickpea named Peter. He's not always a chickpea. Sometimes he's an eggplant and less often he's a carrot. Peter owns a Mideastern food stand on Boston's Fenway near the hospitals and colleges. He says dressing as a vegetable is good for business because people like being served by someone in costume.

As I walk from my office to Peter's stand, my mind jumps back and forth between subjects I don't want to think about. They sneak into my mind no matter how I try to avoid them.

The first is the most pressing. Mother. I haven't the foggiest idea how I'll tell her that I want to marry a human vegetable. She won't understand. Lawyers, doctors, teachers have respectability. Even restaurant owners do, because a restaurant is concrete, but a food stand to her would be flimsy, insubstantial.

She still wants to make decisions for me. When I visit her on our family farm in Concord, she tells me to bring a sweater even it's hot. If I protest, she says, "New England weather is very changeable, you know." When we disagree, she puts her lips together in a way that says, "Don't argue," louder than if she yelled.

She's right about the weather being changeable. Yesterday it was seventy-six degrees. Today it's thirty-three. Wind blows the last leaves off the trees. They swirl around me, a leaf blizzard, which any minute may give way to snow. The leaves remind me of my childhood. Mother calls this leaf-kicking weather.

7

When I was eight, my sister, brother and I watched Daddy rake the leaves into a huge pile. It was a crisp November Saturday with an unreal blue sky, much like today, except the cold wasn't as biting. When he finished, he let us jump in the pile. It was still legal to burn leaves then. What a wonderful smell they made. Autumn isn't quite the same without that odor.

That same night I was in bed and full from our traditional Saturday-night supper of Boston baked beans, hot dogs and cole slaw. My brother and I had divided our apple pie as always. I ate both crusts. He ate all the fruit.

A draft, as well as an over full tummy, kept me awake. I could do nothing about my tummy, but I could change the cold. I got out of bed to lower the window. The wooden floor felt icy on my bare feet.

As I stretched up to shut the window, I saw Mother and Daddy jumping in the leaves, just as I had done that afternoon. In the moonlight they threw leaves at each other, stopping to hug and kiss. I'd been embarrassed, yet I couldn't stop looking. This was a side of them I'd never seen.

Mother never showed affection. I can't remember her hugging Daddy or other relatives. She rarely touched us. Daddy was different. We climbed all over him. He'd give us a cuddle or throw us in the air, then tickle us, although we begged him to stop. He knew we were really saying, "More."

When did Mother change from a woman who jumped in leaves to the nagger she is today? Maybe it started when Daddy died. Maybe penny-pinching wore her down.

When I think about it, I realize that our house was paid for generations earlier. Our relatives had lived there since before the Revolution, so it never made any sense the times she said, "We can't afford it."

Or maybe it was the arthritis that started in her forties. Now her hands are gnarled. She chews aspirin like some people chew gum. She says it came from all the typing she did. Her job as a secretary at Boston University gave us all a free college education. Guilt—the gift that keeps giving. I feel guilty for resenting her demands and complaints. She's the East Coast distributor of guilt. I dislike myself because I buy all she sells. So who knows what changed her? Who cares? Me.

Thinking about Peter is more pleasant. I shove my hands in my pockets because I forgot my gloves. Maybe I'm rebelling against Mother's constant reminders to take appropriate clothing for the worst weather imaginable. At thirty-nine that's just plain stupid.

A tingle warms me as Peter's stand comes into sight. What would my students at Fenway College think if they knew that Dr. Elizabeth-Anne Adams, former nurse, tenured director of the nursing program, author of two textbooks, was acting like a teenager with a crush on a rock star?

My students love me, which is good because my husband doesn't. That's another thing I don't want to think of. It will be almost as hard to tell him I want a divorce as it will be to tell Mother. Pushing the words out of my mouth isn't difficult. I say them all the time to my reflection in the mirror: "David, I'm leaving." Of course, he is never there to hear them.

We see very little of each other, my husband and I. He's a corporate lawyer, always working or off on a business trip. Even when he's home, he's working. He not only has a mobile phone but a car fax, supplementing the two house faxes and three computers.

9

He cares a lot about appearances and labels. When alligator shirts were in, I cut the logo off one of his old shirts and sewed it on top of another alligator on a second shirt. He didn't notice the copulating reptiles until his opponent pointed it out to him in the middle of a racquetball match. He stomped off the court, his Reeboks squeaking, or so his friend reported. I don't regret doing it at all.

He never said he doesn't love me. How do I know? I just do. If I ask for a divorce, he'll feel as if he were losing some property like the time his Volvo was stolen. He was furious that someone dared touch his car. When they found out who did it, he drove by their house and threw a rock through the window. He hates loss as much as I hate conflict. That's saying a lot.

Right now my husband is in California until late next week. I like it when he's away on business because I can spend more time with Peter—although when David is at home he's so busy that he'd never notice if I slipped out. I still feel funny about doing that. More guilt.

As I approach Peter's stand, he sees me and waves. He's wearing his carrot costume rather than his chickpea outfit. I can see his shock of dark hair under the green leaves. He has wide Slavic cheekbones, not like my chipmunk cheeks. The windows are shut, keeping out the cold. A HOT CHOCOLATE sign replaced yesterday's LEMONADE.

Peter lets me in the back door. There's not much room to move between the grill, fridge and counter. His green leaves graze the ceiling.

A picture of Daddy harvesting carrots flashes into my mind. He took pride in culling vegetables from the rocky soil. He never expected me to cull a relationship with a human vegetable. I wonder what he'd say. He might be supportive as he was every time I suggested something I wanted to do. We'd discuss the whys and the why nots like two adults. Peter is the same.

"I spilled chocolate on my chickpea outfit," Peter says. His arms stretch out the holes, and his dark shirt makes his arms look like roots. His hug brings me back into the present. It's like cuddling a stuffed animal. "We'll leave as soon as Mohammed comes." Mohammed has worked for Peter for a year and is taking the 4:00 p.m. to 6:00 a.m. shift, leaving us the night together.

A customer, probably a doctor judging by the stethoscope around his neck, knocks on the window. Peter slides it open to take his order for hummus and hot cider. I dish it up as Mohammed comes in. Leaves swirl in after him.

"Sorry I'm late." He's the same age as Peter, twenty-nine. Not only do I love a vegetable, I love one ten years younger than I am. Mohammed steps into his celery outfit as Peter cashes out and metamorphoses back into a human.

My lover lives within walking distance of the stand. He refuses to own a car, saying he won't add more pollutants to the air. We walk to his place, taking the shortcut across the Muddy River. A few ducks waddle onto the bank to mug us for the bread that Peter brought them. We hold hands and forget there's a major city nearby.

My chickpea owns a converted carriage house. His key is so huge that it looks like a Western jail key. He has to jiggle and wiggle the doorknob at the same time to make it work. The lock finally gives, and the front door swings open into a huge room.

Books cover the walls. I never trust people who don't read. Many of the couples David and I know use books as decoration.

David at least reads, although it is mostly work stuff.

11

Peter buys me antique books searched out at Ye Antique Booke Shoppe. We both love that store with the smell of aging paper and musty leather. My husband values books as an investment.

Me? I wonder whose eyes wandered over the words before mine. Who did those long-ago readers love? Hate? When I told David this, he just rolled his eyes. When I told Peter, he said he felt the same way.

Boss, Peter's golden retriever, greets us as we enter the carriage house. He says the dog is the only boss he'll accept. She's torn between her desire for affection and the need to go out. Nature wins. Inside Peter opens his half-sized refrigerator, over which is a "Small is better" sign.

Pulling out a bottle of California wine, he searches for his corkscrew. He never can find it, nor his keys, which considering the size of his house key, is amazing. But with all the clutter from books and magazines, they can slip out of sight easily. He calls his decorating style "creative chaos" the way others would say "Early American" or "French Country."

Last month, I bought him a key chain that beeps when you clap, but it also beeps when Boss barks. If I'd found a beeping corkscrew, I'd have bought that too. We locate the opener between *Mother Jones* and *The Nation*.

Peter sees me shiver and rubs my arms. "Would you rather have hot tea?" he asks. I nod. Putting on the water, he reaches for the teapot with his free hand. Although the spout is cracked, he won't throw it out. He says a teapot is like an old friend. His ex-landlady gave it to him to celebrate his buying the carriage house. He still grocery shops for her.

When he finds the tea infuser, he mixes two teas—Earl Grey and gunpowder. "I've a better idea," he says. "How

12

about hot wine with cinnamon?" With David there's never a deviation from a plan. With Peter we might start out for a restaurant in Boston and end up walking a New Hampshire beach.

I'm spending more and more time comparing my husband and my lover. What good does it do me? Make me more dissatisfied with my marriage? And my being dissatisfied would confuse people. From the outside it looks like I have everything a woman could want.

David and I never talk about our differences. I may joke about them, but that's as close as we come to disagreeing. I guess it's the same path I take with Mother—the placating path, the lane of least resistance, the happy highway. Even at work, I shrink from controversy except as a last resort. However, I can handle a bit more professional disagreement for reasons that make no sense to me.

The wine and fire warm us. "We've time to make love before going to Judy and Mark's," Peter says, nodding in the eagerness that I find so cute.

I drop everything and run upstairs. A balcony juts halfway over the living room. Once a tack room, it now holds a sleeping platform. I tear off my clothes and jump between the patchwork quilt and the flannel sheets.

Making love with him is wonderful. We talk and tickle and laugh our way through. The first time we did it, I asked, just as his penis touched my vagina, "Are you sure you want to go through with this?" I was only half kidding. There'd been so much sexual tension between us for so long that any other alternative was unthinkable.

After we'd made love the first time, Peter said, "You know, Liz, you use humor to protect yourself." I'd felt more exposed than I had when I'd stood naked in front of him.

When we've this time, I look down at the face of my

beautiful boy. His eyes are closed. Moonlight from the sky-light shining on his face makes him look even younger. I am shocked by the force of my feelings.

We didn't set out to be lovers. Regularly, I remind myself of how it happened, taking out each detail and looking it over, much like thumbing through a favorite photo album.

We'd met by accident almost a year earlier, when I'd stopped to eat lunch at his stand. Although I'd passed his place for years, I'd never bought anything.

Normally I ate at Puke Hall. The real name was Duke Hall, after a dead college president. I'd been the one to rechristen it. Most of the college had adopted the unofficial name, despite written directives from the current president to show respect for dead ones.

The first day I went to the stand because I was bored and wanted something different. Business was slow. I'd glanced at a book next to the cash register. It was about the Lobi tribe in Ghana. He saw me looking at it. "I worked with the Lobi for my dissertation in anthropology, but I didn't finish."

When I asked why he'd quit, he'd told me, "I was sleeping several nights at the funeral of an old man."

"I don't understand," I'd said.

"That was the custom," he said, "because funerals went on for several days. The longer you're there, the more you show how much you cared. I loved that old man."

I didn't say a word. I was busy praying that a customer wouldn't come and interrupt us.

"Suddenly I was overwhelmed with doubt. Why am I here, I asked myself. I was intruding. So I packed up and went home." There was light in his black eyes.

We talked for so long I had to run for class. I arrived

14

panting just as my students were gathering their books and putting on their coats.

Over time I learned that Peter's home was Seattle. His bank president father had little patience for anthropologists and even less for those who dropped out before finishing their Ph.D.s.

According to Peter, he got tired of being picked at and had come back to Boston where he'd been happy as a student. Odd job after odd job led him into opening the stand more by accident than design.

I had enjoyed our first chat so much that I went back often. On my fifth visit, he said, "Hey, Teach, try my new baba ghanoush recipe."

"I'm safe from vampires." I referred to the amount of garlic.

He said he liked my sense of humor.

After my vampire remark, I ate at Puke Hall for several days. The next time I went to the stand, his face broke into a big grin. When he said, "I thought you deserted me, Teach," I felt all mushy inside.

I compared it to David's return the night before. After a week-long trip, he'd walked through the door, his briefcase in one hand, his portable phone in the other. When he hung up, he said, "Liz, did you pick up my blue suit from the dry cleaners?"

"Hello, I missed you, too," I said. He didn't respond. The mobile phone's ring drowned me out.

Having been raised by an old-fashioned New England Yankee, I never set out to make Peter my lover. Old-fashioned can be defined as moral. Moral means not committing adultery.

I ate more Mideastern food than I ever would have eaten had Peter not been there. I told myself that it tasted better and was healthier. When the lines were too long for him to talk to me, I'd take my pita bread back to the office, a not-so-faint feeling of disappointment fighting with the larger one of stupidity. Finally, I started going for lunch at two because most people had finished eating, and Peter was freer to talk.

I fantasized about him stripping away his costume in slow motion, sweeping me up in his arms and carrying me away. I never finished the fantasy, just like I never worried about traffic hitting us as he carried me across the street. Even if it weren't the best fantasy, it was mine, and as mine I put what I wanted into it. Only I really didn't know what I wanted in it. I was a failure at fantasy.

Had it not been for *The Christmas Revels*, I doubt if we would have become lovers. Peter says we would have, but I don't see how. My secretary had given me two tickets. A miracle, *Revels* tickets being almost impossible to get.

David said he couldn't go. He had to finish a report, which was too bad, because theater was something we enjoyed together. Previous commitments abounded when I finished my list of people who might go without a spouse. So rather than miss it, I went alone. Some people hate going places by themselves. I enjoy it, missing only the discussion of whatever "it" was afterwards.

"The Lord of the Dance" is a *Revels* tradition. Before intermission, the performers lead the audience into the entrance hall. Hundreds of people sing as they wend in and out in a snake dance.

I watch my feet when I snake dance, because I'm clumsy. There I was chanting and watching my feet, thoroughly enjoying the comradeship of strangers, when I glanced up to see Peter sans chickpea costume. He was thin without his padding. Wearing an Irish knit sweater, he

16

looked like a professor, a very, very, very handsome professor—better than any of my fantasies.

His eye caught mine. He smiled. No, it was more than that. He beamed. Deserting his place in line, he broke into the spot next to me. When the dance stopped, we hugged each other as most of the dancers did. "Who are you with?" he asked.

"Myself."

"That's a sin. We'll correct that."

He introduced me to the couple he was with, except I already knew Judy and Mark Smentsky. Judy was Fenway's doctor. Mark was a sculptor, whom I met at campus affairs. I didn't socialize outside work with people from Fenway. David had little use for anyone working in education. They couldn't do anything for him.

I'd always liked Judy. She'd never mentioned that she knew Peter, but then why should she say, "My husband's cousin was roommates at Northeastern University with the vegetable of your fantasies"? She had no way of knowing I was going through a premenopausal teenage crush.

When the curtain rose on the second act, Peter sat in the empty seat next to me. Afterwards we walked through Harvard Yard.

Judy and Mark went home because they didn't trust their teenage daughter to properly care for their seven-year-old. I reveled, no pun intended, in their teenager's irresponsibility. It was the first time I was alone with Peter without someone saying, "Do you have any of that good cucumber and yogurt stuff?"

"Let's go to the Casablanca for something hot," he said.

We entered the small café under the Brattle Street Theater. We both ordered hot chocolate with mint at the same time without checking with the other. I seldom remember names, but I remember what people wear and what they eat.

Two men, probably in their thirties, one bearded and the other clean shaven, played Othello at the next table. The slap, slap, slap of the pieces disturbed the quiet. The only other patron was an elderly man writing in a notebook.

A waiter cleaned the huge espresso machine, rubbing the copper with a cloth. He made shutdown noises, although the place was not scheduled to close for another half-hour.

We talked over a table barely large enough for our two glass cups. When Peter made a point, he'd touch my hand with his finger. He had hot fingers. "I lived with a woman for four years. One day I came home. She was gone, leaving a note that she wanted to find herself."

"Were you hurt to have her disappear without warning?" I asked.

"Looking back, the signs were there, but I'd ignored them. I hurt for a long while," he said.

"How long?"

"Eight months, three weeks, two days, twenty minutes, and thirty-three seconds."

"Exactly?"

"No, but I learned how to recover from a cracked heart." When I looked confused, he said, "A cracked heart isn't as serious as a broken one. I was in-like, not in-love with Laurie."

"So how did you recover from a cracked heart? Don't tell me glue and Scotch tape," I said.

"I concentrated on what was wrong instead of missing what was good. Now I can let the good memories back in."

I told him about my work. When he asked about men, I mentioned David.

18

He leaned back in his chair. "Is it good?"

"Is what good?" I asked.

"If you have to ask, you don't know." He changed the subject to safer topics: movies, food, restaurants, the Celtics.

As the Othello players put away their pieces and the writer closed his notebook, we gave in to the grumpy waiter who wanted to close. As the waiter held the door for us to file out, the bearded player dropped the box holding the game. The black and white stones rolled over the restaurant floor. The waiter sighed. Maybe he thought it was a plot to keep him from going home. Peter and I crawled under the tables along with the players until the stones were all back in the bag. The waiter watched, tapping his foot.

We couldn't say good-bye. We walked around the Square looking in windows. Laila's Toys had its annual display of a cloth pea pod on cotton snow. Five-inch stuffed peas hung at various heights against a black starry background. A sign read "peas on earth."

"I get a chuckle each year when I see this," Peter said.

"Me too."

The Square was almost deserted. Another couple walked briskly and disappeared into a dormitory entrance. The street musicians who braved the weather all year for donations had packed up, but I could see the mark of a violin case in the snow. From an apartment over a store we heard Vivaldi's *Four Seasons*. The outline of someone directing an imaginary orchestra was silhouetted on the shade.

The Congregational Church clock struck two. "I've got to go," I said.

We walked to my car, his arm around my shoulder, but he made no move to kiss me. In my fantasy, he'd have

kissed me and the cold of the Square would have been replaced by the heat of passion, accompanied by Beethoven's
"Ode to Joy" sung by the Mormon Tabernacle Choir.

In reality, my car coughed its unwillingness to start, then
gave in. Peter patted the back of my car, and I could see in
the rear-view mirror as he waved. It took ten miles for the
car to warm.

I resented that we'd gone separate ways. I should have
offered him a ride and wondered why he hadn't asked.
Damn my passivity. Still, that night marked a change in our
relationship, only it wasn't a relationship then. Our friendship had begun.

After the holiday break, I rushed to the stand for lunch
the first day of classes. When we'd exchanged the usual did-
you-have-a-nice-Christmas remarks, he threw out, "Wanta
go to Flan O'Brien's for a beer after work?" Then a couple
of days later, I worked up my nerve to suggest margaritas at
Sol Aztec. The entire day before I asked him, I remembered
my mother's childhood rule of never calling a boy. I told
myself we were friends, nothing more, except that he had
more testosterone than estrogen.

Our meetings fell into a habit. One of us would name a
place.

"Flan's?"

"The Smokehouse?"

"The Squealing Pig?"

"Skip Jack's?"

The other would reply, "What time?" There wasn't a
pub, café or restaurant within a two-mile radius of the
Fenway that we missed. We talked about everything except
"us" as an "us."

He invited me to a reading at the Boston Public Library.

Chickpea Lover

The author had long hair and read several short stories. Peter asked her, "How do you prepare for a reading?"

"I pressed my slacks," she said. They did have sharp creases.

He'd been given tickets to a Celtics game, fifth-row seats behind the players, so close we could see their sweat. Williams had a tear in his shirt.

Peter touched me a lot during our outings, sometimes he hit me playfully, sometimes he draped his arm around my shoulder. If he wanted to hurry, he'd grab my hand and pull me along as we ran, but he never kissed me or made a real pass.

In spring, May 5th at 11:57 p.m. to be precise, after the first Boston Pops concert, we were walking through the Christian Science Park. Although the trees were in first bloom, they'd been clipped to form perfect green bubbles. Peter took off his sandals, then knelt to take off mine, before pulling me into the long pool. The water only came to our ankles, but it made them prickle like the ocean in Maine, when even on the hottest day the sea numbs the body.

"What are you thinking about?" he asked.

I couldn't say that I imagined him kissing me, so I turned away.

He turned me so I faced him and took his finger to lift my chin. Softly he brushed my lips with his. "Come to bed with me. We've waited long enough." Those nine words hung between us until I nodded.

We took the T to his place. The trolley took longer than ever before.

I was scared. David had been the only man I'd ever gone to bed with. The sexual revolution had gone on without me. Even David and I only made love sporadically. I'd never

21

quite understood what the fuss was all about.

Peter held my hand tightly since I'd agreed, as if afraid I'd change my mind. Little did he know there was no danger of that. I hung onto him in case he changed his.

Once inside his house, Boss jumped all over us. In none of my fantasies did I imagine a *ménage à trois* with the third party being of the canine persuasion. Peter shoved the dog into the garden and led me up the staircase. I thought of Rhett carrying Scarlett up the stairs, but Southern plantations have wide staircases. Peter's spiral one could have killed us both had he tripped. More to the point—this wasn't a fantasy. This was the real thing.

As Peter unbuttoned my blouse, I wished I'd worn prettier lingerie. Mother never told me to wear clean underwear in case I had to go to the hospital like all my friends' mothers did. She said, "Wear pretty underwear in case you meet Patrick." We both had a terrible crush on him when I was in high school.

Since Mother guarded my virginity all through school, I wondered why she thought I might let Patrick see my underwear even on the off chance he came to Concord, Massachusetts. He was too old for me anyway.

One night when we watched a *Dallas* rerun on television, I asked her, "Why did you tell me that about my underwear?"

"So you'd have clean underwear, if you ever had an accident and had to go to the hospital," she said.

When Peter reached my clean cotton panties, he found a lion and the word Tuesday. It was Thursday. "Sexy," he said and kissed the lion. My hip quivered. I wanted more. I got more.

Judy and Mark Smentsky own a Victorian mansion, ten

minutes from Peter's. A five-foot metal tree with square metal leaves dominates the front yard. Mark's work is all over both inside and outside. Entering the front hall, I see a green suit of armor. Tonight a paper turkey hangs from one green metal glove. It's not one of Mark's sculptures, but a Mexican fake that Judy bought and painted green. She named it Gerlach Hauptdesert for the knight in Sir Gawain and the Green Knight.

"Sable put it there," Judy says, pointing to the turkey as she takes our coats.

"Hi, guys," Sable calls from her chair in what Judy calls the sitting room across from the entrance hall, one of four such rooms. Large arches make this house seem very open. Judy could shut the rooms off with the sliding wooden doors, but she likes to be in touch with all the activities of kids, dogs, birds, cats and gerbils that make up this household. Sable is in the middle of a giant economy pout because she's been grounded. Judy warned me yesterday when she invited us over. Sable likes us enough to forget her sulk long enough to hug Peter and me. Then she bats the turkey before stomping off. Mark, who is almost twenty years older than Judy, who is my age, brings four Amstel beers. "I'm out of Sam Adams," he says. He wears his white hair sixties-long. Unlike a lot of ex-hippies, it is not thinning, but Santa Claus–full. He is dressed in jeans, a plaid flannel shirt and work boots.

"What did you think about the latest Israeli attack?" Mark swigs his beer from the bottle.

"I am just tired of all war talk," Peter says, sipping his beer.

Sasha wanders in dressed in faded pajamas, dragging a teddy bear behind her. On her feet are fuzzy slippers with bunny rabbit ears and faces. "Can we have a sing-along?" she asks.

"It's too homey for company," Judy says.

"Let's," Peter says. "We like homey stuff." The "we" grabs my heart.

Sable walks through the kitchen and says, "That's so tacky I could just die."

"Death threats are everywhere Sable is these days," Judy says so softly that Sable doesn't hear.

It feels good to sing the Dylan and Seeger songs. Mark says it brings up memories of marching down Commonwealth Avenue. Despite my goody-goody youth, I did my share of demonstrations, mostly on women's issues. Only I could never participate at the price of my grades. A low mark was the same thing as a dagger in Mother's heart, and flunking out wasn't any more of an alternative than giving her a glass of water with arsenic. In fact, the latter would have been more acceptable.

David never protested. He can call the governor and our senators and get put through immediately. He is politically conservative. He would have joined the Army and served his country like a man. He liked Reagan and both Bushes. He hated Clinton. Since politics is a taboo subject in our marriage, it's fun to be with those who see the world from my view.

We swing into "If I Had a Hammer." When we sing out what we would do with our bells, Judy moves across the room. As soon as we stop singing, she marches a protesting Sasha to bed.

When she comes back, she announces, "He's dead."

"Who?" Peter asks.

"Frank N. Stein."

Mark looks at the Habitrail that covers a long bookshelf with plastic boxes filled with wheels, tunnels, and miniature staircases. A gerbil, the sole inhabitant of his rodent apartment complex, lies motionless in his wheel. I didn't know they still made Habitrails, but Judy is into scrounging old things so she might have picked it up anywhere.

"Go get another," Judy says.

"Sable should learn to cope with death," Mark says.

"She already did when my mother died. Gerbils don't have to die when you're seven."

"Come on, Mark. The Chestnut Hill Mall is still open. I know where the pet store is," Peter says.

After the men leave on their gerbil safari, Judy and I shake old Frank out of the cage into the toilet.

"When I was a kid, we used to hold funerals for goldfish before flushing them," Judy says.

"We buried ours in the backyard," I say.

She looks at Frank floating in the water. "Go to God." She flushes.

We disinfect the cage. Because the men still aren't back, we start stringing popcorn and cranberries, which was the original reason we were invited. It's still early, but Judy likes to do things in advance. We've a standing invitation for anytime I can escape my real life.

The kernels and berries resist our needles until we wax them, then they glide through. We giggle about being so domestic and glance at our watches, worrying that the men can't find a replacement.

"What are you going to do?" Judy asks, but adds, "We don't have to talk about it."

I smile at the way my relationship has turned Judy from a colleague into a friend. Jabbing my finger with the needle, I suck the blood. It has stained a popcorn kernel.

Judy has made me realize how much I miss having close women friends. After I married, David didn't like my college friends and we drifted apart. "Our friends" are all related to his law and business interests, and I constantly have to remember which messages to share and which not to. He talks about our evenings out in terms of commercial interests.

"How should I know," I answer Judy's question. "I want Peter. I want this life. But I don't know how to leave the old one." My finger is still bleeding, and Judy gets me a Band-Aid. "There's all sorts of how-to books on getting jobs, raising kids, but none on leaving a husband."

"How about the old song, 'Fifty Ways to Leave Your Lover'?"

"I don't want to leave Peter."

"You know what I mean," she says.

Before I can answer, the men return with the new gerbil.

After we leave the Smentskys, after we make love, when we're almost asleep, Peter whispers, "Did you have a good time tonight?"

"Hmm." I'm too sleepy to say more.

"It could always be like this." He touches my cheek and rolls over.

I lie awake, sleep banished, listening to him snore on my right. Boss snores to my left.

I change worlds the next afternoon. I could stay at the carriage house, but I need to get ready for next week. After I get my stuff together, I'll head back to Peter's. Maybe I can spend part of the week there—a luxury.

Usually I go home so the neighbors will see me. Not that we associate with them, except for David's sister. She lives three houses down the road. I heard her say she doesn't think I'm good enough for him. In a way she's right. For all our incompatibilities, he doesn't deserve an unfaithful wife.

Driving back to the suburbs, I ask myself why do I keep procrastinating making a decision. I don't procrastinate chores. At school my papers are always done at least a day early. My Christmas shopping is usually done before Thanksgiving, except for this year. Dirty dishes go straight into the dishwasher. I've a reputation for being the professor who hands corrected work back faster than anyone.

It's only personal decisions that I put off. When David proposed, I didn't answer for weeks. A graduate of Harvard Law School, he was so handsome he could have been a refugee from *Cosmo*'s most eligible bachelor column. Yet, I couldn't make up my mind.

Mother had a fit. She was convinced I'd lose an excellent catch. "He's even four inches taller than you," she reminded me. She had found my growth spurt at the age of fourteen to my current five-foot-eight a bit overwhelming. I tower over her and my older sister, Jill.

"You won't have to work, unlike me," Mother had said.

Right up to the moment when Uncle John delivered me to David in front of the minister, I kept thinking I could still back out. When the minister asked if there were any reason this couple shouldn't be joined together in holy matrimony, I almost said, "I do." For a crazy moment I pictured Mother, who had spent much more than she could afford on the wedding, fainting. I didn't do it because I had no idea of what I would say to her when she revived.

My fears seemed unfounded in the early days. David was touchingly excited about his career. "How would you handle it?" he'd ask over dinner, and we would talk strategy. It changed so gradually, I never noticed.

I pull into our driveway. The house looks like a feature in *Architectural Digest*. My husband drove our architect, builder, plumber and everyone else who worked on it crazy getting it just so. It's modern with lots of glass and wood. We've three acres of forest overlooking a pond.

As I unlock the door, I see through the house to the large glass wall in the back. The Canada geese swim on the pond. If I feed them, David will lecture me. "They'll stay all winter because the pickings are too easy." He's more worried about goose shit on the lawn than their welfare.

One year when a family decided to nest for the summer, he broke their eggs to make them leave. I didn't speak to him for a week, which didn't make any difference. He was in Florida.

Our house is furnished with antiques and Oriental rugs, a striking contrast to the modern design. David has excellent taste, but his house has never felt homey to me.

I'm not allowed to mess things up, like spreading the Sunday newspapers around as I lie on the living room rug with a cup of coffee that David has made. His Sunday breakfasts are works of art. "Food belongs in the kitchen or dining room," he will remind me. A stained carpet may be a greater sin than my adultery.

Everything, and I mean everything, is exactly as David wants it. Even for the room I use as an office he chose all the furniture. When I make a suggestion, he looks at me. Those four inches make him seem a lot taller as he says in a tone implying my taste is questionable: "(sigh-pause-sigh) Well . . . (sigh), if you really . . . (sigh) want it." Then his breath trails off.

Liz, the wonder wimp, always backs down. Well, almost always. Once I insisted on buying a vase we found in an antique store. He didn't like that some of the gold leaf had worn off the edge. It was pink Sandwich glass made on the Cape around the time of the Civil War. I loved its luster and pictured my roses, which were almost the same color as the vase, in front of the hall mirror. I loved putting bouquets in front of mirrors because they look double. That had been David's idea. Although I've found fault with him, especially lately, I have to give him credit when he deserves it.

As for the effect of the flowers, I never got to see it because David dropped the vase as he carried it into the house. Smithereen City. He said it was an accident. I have my doubts. Too many accidents happen to things he doesn't want.

We've four bedrooms, three for children never conceived. After seven years of marriage, my biological time clock went off with a vengeance. Walking by a baby carriage without staring was impossible. Between classes, I'd stroll through the Coop's baby department picking up little clothes.

When my body betrayed me monthly, I'd cry. I'd rail at God, convinced he was punishing me for my faithful use of birth control as I worked on my Ph.D.

"Hey, God! I've changed my mind," I screamed silently. God didn't get my new messages. Sex, usually regulated by David's energy and business trips, became a timed maneuver, bearing no resemblance to love. I took days off from work to fly to wherever he was if it corresponded with my egg production.

Finally, I went through all the tests, and the doctor said I'd less than a fifteen percent chance of conceiving. David was never tested. The night I came home with the results, he held me until I stopped sobbing. I remember how tenderly he stroked my hair, saying, "It's okay, it's okay. We have each other."

His car keys are on the kitchen counter. Shit. I'd left my car in the driveway without checking the garage. "Hello," I call. The kitchen has an all-glass sliding door looking into a greenhouse. My voice echoes against the glass. Glancing around I notice dirty dishes from at least two meals. Our housekeeper works Monday through Friday. When I left Saturday morning, the kitchen was spotless.

"Where the hell have you been?" David storms into the room. He's dressed in the red flannel bathrobe we bought at L.L.Bean the last time we drove to Maine, not the silk one he prefers. He looks terrible with at least a two-day beard. Normally he's a manic shaver.

"What are you doing home?" I ask.

"Flu." My husband is a terrible patient. During his last cold, he kept moaning, "I hope you never suffer as I'm suffering." When he caught poison ivy, he was positive it was leprosy. He'd returned from Africa on a Friday, but we'd gone camping over the weekend. Since his hand didn't fall off and the rash disappeared, I assumed my diagnosis was correct.

I feel his head. It's hot. He stiffens at my touch. "I asked where you were." David never yells. When he's angry, he lowers his voice and enunciates each syllable. This time he clips each letter.

"I stayed in town at Judy's."

"You should have left a note. I was worried sick."

Instead of my usual apology, I snap, "Who'd I leave it for? You weren't supposed to be home." I feel like a bully.

The phone rings. I answer.

"Elizabeth-Anne, where have you been?"

Double shit. Mother!

She sighs. "I didn't sleep a wink after David called. I was positive I would read in the *Globe* that they'd found your body." She watches too many crime shows and is convinced that you risk your life if you set one foot into a city. *Boston*

30

Cop, 911, NYPD, and *Columbo* reruns are, to her mind, proof of the danger.

"I'm really sorry you were worried, but I'm fine." We go a few more rounds as once again I catch all the guilt she gives.

David sinks into a chair as I talk, his head in his hands. Hanging up, I tell him to go to bed. He does, falling asleep even before I leave the room.

I'm angry at myself for the way I dealt with Mother and David. I hang up my coat. It falls off the hanger, and I have to do it a second time. A cup of tea. I need a cup of tea. Tea soothes me when I'm upset. I push the intercom to the bedroom and hear David's steady snore. I call Peter to tell him I won't be back.

"Anything wrong?"

"No. Yes." I explain.

Peter's funny about my husband. He refuses to push me because he wants the decision to be mine. "I don't want you to throw it back in my face after we're married." He said that at least a dozen times. His pressure is different from Mother's or David's. With them, I'm pushed where they want me to go. Peter makes me want what he wants all by himself. Why do I hold back?

As I wait for the water to boil, I realize how much more I see of Peter than of David. We talk over unimportant and important things. Maybe Peter will grow tired of waiting. That idea frightens me.

The tea doesn't calm me. My thoughts, like my life, are out of control.

CHAPTER TWO

As I unlock my office door, the phone rings. I knock over books, papers and my bell jar clock as I throw myself across the desk to reach the phone on the bookshelf.

"Professor Adams, how can I help you?" I ignore metal and glass bits on my floor. That clock will never chime again.

"What was the crash?" Peter asks, knowing my office is so tiny I can almost reach all four walls from my chair.

"I'm glad you don't love me for my grace," I say before explaining.

"I'm glad I don't love you for your grace, either. Can you meet me at the museum for lunch? I've a surprise."

"What surprise?"

"If I tell, it won't be a surprise."

"Yes, it will, at least when you tell me."

"I've two Helga tickets."

"What time? My last class is at one." Why I tell him this I don't know. He knows my schedule by heart.

"Two for lunch. Mohammed is covering for me. The tickets are for three."

"Great."

"I'll stop by your office."

I almost say no. I'm afraid my colleagues will discover he's my lover, but if I had a lover I wouldn't be so bold as to have him meet me at my office, would I?

"How's David?"

"He didn't go to work yesterday or today, so he's really sick."

Peter didn't call me Monday. I'd have wondered if he were angry about my not coming back on Sunday, except Peter doesn't get angry about things like that. Politics, stupidity, Republicans, famine—these things make him angry. Cruelty makes him furious. Normal life situations he understands. Yesterday, I'd tried calling him a couple of times, but the line was always busy.

"Would you rather go home?" There is nothing but concern in his voice.

"And waste my ticket?" I feel warm because he knows how much I want to see these paintings. "Where did you get them?"

"I've my sources," he says. I don't doubt it. His stand is now a Boston attraction. Since he won the Best Mideastern Food award in the *Boston Phoenix* three years running, he's drawn customers from all over the city. Thus, he's on a first-name basis with the mayor, most of the city council, the dancers in the Boston Ballet, and a number of other local celebrities.

The Museum of Fine Arts is a three-minute walk from Fenway. One of the improvements the directors made when they built the new wing was to add two places to eat. A café offers snacks with fruit, cheese and fattening pastries.

"I made restaurant reservations," Peter says. I look at the long line at the café and appreciate him even more. The restaurant is on the second floor. Trout and scallops are featured on the menu posted outside. The last time we ate trout here, Peter had told me how two summers ago he'd backpacked through the Pyrenees investigating Cathar castles and sleeping in his tent. He'd found a friend and they'd caught a trout which they'd roasted in the ashes of their fire.

Listening to his story, I'd felt jealous—jealous for the taste of fresh-cooked trout and jealous of his friend because he'd wandered through France with Peter and I hadn't. When I told Peter, he'd hugged me and said, "Feelings aren't ever stupid. Only the actions they create are stupid."

"Please give us one of John's tables," Peter asks the hostess. When you look at her directly she looks bald, her chignon is done so tightly. She seats us at a table next to a statue of a drunken Greek goddess. The statue's hand is filled with grapes with the bottom grape over Peter's left ear.

John, whom we've dubbed "our waiter" from our last six visits, comes over. "Hi, folks. Nice seeing you."

"What's good today?" I ask.

"The scallops are fresh off the boat. Had some myself," John says. The last three times we ate here he gave his opinion about everything we ordered. While we wait for our food, Peter fiddles with the vase that holds a single carnation. I toy with my wineglass. We keep our hands busy because we really want to touch. Instead we hold glass, keeping our hands occupied in a socially acceptable fashion for adulterers.

John brings our lunches. The broccoli has hollandaise, and the mashed potatoes are piped onto a slice of pineapple. They are real, not instant. As I look at the food, my stomach turns. I barely make the bathroom. After washing my face and rinsing my mouth, I feel better.

Peter waits for me at the door. "What happened? You OK?"

"I threw up. The smell, I guess."

Peter asks John to bring me some clear broth. Chives float on the top. After a few mouthfuls, my hands stop shaking. We sit there until just before three. Peter orders a

Coke, figuring between the salt and the sugar, my system will get back to normal. I do feel better. Damn, I don't want to get David's flu.

Outside the exhibition hall we rent tape recorders. A soothing announcer points out the not-to-be-missed highlights. The exhibition is exactly what I expected. Helga's braids remind me of two years ago when I gave a paper in South Carolina. Having an hour to kill, I'd wandered into a Wyeth exhibition at the local museum. I went through half the gallery before starting to leave. Unlike the crowds today, I was the only person there.

The guard, a man in his seventies with gray muttonchop sideburns, said, "You didn't see it all, ma'am."

I'd looked at my watch.

"You Yankees rush too much." He shepherded me back into the museum. Being polite made me five minutes late for the lecture. Because I was the speaker, the group noticed I wasn't there and waited.

Periodically Peter asks me how I feel. I tell him, "OK." Although I'm enjoying myself, I'm tired.

A woman in her late twenties stands before us wearing tattered jeans and a T-shirt, carrying a full-length mink coat. She cocks her head as she listens to her rented tape recorder. I watch Peter watch her. I resent her youth and wonder if I'll ever stop being jealous of younger, prettier women.

Peter whispers to me, "Cultural coding," a term he uses to describe what people wear to make statements.

"What code?" I ask. My lips brush his ear.

"Disdainfully rich." He wasn't thinking what I thought he was. I'm so glad I didn't say anything.

The president of the college and his wife are behind us. There's no chance to speak to them, but we nod. Peter and I keep a friendship distance from one another as I pray they didn't notice us a moment before.

While we were in the exhibition it rained, leaving a special smell of wet leaves that differs from the smell of spring rain. Just as we enter the parking lot, the streetlights go on.

"Do you have to go home?" he asks. I should, but I don't want to. Guilt with Peter is better than non-guilt with a sick David. Besides, I really don't feel up to driving. We pick up my car and check the stand. Mohammed tells us not to worry.

Peter's key sticks and he mutters under his breath. Once inside he takes the dog's lead just as the phone rings. "Get it, will you?"

I adore how he lets me answer his phone and get his mail. It shows he's not afraid I'll discover another lover.

It's Judy. Peter and Boss come back in and he starts to make tea as I sit on the cushion chatting. "Did Sasha notice the new Frank N. Stein?" I ask.

"She commented he was nicer, but this morning she knew for sure we made a switch."

"How?"

"Even a seven-year-old can figure out that a male gerbil living by himself for a year can't have a litter."

"Hold on." I cover the mouthpiece. "Did you realize that you guys bought a pregnant gerbil?"

Peter takes the phone to tease Judy about her new grandmother status. He refuses to take any of the offspring but suggests names.

"Mark says anthropologists should know more about gerbils than artists," Peter says when he hangs up.

While I call David, Peter goes to get more wood even though there's plenty in the polished leather trunk where he stores the cut logs. Never has he stayed in the room when I talk with my husband. I'm not sure if it's privacy, courtesy or not wanting to admit my marital status. Every time I start to ask which, I stop myself.

David says, "I'm going to the office tomorrow, and I should be able to make my trip later this week." He tells me he worked on his computer, but it kept crashing. He sounds impatient.

"Why aren't you home?" he asks, but accepts my explanation that I'm tutoring a student. "Don't be too late. Drive carefully." The phone clicks in my ear.

I'm home by nine. As I turn the car into the driveway, I see no lights in the front of the house. I use the automatic door opener and, by the light of the moon shining in the window, I find my way.

Taking off my shoes I enter the bedroom. The housekeeper has changed the sheets and aired out the room. The sick smell is gone, but there is no one in the clean bed. My husband's whistled version of "Memories" combines with the sound of the shower. A little steam escapes through the master bathroom door, which he has left slightly ajar.

I put on my green terry-cloth robe. The bedroom has a chaise longue where I flop to wait my turn. David comes out. A bath sheet, wrapped around his waist, touches his ankles. The steam behind makes him seem like a monster coming through the fog in a horror movie. Drops of water glisten on his chest hair. He greets me with, "Ah, you're home. Can you get me a cup of hot chocolate?" He kisses my head.

I tell him I will after my bath. Padding into the bathroom, I step around damp footprints on the carpet. To get into the tub I have to go down three steps. Usually I shower, which is separate from the tub, but tonight I want to soak. The bubbles, which I make with abandon, hide my body like some TV commercial.

The warmth feels wonderful as I relax. For once I think of nothing. The next thing I know, David shakes me, saying, "Wake up, sleepy head."

I slip on my Fenway College Spring Fling T-shirt and enjoy how the electric blanket has warmed our bed. David reminds me about the hot chocolate. Throwing off the covers I go to make a cup for him and another for myself. We drink them in bed as we read. He has *The New England Lawyer's Journal* as I lose myself in Linda Barnes's latest mystery.

He kisses me good night and rolls over to his side of our king-sized bed. Peter and I sleep curled up like spoons when we spend nights together. Wondering if we would still sleep as close if we slept together every night, I drift off.

The bedroom drapes go up eight feet, but light streams in the glass wall that goes even higher to the wood cathedral ceiling. David's already left. I gag, barely making the bathroom. After going back to sleep for a couple of hours, I wake feeling fine. Having no temperature I dress for my noon class.

Sometimes I think I should pay the college for the privilege of teaching. It's a lot like performing. My students pick up my energy and recycle it back for me to reuse.

However, the college should pay me double for the administrative work, which I hate as much as I love teaching.

Fenway is very parental. I might say it is because it is an

38

all-women school, but it isn't parental in a chauvinistic way. The philosophy, which most of the administration and faculty believe in their heart of hearts, is that we should do everything possible to give these bright young women every chance to get a good start in life. We are expensive, but we also have a deep commitment to the local community with scholarships for students who could never afford the tuition. It is only one reason I love teaching here. With all the recent scandals in politics and business, I feel as if I can make a molecule of difference in the world. Well, maybe a molecule of a molecule. It makes me proud to be able to work here.

A lot of our girls have real problems. Right now I'm watching two girls who may be in the early stages of anorexia. Their grades get higher as their bodies get thinner. After Thanksgiving vacation, I'll send them to Judy at the health center.

There's another student, Mary O'Brien, who worries me even more than my potential anorexics. I've asked her to come to my office. This is the second year I've had her in my classes. She's a scholarship student from Mission Hill, one of nine kids, the first in her family to go to college. She has gone from an all-A student to one barely passing. Looking into her eyes it's like the lights went out. That worries me more than her dropping grades.

Hiding her ample breasts with her books, Mary enters my office. Her long red hair, that she once wore loose, is tied with a single ribbon at the nape of her neck. She's pale, but she has the type of skin that is always pale. Last year she almost strutted when she walked, not stooping and scuttling as she does now.

"You sent for me, Dr. Adams?" She shifts her weight from foot to foot.

I point to the free chair that makes my office even more crowded. "Your grades are way down."

She doesn't look at me. "I know," she says after a long while.

I say nothing, letting a new silence hang between us, hoping she'll fill it. My new clock, bought at the drugstore around the corner, ticks away.

Mary looks everywhere but at me. In an office the size of mine that's difficult. A tear runs down her cheek. I rummage in my drawer for the tissues that I always have for these types of conversations.

"What's wrong?" I reach out and put my hand on her arm. She takes the tissue and twists it between her fingers. She says nothing. I wait. And wait. And wait.

"I think I'm pregnant."

I place myself in front of her and she buries her head in my stomach. What I catch between her sobs is, "Can't tell . . . da . . . will kill me . . . abortion's murder . . . rape . . . black . . ."

I hold her. When she pulls away, some of her red hair is matted to her cheeks.

"What about a rape?"

"On the Fenway."

"When?"

"Three months ago," she hiccups.

"Did you report it?"

She shakes her head. Her hands tremble as I hold them between mine. They're cold. I brush her hair from her face as I guard my anger. The Fenway is dangerous. Each year we warn our girls. Each year at least three students we know of are raped. Mary is a local. She should have known better, but blaming the victim isn't what she needs to hear. "Why do you think you're pregnant?"

40

"I haven't had my period since. I throw up every morning. I want to sleep all the time."

"Have you been tested?"

"No," she says.

"OK, that's where we'll start. Mary!" She looks up. "You're not alone. The school has ways to help. Do you believe me?" She looks away. I take her chin and force her head up. Her eyes avoid mine, but I clear my throat, making her look at me. "Do you believe me?"

"I can't think."

"That's normal." She almost relaxes. I've given her permission for her feelings or at least her confusion. "I would like to call Dr. Smentsky. Do I have your permission?"

Handing this to Judy will be a relief because I know she's dealt with every teenage female problem possible, all far better than I could have. Despite her small build, Judy rules the five-bed center with an iron hand. The iron is covered with velvet. Students and staff adore her.

While Mary changes in the examining room, we go into Judy's office. Some doctors have diplomas on their walls. She has photos of her kids, biological and professional. I brief her.

"Poor kid. She's too Catholic for an abortion." Judy lights a cigarette. Few faculty smoke. Judy only does at work and only when she's upset. She smokes Camels, unfiltered, and picks a piece of tobacco off her tongue. "What I know of her father, he'll disown her if he finds out she's pregnant, no matter what she does," she says.

"Did you meet her parents?" I ask.

"Never, but we talked a lot about her family last year when she worked in the clinic," she says.

Judy admits Mary to the center for the night. She's in no

41

condition to go home. She yawns, rubbing her eyes with her fists.

Judy tucks her in. "We'll call your parents and tell them you've the flu."

As I tiptoe out leaving them alone, I hear Judy talk about validity of feelings.

Judy and I call a Crisis Council meeting for the next morning. That's a forum to help students in trouble. Theoretically, everyone on the faculty and administration is on the council. Usually, it's the Dean of Students, the head of whatever department the student is in, and the staff needed to help the kid. I don't claim it is perfect. We have all the same problems as other places: people playing power games, mismanagement, normal stupidities. However, when one of our girls is in trouble, they seem to melt away.

Crisis Council meetings are held in the Dean's Conference Room at Victoria Hall.

Entering the oak-paneled room is like changing centuries. In the center of the ceiling with all its original moldings, a chandelier hangs over an eight-foot table dating to the Spanish-American War. Gold-framed portraits of past college presidents decorate the walls.

A fire crackles in the marble fireplace. The janitor must have lit it. I mentioned to him there was a meeting when I saw him this morning in Puke Hall. A branch keeps tapping at the window, an unofficial call to order.

Judy arrives after me with Bob Ivers, the college shrink. Moving like a wraith, he drops a manila folder on the table. Like always he wears cords, a turtleneck jersey and tweed jacket.

Dean Whittier, who is approaching retirement, bustles around the room, putting out pads and pencils. Notes are always taken on pads but never removed from the room. In fact, they're shredded to preserve confidentiality. Her mane of white hair is brushed back from her face. I hope I look that good at sixty-four. I should look that good at thirty-nine.

Aging scares me, more now than ever. Peter is so much younger than I am. Mary Tyler Moore married a younger man. So did Joan Collins and paid dearly. I'm not a glamorous star, just an ordinary woman. I put Peter out of my mind yet again to concentrate on Mary O'Brien.

Dean Whittier asks, "Who's the student?" Since Crisis Council meetings have precedence over everything else in the college, the invited people often show up without information. I tell them.

Bob looks up from the papers he's reading. He shoves them back into the folder.

"Mary? She's such a together kid."

Judy pours coffee from the coffeemaker into a china cup. An unused silver tea service sits next to the machine. The room is used for teas, a relic of the past. We teach our girls computer science and drawing-room manners, preparing them for every eventuality. The smell makes me feel slightly sick to my stomach. Usually I love the smell of fresh coffee.

I outline the situation. "She was a virgin."

Bob says, "That's a suck introduction to sex." He glances at Dean Whittier who looks too proper to know about sex. He blushes.

Her eyes twinkle. "Don't worry, Bob. I do have three daughters. Maybe I did it more than thrice, but that's my secret."

A twitter breaks some of the tension that always runs through these meetings.

"This kid is a scholarship student. She can't afford an

abortion or even a bus ticket to Worcester," Judy says.

Dean Whittier says, "We can activate the Althea fund." That is money used for student emergencies. We've bought airline tickets and paid off gambling debts. Althea Jones, the daughter of a very conservative British family, named the fund. She'd been arrested during a demonstration to free three Irish terrorists. A faculty member, Liam O'Shea, professor of Irish Literature, had bailed her out of jail. After graduation, Althea created a weight-loss clinic with franchises all over England. She'd set up a fund for student emergencies on condition of repayment.

"What about her scholarship?" I ask.

"I'll get the committee to hold it if she decides to take time off to have the baby," Dean Whittier says. She heads the committee. Her suggestions carry about the same weight as the words on the tablet Moses brought down from the mountain. Maybe more.

Only the president overrides Dean Whittier and then only after a bitter battle.

President Baker is probably the only one who doesn't regret Dean Whittier's pending retirement. Rumor has it he disliked her since his arrival five years ago. Rumor has it his hatred is because she's more competent than he is. Baker is one of my least favorite parts of Fenway.

The meeting takes less than fifteen minutes. Bob Ivers pats me on the shoulder.

"I'm glad you caught up with her. I'd hate to lose her. She's got a lot on the ball."

The temperature outside has risen despite the wind. Judy and I unbutton our coats as we cut across campus. Together we enter Mary's room. She's asleep, one hand over her head. Her red hair creates a fan on her pillow. She jumps when the door shuts and then sits up.

"OK, Mary," Judy says. "We've come up with a number of ideas, but you decide which will be best for you." As I watch Judy talk with Mary, I can see the muscles in the student's face relax. "Now, you choose, but you don't have to sacrifice your education."

Both Judy and I hug her and tell her we'll support whatever decision she makes.

Leaving the center, I remember I've not eaten lunch and go to the stand. Peter opens the door for me. "You look beat." He rumples my hair. He's back in his chickpea outfit, and he feels soft and squishy.

"I am." I tell him why without mentioning the name.

"Poor kid." In a couple of weeks he'll ask what happened to the pregnant girl. He still asks about my student who joined AA last spring. "Meet me for a drink tonight, we can talk more."

"I better go home," I say, but accept a salad with extra feta cheese on pita bread to tide me over.

David keeps mincing onions as I walk in. I see thin sliced beef and decoratively cut veggies. The wok is out. Rice is cooking in the microwave. Without looking up he asks, "Can you pack for me, while I finish dinner? I'll be gone 'til the day before Thanksgiving. Miami, California and Atlanta. I'll need golf things."

As I reach for his suitcase I mutter to myself about his lack of greeting. Maybe because we've been married so long he doesn't see a need for small talk. I should tell him how I feel, but I wimp out.

At dinner, which is wonderful, I say, "I've a student who looks a lot like the first Queen Elizabeth. We had a

Crisis Council meeting toda . . ."

"Another one of your rich brats got herself in a scrape? By the way, do you like this new version of Beethoven's *Ninth*?" He refers to the CD playing in the background.

"Very nice. Mary's not rich."

"You're obsessive about your students. Check the kitchen calendar. I marked a number of dinners we have to go to before Christmas. Also our Christmas open house . . ."

"I would rather not entertain this year," I say.

"Hire a caterer. The office will pick up the tab. Just make the arrangements by the time I get back."

I pick at my beef teriyaki and wish a Crisis Council meeting could solve everything for me.

CHAPTER THREE

I spend every night that David is away at Peter's. We talk about Mary, who has decided to go to Ohio to have her baby at a Salvation Army home for unwed mothers. Her parents have been told she's doing an internship. She'll give the baby up for adoption.

We talk about politics, about his food costs, about movies. We talk about everything except us. If he starts to talk along that topic, I change the subject. Wednesday night we go to rent a movie. Hand-in-hand we walk around the video store playing what-do-you-want-no-what-do-you-want. We decide that I'll select the category, he'll choose the movie.

"Disease movie," I say, knowing he hates movies when someone gets sick and dies. The last one he saw was *Terms of Endearment*, and he only went because he thought it was a Jack Nicholson film. Debra Winger's cancer took him by surprise. He told me that after she died, everyone in the theater sniffed. He couldn't stop laughing, not at the death scene but at the group sniff. He walked out and didn't go back.

"No way," he says.

"Comedy?" I say.

"*Men in Black II.*"

"No way! Unless it's a disease movie and all the actors die so there'll never be a *Men in Black III*," I say.

He picks up *Runaway Bride*. I agree.

We take the empty box to the counter and the clerk gives us the tape. As we leave the store, still walking hand-in-hand and as I nuzzle Peter, Dean Whittier comes in. She's wearing jeans and a down-filled coat.

"Hi, Liz. Hi, Peter," she says as if we belonged together. Not a flicker of her eyelash gives away any sense of disapproval. She knows David, having met him the few times I cajoled him into escorting me to a school event.

"How do you know her?" I ask, shocked at seeing her, shocked that she knew him by name.

"She likes my food," he says.

"I've never seen her at the stand."

"She stops mornings to buy breakfast."

We walk back to his place without touching, without speaking. The frost-covered leaves crunch under our feet. The sweet smell of autumn is frozen out by the cold. I stop to tie one of my sneakers and retie the other so they feel identical. As a child I'd insist Mother tie both of them even if only one needed it. I like to feel even.

Seeing Dean Whittier makes me feel uneven inside, like a teenager, caught by the principal. When I was sixteen, my best friend and I snuck into the room where the timing mechanism for all the school's clocks was. My friend looked at me. I looked at her. Before I could say, "Don't," she'd spun the hands to the end of the period, which was also the dismissal bell. As we came out of the closet, the principal grabbed me. My friend got away. I spent afternoons for the next month in detention. Every time I do anything close to wrong, I get caught.

Once again the key sticks. Once again Peter walks Boss then starts a fire. I put water on to boil and try to think about the patterns in our lives, because I don't want to worry that Dean Whittier will think less of me. It doesn't work. Peter's voice interrupts my thinking about not thinking about Dean Whittier.

"Liz?"

"Hmm?"

"Have you a morals clause in your contract?"

"Yes. No one has ever been fired on one, though." I feel myself drawing inwards. Going to the refrigerator is a good way to avoid talking about it.

Peter's eyes watch me. I can't see them, but I feel them. Maybe he's letting the silence work as I let it work with Mary.

"I love you. I want to marry you."

"That's safe. We can't. I'm already married." I hate my bitchy tone, but bitchy gives me the distance I need.

"That's a cheap shot." He's right.

"I'm going home." I put on my coat, which I had thrown over a chair.

"Home? Where is that? Where David is? Or isn't most of the time?" he asks.

Boss looks up from her bed in front of the fire.

She's not used to an edge in our voices. I want to tell the dog, I understand, I'm not used to it, either.

"You're not running away this time, Liz." He stands between the door and me.

"Who's running?"

"You," he says.

"So talk. I'll listen." I plunk myself down on the couch, my arms folded across my chest. Peter paces in front of me.

"I'll talk. Look, a year ago this terrific woman kept coming to my stand. We chatted. She wore a wedding ring. Lonely oozed out of her. Lonely recognizes lonely. Know what I mean?"

I say nothing. He pulls a stool in front of me and sits there, looking up at me.

49

"Then accidentally we meet at the *Revels*, which saves me figuring out how to see her outside the stand. The more we talk, the more we discover we have in common. Since she's married and gives me mixed signals, I don't make a pass for months. Lord knows I wanted to."

"I wanted you to, but I couldn't make a move. Remember, when I grew up calling a boy was a punishable offense," I say.

"I'm sure married women kissing single men ten years younger had to qualify for the death penalty," he says. "So finally we go to bed. We spend more time together than most married people. She acts like she loves me. I fall more in love with her, but we never talk about us. Everything else in the world, but never us. That's off-limits."

I get up and head for the door. "It's still off-limits." What am I afraid of? Why am I going home? I wish I understood me.

"Liz." His voice cuts me. I'm afraid to turn, but I pause, holding the doorknob, a lifeline. "We have to talk about the U-word and the L-word."

"I'm afraid."

"Of what?"

"I don't know."

"Do you love me?"

I nod, still with my back to him.

"Say it, then."

"I can't."

"Say it." He spins me around and sees my tears. He shakes me. "Say it. Move your mouth. Deal with it."

I seldom told David I loved him. Feelings weren't for discussion. Gagging, I run to the bathroom and throw up.

When I come out, Peter is stoking the fire. "You OK?"

"Yes." I'm not OK and it has nothing to do with the flu.

I don't feel like driving, but I start to leave again. I hate having flu. This has got to be a mild case, because I got my shot.

"Liz."

I pause, my back to him. This is getting repetitive. If I didn't hurt so much, it would be boring.

"I don't want to see you again until we can at least talk about us." When I turn, his back is to me as he faces the fire. "I mean it. I can't take it. I know how you feel about everything except me."

"You never interfered in my marriage before."

He slams his fist against the chimney, rattling the metal tray resting on the mantel.

"Goddamn it! This isn't about your marriage. This is about you and me. Us."

When I get into my car, I picture myself driving home to spend the night alone. I don't want to do that. I'm not sure what to say to Peter. I go back inside the carriage house.

He unzips my coat. We walk upstairs and make love, more slowly and sweetly than ever before. We come almost at the same time. "Don't pull out," I say. Peter stays in me until he slips out.

"Sorry," he says.

"For what?" His hollering? His penis growing small? For our first fight?

I'm not sure.

We look at the stars through the skylight. He rolls over and rests his head on his elbow.

"If you leave David, it has to be your decision, Liz." Lord, he sounds like Judy talking to Mary. "But either way, I need to know you love me. You're here so much of the time, but then your husband comes back from a trip and I have only your memory. You've a pushy memory, lady. It fills the house."

"I love you," I listen to myself say.

"Why do you stay with him?"

"I wish I knew. Maybe I believe in marriage vows, which sounds stupid considering what we just did. Give me more time, please?"

Gently, his lips graze my forehead. He shuts off the lamp next to the bed. We stay in each other's arms for a long time without speaking. I'm not sure which of us falls asleep first.

CHAPTER FOUR

As I drive towards Logan Airport the day before Thanksgiving, I reduce my anger down to a simmer. Zoo is the best description of the airport today when passenger travel is increased tenfold. People go home, people come home.

My sister, brother-in-law and two nieces are four of the people who will traipse through Logan today. They'll spend tonight with me and the rest of the weekend with Mother.

Jill is two years older than I am. She's married to a real estate tycoon and lives in San Diego. My anger isn't directed at her for flying in today. I'm excited about seeing her and the kids. I find her husband a little overbearing, but likable.

It's David who is causing me to cook in my own bile. Although his flight landed an hour before Jill's, he insisted on going straight to his office. It annoys me that I must fight the traffic, when he was already there. As I brake to keep from hitting a cab, which slammed on its brakes to keep from hitting another car, I think of him sitting in his comfy office. I get madder.

When we talked last night, he said he was too busy to wait for them. I stared at the telephone for a second, imagining him stretched on his hotel bed, his golf clubs in the corner as he waited for room service. Maybe it wasn't exactly like that, but I bet I was close, because David takes his personal comfort very seriously.

I wanted to yell at him. I spoke calmly. "An hour isn't long to wait. They'll be on the ground by the time you collect your luggage."

"And then they'll have to collect theirs."

"David, please."

He'd sighed and said, "Liz, I've been out of the office for over a week. The day after tomorrow is a holiday. There are things I must take care of."

"But it's dumb for both of us to fight that traffic. You know how bad it gets."

"Jill is your sister, not mine. I have to go."

"I understand. Have a good flight home." I wimp out because if his plane crashes and my last words to him were angry ones, I'll feel guilty for the rest of my life. Only after I'd hopped in the shower did I remember that the same thing had happened last year when his brother had flown in.

I slam a Christine Lavin cassette into the tape recorder as I watch the traffic not move. It's her revenge song I want to hear. Singing along makes me feel better. I sing about dismemberment, buses falling off bridges, and other mishaps I want inflicted on my husband. I envy Lavin's ability to say how she feels. As we inch forward, I wonder if maybe she couldn't tell someone how angry she was. Being a songwriter let her put it into music.

Inside the airport I push through the masses until I see the metal detector with its sign, "You need a ticket beyond this point." All around me people stand on tiptoe to identify passengers then wave when they recognize each other.

The arrival screen reports my sister's plane is thirty minutes late, which isn't a surprise. Logan has a terrible on-time record. David would have been furious if he had to wait the extra time.

At the Au Bon Pain cart with its red-, white- and blue-striped tent top, I buy a chocolate croissant and apple juice. Taking the bag, I find a *People* and *USA Today* someone has

left on the window ledge. I figure they'll take approximately thirty minutes to read. There are no seats vacant so I sit on the floor, my back supported by a window.

As legs walk past me, I catch parts of conversations.

"Father's the same. Drunk."

"You've gained weight."

"You haven't."

"Wait 'til I tell you what Meg said about . . ."

Sometimes I'm tempted to break in and ask what happens next. Eavesdropping at airports is a bit like channel surfing. From my spot on the floor, I watch the arrival screen. Just as I finish the latest report on Aniston's and Pitt's Thanksgiving decorations, the sign flashes that my sister's plane is on the ground. I offer my reading to an elderly woman and throw the paper from my snack into a trash container.

Jill and Harry look very Californian with their tans and blond hair. We brush lips near cheeks before I hug my nieces.

Michelle, at sixteen, is taller than both Jill and I. She wears her purple-streaked hair short on one side, long on the other. She says, "I dyed it for a school rally. It won't wash out," before I can say anything. I've had enough punk kids in my classes not to be shocked. By Jill's frown I know she doesn't share my reaction. Both girls resemble my sister when she was their age, although she never had purple hair.

Courtney has lost the baby fat. She's thirteen. "Guess who was on the plane and gave me his autograph?" she asks. Before I can, she pulls a piece of paper from her pocket that reads, "Happy Thanksgiving, Courtney, love Matt Damon."

Harry pushes us towards the escalator. Jill, Courtney and I stand to one side as Harry and Michelle pull the luggage from the carousel. I halfheartedly look for Matt Damon. He's nowhere around.

"How long you staying?" I ask as the suitcase pile grows.

"Only 'til Sunday," Jill says. She doesn't make the connection. So far there are eight suitcases for four people for five days. Harry and Michelle wait for more. I leave my family along with the probable contents of their entire home on the sidewalk to get the BMW that is parked too far away in the garage to struggle with ten pieces of luggage. It's David's car, which I have had all week. He refuses to park it in the airport garage so he trades it for my Ford Escort.

Circling back takes forty-five minutes of more stopping than going. I hum curses with Christine Lavin each time I inch forward.

When I pull over to the sidewalk as near as I can get to my sister and her family, a state cop, his boots up to his knees and his belt crisscrossing his chest, taps on the windshield and growls, "Move it, lady."

"I'm picking up those people over there." I point to a heap of luggage dwarfing my family.

"Make it fast."

With strategic packing and by tying two suitcases on the roof, we manage to get everything in the car. Traffic is still backed up. The Big Dig, Boston's ongoing construction project that I bet will go on to the twenty-second century, doesn't help.

"Nothing has changed," Harry says. "Boston is still dirty, inefficient." However, I see in the rearview mirror that there's a twinkle in his eye. He and I always battle about the superiority of the East Coast over the West Coast. Two years ago I sent him a video with Woody Allen saying he didn't want to live in California because their only cultural contribution was making a right turn on red. Using both VCRs I re-recorded that phrase at least fifty times. He sent me back an article from *Scientific American* about how many rats live in the city, along with a note saying, "This doesn't include politicians."

"It's changed, Daddy. It's colder and there's no leaves," Courtney says.

"That's 'cause we usually come in summer, stupid," Michelle says.

The girls talk about the hostess who announced that anyone caught smoking in the lavatory would lose their potty privileges and have to leave the plane immediately.

I notice Jill doesn't smile, although Harry teases the girls and me all the way back to the house. Usually she's right in there with them.

Worn-out from the trip, everyone goes to bed early, everyone except Jill and me, that is. "Want tea?" I ask her. We sit at the breakfast bar in the kitchen. We're in nightclothes. Mine is David's red flannel robe. Hers is a blue silky thing, matching her blue silky nightie. They cling to her body. She still doesn't have an extra ounce of fat.

There's still enough sibling rivalry between us that I feel satisfaction that her skin is more wrinkled than mine. I examine it to project how I will look in the future.

"Any cider?" she asks. "Remember how we bought it from the Faircloughs' orchard next door right after it was made?"

"I've some from Star Market. You want it hot or cold?"

"Hot. I'm cold." She shivers.

As I pour two cups in a pan and add cinnamon sticks, a twist from the nutmeg grinder, a couple of cloves, and turn on the heat, I swallow the words, If you wore a warmer bathrobe, you wouldn't be cold. Instead I say, "Remember

Mother making it like this after football games?"

"With oatmeal cookies," she says.

"Or chocolate chips," I add.

"Or turtles? The recipe that won the Pillsbury bake-off and had nuts for the feet and head?"

"Brownies?"

"Pumpkin pie?"

"Homemade strawberry ice cream."

"Stop! We'll get fat," Jill says.

"We can't get fat talking about food. Besides, you've lost weight." I think of the person at the airport who said the same thing.

"Worry," she says.

"The girls? They seem fine."

"They are. Despite purple hair." Jill swings off her stool. Holding her cup in two hands, she walks over to the glass door. Leaning against it, she looks into the dark. "Harry's having an affair." She takes a long drink of her cider.

Any hope of confiding in my sister about Peter disappears. I look at her more closely than I have in decades, this woman who fought with me about sharing clothes until I grew too big to borrow hers. We fought over time in the bathroom, but she typed my first term paper so I could ski in New Hampshire with the church youth group. Of course, I had to listen to her lecture about doing things in advance. I never told Mother about the night I found her passed out drunk on the front step. Instead, I smuggled her into bed and talked loudly whenever I was near her the next day.

I feel selfish thinking only of myself. My sister is hurting. I put my arm around her and lead her back to the stool. She puts her cup down and picks up a spoon to stir the cider.

"Is it serious or a fling?"

"He's had lots of flings." She licks the spoon. "This has

58

lasted since spring. She's younger. Prettier. She's told me she's going to win."

"She told you!" I try to imagine Peter confronting David. I can't.

Jill shrugs. "Would you believe she came to the house to convince me to give him up? She wanted a tour, I suppose, so she could plan what she'll change."

"Did you tell Harry?"

"No. And if she said anything to him, he never mentioned it. He hasn't said he wants a divorce. My only hope is that since California is a community property state, he'll think it's too expensive to leave me." When she looks up, her mascara is smudged. "I don't know what I'll do. I haven't worked since Michelle was born." We hold each other, standing up and swaying. Then she relaxes and adds, "Don't tell anyone. Especially Mother."

I promise I won't.

Thanksgiving Day is rainy and raw. While I bake mincemeat, apple and pumpkin pies, everyone sits at the kitchen table talking.

"Any chance of Celtics tickets? They're playing the Lakers at the Garden this weekend," Harry says.

"Not a prayer," David says. I don't tell Harry or David I've a friend who could get tickets. With an amazing double standard I find myself angry at my brother-in-law for doing to my sister exactly what I'm doing to my husband.

"Make more coffee please, Liz?" David asks. Michelle offers to do it.

As I roll the crust I tell her where the coffee we order from Sweden is. "Dark roast," I say, pointing to a special airtight porcelain canister. Coffee is to David as Christ is to a born-again Christian. The crust doesn't work. I put it in the refrigerator to let the gluten relax while I work on a second batch. This one comes out round and doesn't tear when I roll it around the rolling pin and place it perfectly over the pie plate. The smells of coffee and pies mingle. I must be getting over my bug because I don't feel sick.

"You guys go to the Celtics?" Harry asks.

"My firm has season tickets. We get 'em a couple of times a year. Liz threatens me with divorce if I take anyone else." I tune the men out when they begin arguing about the Lakers versus the Celtics.

The phone rings. Jill answers it and calls me. She holds it to my ear because my hands are flour-covered.

"Happy Thanksgiving," Judy says. "Someone wants to wish you a great day." Despite the flour I grab the phone, afraid Jill will hear Peter's voice.

"Sorry to call you at home, but I needed to share a minute of today with you. Hope you're not angry," he says.

"Just the opposite. I'm thrilled," I say.

"I love you."

"Me too." I look around, but everyone is paying attention to something other than me.

"You love yourself. That's good. Everyone should love themselves," he says.

"You know what I mean."

"You mean you love me?" he asks.

"Exactly. Listen, I have to run, Mark."

"Very good. Just in case someone hears a male voice. Want me to yell I love you?" he giggles.

I want to ask him if he's been drinking. Or smoking, but I don't dare.

"Give Judy and the kids my love. And take some for yourself. No, wait a minute. Put Judy back on."

"Liz?" I picture Judy pulling off her earring before

placing the receiver next to her ear.

"Thanks, pal. That was sweet."

"I know. Enjoy."

Jill looks at me through half-lowered eyes, the same way she did when I lied to Mother and my sister knew it, but my mother didn't. Maybe it's my imagination. I tell them about Frank N. Stein, carefully deleting the Peter part.

Jill, the girls and I ride in my car. David and Harry go in the BMW with the luggage. Except we have to turn around and go back. Halfway down Route 128, David calls me on my mobile from his. He bought me one, despite my protests, in case I break down and need to call for help.

"Liz, it's me," he says, his voice distorted by static. "Harry says he left the pies on the counter. Can you go back?"

The second time we leave, the girls balance the pumpkin and mincemeat pies in their laps.

"Don't nibble the crust," Jill warns Courtney, shifting the apple pie she holds so the juice won't spill and stain her coat.

"Do you think it will snow? I want to see snow. I've only seen it when we went skiing last year in Colorado," Courtney says.

"It's too warm, stupid," Michelle says.

"They bicker like we did," Jill says. "No wonder Mother sent us to our rooms . . ." Before she can finish we arrive at the family farm, a center chimney colonial from 1756. Two pillars flank the front door. There are wooden additions to the brick house built sometime before the Civil War. We know the house was part of the Underground Railroad, offering sanctuary to runaway slaves. We found the cellar where the fugitives were hidden.

Indoor plumbing was added during World War I, electricity during the Depression and combination windows during the Korean Conflict. The roof was last replaced during Vietnam. In between repairs and national crises, generations of my family have been born, lived and died here.

The land is so stony that Moses Putnam, the first resident, had to be either terribly optimistic or not too bright to try and farm the land. Right now the land is used for an apple orchard. My brother Ben started planting dwarf trees five years ago. A pick-your-own operation supplements his income as a landscape architect. He does more of the planning than the physical work.

When we open the door we see Ben first. Because his house is down the street, he's always in and out, helping Mother.

Janice, my sister-in-law, plump and cheery as always, has five-year-old Samantha on her lap. They sit before the fire in a rocking chair. Sammy jumps off her mother's lap to distribute kisses.

"You look pretty," I say as she twirls and preens, showing off her lacy tights and red velvet dress.

"I had to threaten her with dismemberment to get her out of jeans," Janice says.

Mother is in her glory with all her chicks around. I sit next to the fire, rocking in the chair Janice vacated. The warmth makes me sleepy. The kitchen has the original fireplace. There's still the bread oven to one side and the huge metal hooks from which meats once hung. Today only marshmallows will be toasted over the fire, if anyone is still hungry after dinner and dessert. Wonderful smells surround us.

Janice whispers to me, bringing me back to the present.

"Mother has big news. Please go along with it." Then she puts her finger to her lips. I'm curious.

David, Harry and Ben go for more wood to burn. Through the window we hear muffled chopping. Mother hums to herself. I can't remember seeing her so peaceful for a long time.

The turkey comes out of the oven brown and sizzling. Mother gives me the knife. "My arthritis hurts me too much to carve well. You do it, but remember whoever cuts, someone else chooses the first piece. Including the pope's nose."

"Is that where THAT came from?" Michelle asks. She has come back into the kitchen to check the status of dinner. "Do you boil soapy water in pans when food sticks to it, Grams?"

"Yes, why?"

" 'Cause Mom always did it before we got our house-keeper."

"Let's write a book. We'll call it *My Mother, Myself,*" I say.

The kitchen table is laden with food, a tribute to gluttony. "I read the average American will put away at least seven thousand calories today," my statistic-loving sister-in-law says.

"I'll do my part," Ben says. He comes in with an armful of wood, followed by David and Harry. Rainwater glistens in my brother's beard. All their faces are bright red.

We carry food, walking carefully over uneven floorboards, into the dining room. It's a shame we only use it on holidays because it's a beautiful room with green-flocked wallpaper and wainscoting. All the furniture, china and silverware are antiques handed down from Uncle This or Aunt That. A candelabra surrounded by evergreens and pine cones decorates the table.

"Can I say grace, Grams?" Sam asks. She sits on the Boston White and Yellow Pages. Mother has covered them with a towel so the edges won't cut into her legs.

"Go ahead," Mother says. Sam directs us to hold hands. "God is great, God is good and we thank him for our food. Down the hatch, Amen."

Plates are passed back and forth. Silverware clinks against the china. "Hmms", "goods" and "wonderfuls" pepper our conversation.

I shove a sweet pickle in my cheek, my traditional end to Thanksgiving dinner. One year I had mumps. Agony is an understatement for the pain that pickle caused.

"Liz, swallow that pickle," Mother says.

"It wouldn't be Thanksgiving if Liz didn't look like a lopsided chipmunk," Ben says.

"And it wouldn't be Thanksgiving if I didn't tell her to swallow it," Mother says.

Family rituals, I think. As a teenager I hated them. Now they comfort me, reminding me of who I am. But will I be able to continue if I leave David? Would Peter be allowed to come, or would Mother refuse to accept him? She always clucks when she tells of someone getting a divorce. She'll rage on about how brave the parents are to hold up their heads despite the shame shoveled onto them by their ungrateful children.

Mother hits her fork against her water glass, bringing me back to the present. "Before the boys go and watch football, I've an announcement to make." She ignores the fact that all the boys are over forty-five. Getting up she goes to the desk between the side windows and brings out two pieces of paper, one of which I recognize as her special stationery.

For years she's ordered Wedgwood-colored paper and envelopes with her name and address engraved in a darker blue. I think of the time that she wrote my teacher: "Elizabeth-Anne was out yesterday because she decided it would be more fun to catch pollywogs than sit in class. Do with her what you like." I had handed the note in, sure that it was a normal excuse written by a parent who understood the temptations of a spring day.

Mother picks up a plain sheet. "Listen to Auntie Anne's letter first." Auntie Anne is her sister who lives in Sun City, Arizona, and is two years older than Mother.

Dear Gracie,

As I write this, I'm sitting on my patio sipping mint iced tea. I'd be bundled up if I were still in New England.

Kay, my neighbor, is coming by in a little while, and we're going to play bingo. Last week I won $10 more than I spent. I figure I'm about $100 ahead so far this year. Saturday night there's a barbecue and dance at the clubhouse. We widows go as a group and keep our eyes on the few widowers. Between them and our friends' husbands we get lots of chances to dance. The widowers are usually old farts.

"Tea on their ties and pee on their flies," Kay says. Actually she lies. None of 'em wear ties. I'm afraid to peek at their flies. Mama might rise out of her grave and lecture me on ladylike behavior.

Well, Kay's honking, and I want to drop this in a mailbox on the way.

Love ya,
Annie

Mother puts the letter down and takes up her own stationery. "The day I got her letter I was writing this." She clears her throat.

Dear Annie,

The nights are so cold. I dread winter. Heat is so expensive. The cold is murder on my arthritis.

I have a doctor's appointment next week because I'm having trouble sleeping. The kids are coming for Thanksgiving, at least giving me something to look forward to. I watch my soaps and game shows, but they're getting so boring and . . .

She puts both sheets back in the desk. "I never finished my letter. Anne's was so up, full of things she was doing, and I sounded like a complaining old cow. So I said to myself, if I don't like my life, I better change it. I'm moving to Arizona to live with Auntie Anne." Looking at each of us, she waits for our reactions.

No one says anything for an immeasurable amount of time. I stare at my mother, the woman I've called Super Whiner, never to her face, of course. I watch her eyes jump back and forth between Jill, Ben and myself. "I think it's a wonderful idea," I say, knowing she wants my blessing.

"Right on, Grams," Michelle says.

"You'll be nearer to us," Courtney says, and I see Jill wince a little.

Then we all talk at once and Mother glows in our attention.

"Will you sell the house?" David asks.

"Janice and I are moving in," Ben says. "We'll rent our place. I want to expand the orchard a bit more, add some crafts to the apple stand, and some other products like maple syrup."

"What if you don't like Arizona?" Jill asks.

"I'll come back. That's why Ben is only renting his place."

David frowns. "It doesn't seem fair." His voice is low. I touch him. He opens his mouth and closes it again.

"I don't have a problem with it," I say and Jill agrees with me. I don't want the house. Ben does. Daddy always felt the land should be worked. Ben will do that.

Mother shoves the men into the living room. Before we start to clean up, she brings out pictures of Sun City. As I pick up one of Auntie Anne standing next to a cactus, Mother says, "That cactus is over one hundred years old."

"When are you leaving?" Jill asks.

"Monday. I've my tickets, open return, good for three months. If I like it, I'll come back to pack up. Or if I really love it, maybe I'll just have Janice send what I need. Turn in the ticket. Use it for bingo money."

Mother has never played bingo. She considers it low-class and most games are held in Catholic churches. "I wouldn't be caught dead in a Catholic church," she has said.

"Bingo?" says Jill, giving Janice and me a who-is-that-woman-in-Mother's-body look. I need to readjust my picture of Mother as a whiny old lady, incapable of doing things for herself.

When we finish stacking the dishwasher with the first load and Janice and Jill are quietly talking, Mother motions for me to follow her. We go upstairs to my old room. It's much like when I lived in it, except the floor and braided rugs aren't hidden by clothes, records, papers and books. The spread and curtains haven't changed.

She pulls a large box from under my old brass bed.

Mother is such a fanatic housekeeper there is no dust at all on the box, even though it was there for God knows how long.

"This will be Samantha's room." She never calls her granddaughter Sam or Sammy like the rest of us do.

For years her house has been a storage bin for our childhood possessions. I've thrown out almost everything like my prom dresses. My *Nancy Drew*, *Bobbsey Twins*, Thornton W. Burgesses and *Beverly Gray* books have been given to my nieces. So have my dolls and games. My report cards through my Ph.D. and my textbooks are in my office.

My memory book, a collection of souvenirs from high school, rests on top of the box. I open it. There are ticket stubs from every football game with the final score written in and a program where I'm listed as an alternative to the baton squad. I only marched twice and both times I wore the uniform until bedtime.

There's a napkin that Bill Gilgun touched after asking me to dance. During my freshman year he was a senior. He dated another senior, Corneilia. Her nickname, Neil, seemed to me the ultimate in sophistication.

A large envelope holds senior photos of my chums, most of whom I haven't seen since graduation. My name is written in the upper left-hand corner, theirs in the bottom right. Great wisdom is written on the back like, "We'll never forget homeroom and U.S. History," but I did forget. I wonder if they have, too.

There are diaries, one for each high school year. I open randomly to a page. I read about how Jason ditched me for Barbara Cann. I made voodoo dolls of them and stuck them with pins. The doll is in the box, too.

Mother touches a piece of lavender ribbon from an old corsage. "I remember this. You wore it the night you drove to the Christmas assembly." I'm amazed she remembers. It started to snow during the dance.

"I was positive you'd have an accident," she says.

"I called home to ask which way to turn the wheel if we skidded."

"Which didn't help my worrying at all. Or the time Tommy Marks picked you up. He drove into the yard very carefully and you bounced out of the house and asked him if that was as fast as he could go. He peeled out of the driveway. I thought if you came back alive, I'd kill you." She puts the lavender ribbon back. "Almost every day I wished your father were here to help me. Sometimes I was mad at him as if he died on purpose."

We sit side by side on the bed, my youth spread around us. There's a photo of the Christmas after Daddy died. Jill, Ben and my mother sit on the floor. I'd taken the picture with my new Kodak. A puppy, our gift to Jill, chews on a candy cane. Mother looked so young and pretty. "How old were you?"

She thinks a moment. "Thirty-nine."

My age now. Wow.

She draws in her breath as she does when she has something to say. "I've rehearsed this speech, so don't stop me, Liz. I know I've been difficult, and I want to thank you for putting up with me. I'm going to try and be different."

My mother is sixty-nine years old. For years she has developed moping into an art form. When I call her, it is with dread of the litany of pains and slights she will chant. I pat her hand, feeling closer to her than I ever have in my life.

"You're my mother." It's not much to say, but I can't think of anything else.

"Annie laid me out in lavender for being such a pain to you kids. She says when I get out there, every time I complain, she'll slug me. And when I act happy she'll hug me."

"I'd opt for hugs," I say.

"I haven't been hugged in years. I miss it."

"You never hugged us kids," I say.

"I didn't want to spoil you." She picks lint out of her apron pocket. I reach over to hug her, but she doesn't relax in my arms. Maybe she needs practice.

The late night, the big meal and the conversation have worn me out. "I'm so sleepy. Can I nap?" I ask.

As I stretch out, she throws an afghan over me. It is one she knitted before her fingers grew too stiff to move the needles. Mother pulls down the paper shade and shuts the door.

I look at the room where I spent most every night until I got married. I was born in this room. Mother could never tell us how many hours she suffered in childbirth. Ben took forty-five minutes, Jill came in thirty, and I popped out in twenty while she waited for Daddy to get the car to take her to the hospital.

I think in what good hands Mother will be. I adore Auntie Anne. When we were children she'd take the three of us for weekends. It must have given Mother a break while keeping Auntie Anne from being lonely, but I didn't think of that then.

Auntie Anne's husband had been killed in World War II and she never remarried. According to family rumor, denied with each retelling, she had a three-decade romance with her married boss. Maybe infidelity is genetic.

We did things on those weekends we never did at home, like sleeping in a tent in the living room, or making cookies and eating all the dough raw. One day we played football in the supermarket using toilet paper as the ball. The manager asked us to leave. Auntie Anne stuck her tongue out at his departing back.

I realize that today was the first time I thought of Mother, not as Mother, but as a woman with her own feelings. I have given her far less rights to her own feelings than I give to my students or friends. Sitting up straight, I wonder if I am being equally unfair to David in not granting him his own personality and reasons for it.

A quiet tap on the door and Sammy pokes around the corner. "You asleep, Aunt Liz?"

"No, sweetie." She hops onto the bed next to me and cuddles in.

"How come you're taking a nap?"

"I was tired."

"I hate naps. They're for babies."

"Lots of adults consider it a real treat to take a nap."

Sammy looks at me in disbelief. "Nahhhhh." She lets the h's roll off her tongue and makes a face.

"Do you know this was my room when I was little and next it will be yours?" Maybe the idea of me as a little girl is as hard for her to believe as the idea that some people like naps. "I used to make up stories about those water stains on the ceiling. No matter how often we painted over them, they always came back." I point to one. "That spot there used to be a teddy bear."

We make up a meandering tale about the teddy bear that wants to go swimming but the fish spot on the ceiling keeps tickling him. A knock interrupts. Sammy lets her grandmother in then runs downstairs. For the first time in a couple of years I really regret not having kids.

Mother bustles around folding up the afghan, even though I never said I wanted to get up. "Janice is really looking forward to living here. It really surprised me how she has settled down after all the moving around."

My sister-in-law was a diplomat's kid. She'd lived in eight countries and Washington, D.C.

"Probably she likes the stability," I say.

"I always thought she'd desert poor Ben, and . . ." Mother looks shocked when I hit her.

"Getting you in practice for Auntie Anne." I smile at her.

"Well, Janice has been a good wife and mother," she says.

I hug her and although she doesn't relax, she is a little less tight than before.

The fog has rolled in, reducing visibility drastically. New England doesn't have that many foggy days. It scares me when I drive in it. At least if I skid in the snow I can see what I'm going to crash into. All the drivers have reduced their speed to a maximum of thirty miles an hour. I hunch over the wheel, as if a few inches could make a difference on how far ahead I can see.

I arrive before David, who had been talking to Ben when I left. Once in the house I clean up the remainder of the pie-making that I was too rushed to do earlier.

My husband enters and I know by the way that he moves that he's fuming. If I don't ask, maybe he'll calm down. No such luck.

He starts spitting out words. "Are you going to stop your mother?" He still wears his coat and gloves as he paces around the kitchen.

"I think Arizona will be good for her. Why should I stop her?"

"I don't mean about her moving. The house. With the land it must be worth a million at an absolute minimum."

"What's your point?"

He slaps his gloves onto the countertop. "God, Liz, you're so innocent. Your mother scraped for years while sitting on a gold mine. If she'd sold it she could have invested it and made life easier for herself."

If I'm innocent, David has a one-track mind, and although I know it's useless, I want to explain. Just once I want him to see my point of view. "You don't understand. She couldn't sell it. She had to keep it for Ben. It has been passed down to the oldest son for over a hundred years. My brother wants it."

David unbuttons his coat. He speaks slowly as if I were some child unable to grasp simple facts. "Of course he wants it. It's worth a fortune. And what happens if your mother has to go into a nursing home? Who'll pay for that?"

"Maybe we could sell it then. Or better, keep it and split the payments between the three of us."

"You have no money sense. That house should be divided between the three of you."

That's not how our family does things. For all our bickering we are solid. A unit. When David's brother was in the hospital, we only learned about it after he was out. It wouldn't have mattered because I'm sure David wouldn't have visited. His sister didn't, and she knew. "That's not how we do things. Daddy didn't have to share it with Uncle Archer or Uncle Walter."

"So because of some outdated family tradition you and Jill are going to let Ben scoop your inheritance out from under your noses?"

I want to scream and throw things. Instead, I wimp out once again. "Let's change the subject," I say.

David keeps poking at the topic, following me around as I finish cleaning up the kitchen. Still silent, I go to bed. He doesn't follow me. When he comes to bed, I pretend to be asleep.

I'm sick most of the rest of the weekend and beg off from a Saturday-night dinner with the family. I'd love to be with them, but David is still angry over the house, and going out there would just make things worse, even if I felt up to it.

"But I'm baking beans and brown bread from scratch," Mother says when she calls me to invite us.

"Please, no food," I beg.

Jill and Janice visit Saturday afternoon and sit on my bed and we talk about nothing, everything and Mother.

Janice makes a pot of herb tea and brings me dry toast. "You'll probably lose all the weight you gained at Thanksgiving. I'm jealous." She pats her ample stomach.

When they leave, David, who has been working in his study, complains about my hanging around in bed. He was semi-sympathetic, despite the undercurrent of tension, until he took my temperature and found it normal.

"Are you going to get dinner?" he asks.

"I don't feel like cooking."

"I'll go to a restaurant. I can bring the work I need to do with me," he says.

He leaves Sunday at noon for Dallas. My sister and her family go with him because their planes leave at the same time. Ben drives them to our place where they shift everything to David's car. A man from his office will pick up the BMW the next day. It took a lot of phone calls to work out the logistics.

All I had to do was listen to the plans being made. I have made the effort to dress in jeans and a Fenway sweatshirt over a turtleneck, but I can't seem to get warm. As Ben and I stand in the driveway waving good-bye, his arm around my shoulder, he says, "You look like hell, baby sister."

"Thanks."

"Come on inside. I'll make you some tea." He putters around my kitchen as I sit on the chaise longue in my bedroom. He brings me a tray.

"You're sweet."

"Your husband doesn't think so."

"Why?"

"He said that he thought I should offer you and Jill a cash settlement on the house. How do you feel about it?"

"David should mind his own business. Let's stick with our family tradition."

"Jill said the same thing. Harry was a little upset, too."

Ben brought a cup of tea for himself. He sniffs it. "Did Jill seem unhappy to you?" That's a strange question from my brother. He's one of the few straight talkers in the family. Mother and her sisters talk around situations. For example, when Mother wants to know something about Aunt Ruth she'll call Auntie Anne, who says, "If you want to know something about Ruth, call her directly."

"Why?" I ask my brother.

"I thought she might have said something to you."

God! I hope my brother and I aren't playing the family indirect game. Yet I won't give away Jill's secret. Then it dawns on me that maybe she did talk to Ben, and he's fishing to see if I know.

"I thought maybe if she were having some marital problems, I'd offer to have her and the girls stay with us." Ben dangles his line again.

This time I bite. "She did talk to you."

"I wanted to string the bastard up. I know Jill can be a bitch, but she's still my sister, and I don't want anyone messing her over."

75

"Did you say anything to Harry?"

"God no. If it works out, it's better he doesn't know we know. I didn't say anything to Janice either, except if Harry dies I want Jill and the kids with us."

"And she said . . ."

"My wife adopts any stray—animal, vegetable or mineral."

He gets up to go. "Wanta come back with me so you won't be alone?" I refuse to go with him, because I just want to sleep. He rumples my already messed-up hair.

After he leaves, I feel too lousy even to call Peter.

CHAPTER FIVE

I feel so miserable on Monday that I call in sick, something I almost never do. I make a doctor's appointment before calling Peter to share my misery.

"Too bad you're not here, I make a great borscht. Good for what ails you," he says.

"It's chicken soup that's healing," I say.

"Can I help it if I'm Russian, not Jewish?" He tells me how his grandfather was a chef for the Russian aristocracy until the Revolution. "He ended up in Seattle, opened a restaurant that my uncles have expanded into a local chain."

I knew why he hadn't wanted to be a banker like his father, but having a ready-made restaurant seemed to me to be perfect for him. "Why didn't you join the business?"

"I had to come to Boston to meet you. There's a line forming. Call me after you see the doctor."

Finding a spot in the Reading Medical Center parking lot is difficult because the Boys Club annual Christmas tree sale occupies half the space. The evergreen smell is tantalizing. Pine needles form a green carpet as I walk into the building.

A fake tree in the foyer of the medical center is a poor substitute for the real things outdoors. Someone has sprayed a fake pine odor that makes me feel woozy. I win the battle not to throw up.

Mrs. O'Connor, the receptionist, is seated at a desk next to the tree. She's bundled in a sweater, probably against drafts, which she always cautions others to avoid. She may send patients to the wrong doctor, but she'll also hand them homemade cookies as they leave. Four or five years ago, the doctors decided paperwork and Mrs. O'Connor were a recipe for disaster, so now all she does is knit sweaters and scarves and misdirect people.

A central waiting room has toys for children. *American Baby* has been contributed by the gynecologist. The orthodontist donated *Sports Illustrated*, *McCalls* and *Newsweek*. I pick up the same issue of *McCalls* I read at my last two annual checkups. Although I need to piddle, I wait, knowing the doctor will want a sample.

My turn comes and the nurse redirects me into the changing room. She hands me a paper johnny that ties in the back.

Dr. French looks like a very old Mr. Spock from the first *Star Trek* series, only with normal ears. Come to think of it, probably Mr. Spock looks old these days. French has been the Adamses' family doctor since my husband was a little boy. It was from him that I learned David's mother ran off with another man. David always changed the subject when I asked about her.

I list my complaints as Dr. French does his usual weigh-in, blood pressure and urine tests. Everything is normal. So is my temperature. "Let's try an internal," he says.

I want to say let's not, but I don't. The paper johnny crackles as I slide to the bottom of the examining table and place my feet in the stirrups. Looking up, I see a smiley face on the ceiling. Dr. French, having iced his instruments, attacks.

If I'd a choice of going to the dentist or having an internal, the dentist would win every time. Thinking of the dentist keeps my mind off what is going on in my pelvic area, not that I like dentists either. My childhood dentist never used Novocain. After my breasts developed, when he wiped his fingers on the towel around my neck, he pinched my nipples. I told Mother, who wasn't sure I was telling the truth until Jill said he'd done it to her, too. Our new dentist used Novocain and kept his hands in my mouth. By the time I finish these memories the internal is over.

"Hmm," Dr. French says. Hmm during sex has one meaning. Hmm during a physical can mean lots of things. "Get dressed. I'll see you in my office."

Back in my jeans and sweatshirt, I knock on his door. He types notes onto his computer. High technology doesn't belong with his desk, which has a hunting scene with deer and bears carved into the almost-black wood.

Looking over his half-moon glasses, he motions for me to sit.

"When did you have your last period?"

I think. I've always been irregular. Once the possibility of pregnancy was ruled out, I never paid much attention. When they come they leave me doubled over in agony. "Maybe after vacation in July. Before that sometime in May."

"I'm going to run another test, but I think you're pregnant. Somewhere between two and three months, I'd guess."

I've heard of people saying their mouth dropped open, but I never gave it much credence until my mouth dropped.

"You're a nurse, you must have thought about it," Dr. French says.

He waits for my reaction. Five years ago I'd used up half a box of tissues when he told me I probably couldn't have children. It happened after I'd thought a case of flu was a pregnancy. He had the GYN in the practice run some tests.

My ovaries weren't good egg producers. Dr. French as my main doctor elected to tell me himself.

I sit there blinking.

"Maybe it's fibroids." Getting fibroids is like getting gray hair. What's a good present for a fortieth birthday? Fibroids. Gift-wrapped in a womb.

"Possible. Not probable." He gives me instructions on giving him a clean urine sample. "I'll want to do an amniocentesis. At about fourteen, fifteen weeks, if we can guess when that will be. I'll try doing a sonar to help determine how far along you are."

Back in the car I sit stunned, my hands on the wheel, my knuckles white. The key dangles in the ignition. I try and remember when David and I last had sex. Considering how infrequently we do make love, I shouldn't have a problem. In July we did it three times. We were on vacation. It had been so much like the early days of our marriage that I almost broke off with Peter when I came back.

But once I saw Peter after he came back from his camping trip out west in mid-August, I ran into his arms. We'd made love for hours. After years of only occasional sex with limited enjoyment, I relished Peter's lovemaking. According to the sex manuals, a woman peaks at thirty-nine. Peter is benefiting from my age-driven lust.

Did David and I make love after that? I think back to Labor Day when we had been to a barbecue at his sister's. I'd had too much to drink. David kept caressing me. I just wanted to fall asleep. I couldn't have been so drunk that I forgot having sex with my husband.

I touch my stomach. Another life may be inside me. Instinct tells me I'm touching Peter's child. Common sense tells me it's time to make a decision.

The radio comes on when I start the engine. A talk show

has replaced the music program on when I left the car. The Right-to-Lifers battle the Right-to-Choosers. "People who want and need abortions will get them. Women should be safe, not the victim of some back-room butcher," someone says.

I remember reading an article by a woman who, in 1970, flew with a pregnant co-worker to Montreal. She couldn't face an abortion alone. That was before *Roe* v. *Wade*. The arrangements had been made by The Clergy Council, a group of ministers and rabbis, who felt women were entitled to safe abortions. They sent girls all over the world to qualified doctors. I fall on the pro-choice side. I have enough trouble making my own decisions. I have no right to make them for others. For a time when I was trying so hard to get pregnant, I wondered if God was punishing me for thinking that way. As a nurse I know guilt and ovary functions have little correlation. As a woman who considered every period a denial of something fundamental in me, I reacted irrationally.

If I am truly pregnant, I don't have to have the baby. I can get a safe abortion.

Peter and I discussed birth control after the first time we made love. We decided it wasn't necessary after I told him my medical history. I'd been at the stand and halfway through the talk, I'd giggled. He asked me what was funny. I said, "I'm talking about birth control with a chickpea. Would our children be human or vegetable?"

"They'd be beautiful but we couldn't let them near the Jolly Green Giant at harvesttime," he said. Then he'd taken my hands and kissed the palms. "I wish we could have a child together." The conversation ended when a customer wanted coffee and couscous. Saying someone wants a child is one thing. Having a child is less romantic than the idea.

★ ★ ★ ★ ★

At home after giving the housekeeper the afternoon off, I wander from room to room. Using the remote control I try every television station. My maximum attention span is approximately nineteen seconds on any one of my sixty-three possible selections.

Mother told us if we had to make a choice, list the pros and cons on a sheet of paper. I shut off the television and go to my study. My computer juts out on a stand. I bring up my word processing and make two columns marked ABORTION and NO ABORTION. I use boldface, underline and capitalize them. There are no more options to delay my list-making. I move the cursor to the NO ABORTION column halfway across the screen.

ABORTION	NO ABORTION
Don't have to tell David	Fenway has maternity leave
Don't have to tell Peter	I want the baby
Don't have to tell Mother	I want the baby
No career interruption	I want the baby
David won't think it's his	I want the baby
Peter won't think it's David's	I want the baby

I couldn't have an abortion, no matter what the consequences. I want my baby.

Labeling two new columns DAVID and PETER, I underline, use boldface and capitalize. I wish I could buy a software package to make my personal decisions for me. If I were a programmer, maybe I could create one. It would sell better than Microsoft. I don't make the list. I'm not ready to deal with it.

After deleting the document, I drive to the next town to

buy a pregnancy kit. I don't want to wait for the doctor's call. The box has a photo of two women and two men. All four people are happy. One couple is delighted that she is pregnant, the other is equally happy that she's not. There is no woman with two men. The test is positive.

To stop morning sickness, I try eating saltines before getting up. I throw up anyway. So much for the cracker idea. When this is all over I will have something for this discomfort. Knowing a baby and not the flu is why I'm sick, I go to work.

My Wednesday course, "Philosophy of Nursing," is required for all nursing students. After so many fact courses, it's fun dealing in concepts. It's taught once every four years so all the nursing students take it at the same time. I like students of different levels sharing the same material. Because of the size, I lecture in the amphitheater, the only room large enough to hold 200.

The amphitheater has just been renovated. Blue corduroy seats have replaced the old torn red plush. Fake teak boards on the right sides of the chairs are for note-taking. Tough tutus to lefties. This was a battle that Dean Whittier lost to President Baker.

The idea of information going from my notes to their notebooks never appealed to me. I owe my students more. As a teenager I pretended I was a rock star, singing to my image in the mirror and using a carrot for a microphone. I incorporate techniques I've stolen from storytellers and singers, striding about the stage, posturing and doing whatever will stimulate my kids.

The students never know when I'm going to call on them, start a debate or make them role-play. Despite the possibility, students tell me this is their favorite course.

They even tell me that after I'm no longer in a position to grade them.

One of my suspected anorexics is seated in the first row. When I ask how she's doing, she says fine. I want to say, "No, I mean REALLY, how are you doing?" but I don't. Instead, I tell her I'm available if she needs me. She won't come to me. I know the pattern too well.

Onstage I push a pile of blue exam books aside to write myself a note to call Judy about the anorexics after class. If all the words written in blue books were placed end to end, I bet they would cover the world. Whoever sells blue books to universities must make a fortune.

These test books belong to Dr. Henry Sumner, who taught the class before mine. He's nowhere to be seen.

Melissa Greenbaum runs from behind the curtain where there are three dressing rooms. She's crying. A few minutes into my lecture Dr. Sumner collects his stuff. He avoids looking at me, but he never looks anyone in the eye.

I act my way through my first hour and a half. Eat your heart out, Meryl Streep. Then I ask the students to role-play. A nurse has to deal with a father and mother who can't agree on approving a treatment for their child.

Amanda Silver, daughter of a Broadway actor and actress, volunteers. As a child she acted in several plays, TV commercials, and a movie where she was possessed by the devil. She told me that film paid for her four years of college education. After she finishes playing the distraught mother, the kids clap. I wonder if maybe she should have stayed in acting. Her grades are only mediocre. But when she did her internship on the wards last semester, she was brilliant with patients.

After class, Mary O'Brien waits outside the amphitheater. My eyes stray to her tummy hidden under a bulky sweater. We are in the same situation—pregnant—with a man in our lives who won't take the news well. The difference is that my baby was created in love, hers in violence.

"Come to my office," I say.

"I want to thank you for all you've done, Dr. Adams," she says.

"It wasn't all that much, Mary." I'm not being modest. Judy and Dean Whittier did most of what Mary needed. "When are you leaving?"

"Next week after I finish one more paper. I'm getting full credit for this semester."

I can just imagine Dean Whittier cajoling professors to give Mary as much consideration as possible. The phone rings.

"Can you come to Atlanta?" David asks.

"Thank you, I'm feeling much better." My doppleganger takes over, shoving the words right by my teeth. I love my coward's tools—sarcasm and wisecracks in place of serious discussion. I wish I could say, "I want you to show me the same civilities you show your clients." I can't.

"Don't start, Liz," he says. "My client has a daughter who wants to be a nurse. He wants to know about opportunities for her. He really doesn't approve of her choice, but I said that you'd give him the big picture."

"When?" My husband doesn't want me: he wants my value-added service to his client.

"Thursday night."

"My last class finishes at one, but I have Friday classes."

"Find someone to cover Friday. Fly down Thursday afternoon. We've reservations at the Czar's Palace at nine. You'll have an incredible meal."

What I want to say is how pissed off I am that he left me

sick, that he didn't call to see how I was doing, but called only for a business need. I hate it when he tells me how to handle my own job. My work means as much to me as his does to him.

What I say is, "OK."

"Good. Call Sylvia and let her know. She'll book it for you. Also ask her to fax me the copy of the Wilson contract. Have her call the Atlanta Marriott first so they can put it in an envelope marked confidential the second it comes off the machine."

"I thought you were in Dallas?"

"That was yesterday." The phone clicks.

"Good-bye," I say, remembering when David had time for amenities.

"I'm sorry, Mary, for the interruption." She looks so vulnerable. Her hair is fastened back with two barrettes. Mary only needs a ruff to pass as the young Queen Elizabeth I's double.

"I guess I've made the best choice out of all the bad ones." She speaks fast as many first-generation Irish do, totally free of a brogue but combining the Boston accent with the Irish lilt.

During our conversation, we start to sweat. The heating system has major problems. In my tenure three janitors have failed to regularize the temperature that within five minutes can vary by twenty degrees. Mary fans herself.

"I'll open a window," I say. For a minute she thinks I mean it until she realizes that I haven't any windows. She smiles. I'm glad she still can. "Write me and tell me how you're doing—if you feel like it. And I'm really looking forward to seeing you next fall."

She gets up and puts out her hand to shake mine. "I don't know how I'll ever repay you."

"Easy. Do what you have to do and come back. Finish your education. Become the best damned nurse you can." She starts to leave and I say, "I know it sounds sappy, but my dad had a philosophy. When someone does you a good turn, pass it on."

Mary has been gone less than two minutes when Melissa Greenbaum appears at the door. "Can I talk with you, Dr. Adams?"

"Sure." Since she's an excellent student it can't be academic. She sits down, arranging her designer-everything-clad body in my free chair. I mean real designer. Yves St. Laurent, not just Liz Claiborne. This is one rich kid, although not a spoiled brat like some students. Her father is president of a pharmaceutical company where Melissa works summers. Last August one of the deans had to call her, and he went through three of Melissa's secretaries before he reached her.

I love the variety of kids in my classes. In the amphitheater I saw a sheik's daughter sitting next to a scholarship student from the ghetto whose parents were drug addicts.

"I don't quite know how to start." She picks up the paper clips from a magnetic holder on my desk and rearranges them. I wait. "I'm not doing well in Dr. Sumner's class."

Sumner teaches chemistry. He's a hard teacher, but the kids learn their stuff. That Melissa isn't doing well surprises me. "Why didn't you go to your department head?"

Melissa blushes, the first time I have ever seen her do that. "I needed to confide in a woman."

"Which means you haven't talked to Dr. Sumner, either."

"He's the problem. I definitely couldn't go to him."

The phone rings. I tell Peter I'll call him back after I

finish with a student and prepare my next class.

Picking up on my answer, Melissa mouths, "I can come back another time."

I motion for her to sit down. Then I promise Peter that I really will call back.

Before Melissa can start her next sentence, Tina Masters, my graduate assistant, pops her head in the door. Tina's nickname is Chunky Butt, which she accepts as a reasonable description of her body, not a racial slur.

"Excuse me, Melissa," I say. "Tina, can you monitor my classes Friday? David wants me to impress some clients Thursday night in Atlanta."

Tina claims to be five feet. I bet she doesn't hit four-foot-eleven. Despite her proportionately large rear end, she's ninety pounds of energy. Raised on Blue Hill Avenue, one of ten children, she fought her way through Boston Latin, graduating tops in her class. She won a full scholarship to Boston University and is now working her way through graduate school. Tina agrees to show my classes a film and to pass out study guidelines for the final.

"Never mind, Professor Adams," Melissa gets up. "I'll work it out."

"Are you sure?" I ask.

She nods and picks up her books, which she carries in a French schoolchild's book bag. The label says NafNaf. She hoists it onto her back.

"I'm sure."

I call Sylvia and give her David's list of things to do.

Fighting to stay awake while driving home, I land on the sofa where I fall asleep. My coat substitutes for a blanket. The phone wakes me. I'm barely aware of where I am. It's dark outside. When I'd fallen asleep the sun was pouring in.

I grope for the phone, knocking it onto the floor.

"What's wrong?" Peter asks. "Are you avoiding me?"

"No," I say.

"Liz, lie to me if you will. Don't insult my intelligence. I haven't seen you since before Thanksgiving."

"I've been sick. I'm behind in my work. I have to go to Atlanta tomorrow."

"Come spend the night with me?"

"I'm exhausted."

"What if I catch the train out and drive you back?"

I say no. I tell him I'm going to bed and will call him the second I get back from Atlanta.

"I love you," he says.

I tell him I love him. Saying it is so natural now. I wonder why it was so hard the first time. He hangs up first and the click severs something inside me. I want to call him back, run to him, ask him to protect me. Leaving my coat on the couch, I go to bed.

CHAPTER SIX

We take off over the harbor then turn back inland, heading towards Atlanta. After the safety film about exits, oxygen and life vests, I realize that I've never, ever checked to see if a life jacket was really under my seat. Maybe all these years the attendants have lied and the only vest is the one used for the safety demonstration.

I ride in first class, as I always do when I travel as David's wife. The stewardesses or attendants, whatever their title is these days, keep putting the drink carts away to strap themselves into their seats.

The pilot's voice comes over the intercom. His drawl tells of magnolias and mint juleps. "We're experiencing some turbulence and I'd like y'all to stay in your seats."

When the plane drops, I reach for the barf bag. Normally, I take pride in being a good bad-weather traveler. Last summer when Peter and I went on a whale watch, we were caught in a sudden storm. Everyone else was green, hanging over the railing or lying on benches retching into bags. I watched the waves crashing against the deck, loving the power of the storm.

Once on the ground, I stagger toward a man holding a sign with my name on it over his head. He's wearing a riverboat gambler's hat, boots and a blue pinstripe suit. He introduces himself. "Ah was sent by your husband, ma'am. He couldn't get away . . . meet you . . ." Some of his words get lost in his curly red beard. Since I'd been planning to take a taxi—and considering how woozy I feel—this service is a delight.

"Luggage?" he asks.

"I've only this." I hand him my carry-on bag. It's brilliant red and not much larger than my briefcase, but lighter. Of course, I don't have my briefcase. He throws the strap over his shoulder.

"Most women bring lots of suitcases." He leads me to a stretch limo. My suitcase looks like a drop of blood in the empty trunk that would have held my sister's ten pieces and still have room left. The chauffeur holds the door for me, tipping his hat to the policeman, who smiles and tips his cap in return. I guess he didn't take the growling course that the Boston airport cops seem required to take.

The area between the airport and downtown Atlanta looks like Berlin must have after the last bomb fell. Everything is under construction. Then again it looks like Boston during the Big Dig.

"We want to expand our convention capacity," he explains. "I've my doubts that we'll ever get back the money." Only he says, "Ah've ma da-outs." If we were in Boston, I'd say he had an accent. If I am in Atlanta I am the one who talks funny. "Anyway, ah'm not shur we need all them politicians running 'round the city."

"Does anyone?" I say as we pull into the Marriott. The doorman has the door open almost before we stop. Like a woman in a perfume ad, I strut into the lobby where the desk clerk gives me a magnetic key card to David's room.

Standing in the lobby I look up seventy stories. Rooms edge the balconies. A glass elevator takes me to the thirty-fifth floor. My key card inserts into the door slot of 3508, only nothing happens. I rattle the knob. I push against the door. I check to see if it is the right card. As a security measure there is no number on the card, but I have a separate guest slip that says my room is 3508. When I read the directions telling me to remove the card before opening the door, the key card works just fine.

Petals from a bouquet of mixed flowers litter David's papers, which are spread out around the coffee table. His laptop sits on the desk. Spying the king-sized bed in the next room, I take off my clothes and crawl between the spread and blanket, too sleepy to pull out the sheets locked between the mattress and the box spring.

David shakes me awake. "Am I glad to see you. We have to hurry."

I stretch like a cat, slowly, extending each body part in turn, then rub my eyes.

"You look like a little girl when you do that," he says and pats me. He goes into the bathroom. I hear the buzz of his shaver as I unpack my never-wrinkle-so-let's-wear-it-to-client-dinners dress and throw it on the bed.

In the bathroom there are flower-shaped soaps in a shell-shaped dish. I choose the rose. "Have I got time to shower?" David doesn't hear until I touch his arm to get his attention. He shuts off the razor, and I repeat my question.

"If you hurry. If you don't need to do your hair."

I'd washed my hair that morning. It's frizzy from sleeping on it. David is irritating me more because of the past annoyances than from anything in particular he's doing at the moment. His tone is quite gentle and not the least barking. I tell myself to be more adult as I strip for one of the fastest showers in history. After I dress, I pin up my hair, hiding the frizz.

The restaurant is a memory restaurant that forever will serve as a benchmark for me against which I'll measure all other restaurants. I feel as if I've entered a palace with gold-trimmed moldings and parquet floors. The decorator must have taken Versailles as his inspiration. No menus are given as we are seated in gilt chairs upholstered in a light green silk. I wonder how many glasses of wine have been spilled on them. Do they keep extra fabric to replace stained?

A man, dressed in a Russian peasant blouse with buttons on the shoulder and flowing sleeves, approaches our table. He has one hand behind his back. "I'm Omar, your waiter. I will take care of you and only you this evening."

He brings out two yellow roses, one for me and the other for Aggie Lou, the wife of David's client. Then Omar recites the five courses. Standing with both hands behind his back, he listens to each of us order. Waiters must have to pass a memory test before being hired.

Although I want to ask Omar where he's from, I don't. David hates it when I talk to people other than the transactional type of conversation required. He doesn't care that our bank teller is newly engaged, or Angela at the supermarket feels better since she started wearing elastic stockings. I love to delve into bits and pieces of other people's lives, but I know better than to do it in front of a client.

Tom Freeman, Aggie Lou's husband, suffers from PMS—Petite Man Syndrome—a condition peculiar to short males who compensate for lack of height by dominating everyone and everything around them. Even though I've never seen it written up in a medical text, I know it exists. Freeman is proof.

I keep myself amused by trying to pin down which thing about Tom is the most disagreeable. In the top three is his constant motion. He shifts in his seat, drums his fingers on the table, picks up and puts down his silverware repeatedly.

"Let's get this show on the road," he says when the drinks don't arrive seconds after we ordered them. Fortunately, Omar appears in less than three minutes with four small glasses of vodka.

"Which flavor did you order, Liz?" David asks.

I know he knows, but it is his way of being social. "Lemon."

"Mine's tea, do you want to try it?" I tell him yes. We exchange swallows.

"Mine is . . ." Aggie Lou starts.

"Cherry. You ordered cherry," Tom says. He reaches over and tastes hers and puts his glass in front of her. She obediently tries his before he grabs it back.

Although I've never been overly fond of vodka, this is wonderful. Alcohol may not be good for my baby, but dimming my senses against Tom and Aggie Lou has merit.

"Is Liz short for Elizabeth?" Aggie Lou asks and when I nod, she says, "My real name is Agnes . . ."

"Agnes Louise. She's named for her two aunts," Tom says. "Aunt Agnes. Aunt Louise."

It's going to be a long evening, I decide, a very long evening. I tune out the conversation. Aggie Lou's hair is only a slightly modified version of a Dolly Parton wig. Maybe she stole one from Dolly.

Before the first course arrives, I need to use the bathroom. Although I'd have preferred going alone, Aggie Lou and I wend our way between the tables locked in the well-known women's ritual of a group piddle. Men go by themselves.

Standing in front of the ladies' room mirror, she compliments me on the naturalness of my skin. It sounds like an insult that I'm not wearing makeup.

When she starts on my hair, I tell her I had it cut in

Paris. It's not a lie. My beauty salon is named Paris Dreams. Aggie Lou pokes at her curls and wonders if she should simplify the style.

"I'll ask Tom," she says. This will be a very, very, very long evening.

Sometimes I think David's clients come from a cookie cutter. They're all rich and successful. Their success has erased their need to listen to anyone except themselves.

Through the hors d'oeuvres, salad and soup, that tiny man tells me all about nursing and what his daughter faces both in her courses and work afterwards. He keeps jabbing me with his finger to make his point. I resist the temptation to bite it.

David at one point puts his hand under the table and pats me on the leg. I appreciate his show of sympathy. The rest of the evening is lost in a haze of smugness of getting out of the market before the crash and some of the best food I have ever eaten in my life.

Back at the hotel elevator, as we rise to our room I watch the floors fall away. David put his arm around me. "I'm really glad you came. I know you hated it."

"I really did. Except for the meal, that is."

"You're so good with my clients. Do you know what Tom said when you and Aggie Lou went to the little girls' room right before we left?"

I shake my head.

"He said you confirmed all he thought about nursing. He was glad you came so he can go home and tell his daughter she should find another career."

"I never said anything about nursing. He told me about it."

"I know. But he thinks you did. That's what counts." He

95

puts his hand on my head and pulls it to his shoulder. "Let's not talk about business."

We walk like lovers, hand in hand, from the elevator to our room. David has no trouble with the key card.

The bed has been turned down. There's a chocolate-covered mint in a black envelope on each of our pillows. David unwraps his and puts it in my mouth. The black chocolate is bitter against the tingly mint. He kisses me. "Thanks for tonight, Liz." He unbuttons my dress without my asking. I'm convinced that buttons on the back of dresses are a designer plot to make women feel incompetent. My husband slips the dress off my shoulders and caresses my breasts. "Let's make love. It's been too long."

I agree with a kiss, ignoring the part of me which wants to say no. I've never said no to him in all our years of marriage. Sleeping with my husband makes me feel unfaithful to Peter. Spiritually unfaithful. Sleeping with Peter makes me feel unfaithful to David from the perspective of what society says is right and wrong. It shouldn't be a sin to make love with the man you're married to, but it feels like it.

His lovemaking is gentle and silent. The earth doesn't move or anything, but it's not repulsive. "Was it good for you?" he asks.

I say yes. He always asks the same question and I always answer positively. It's too late to start being honest with him. My lies make him my victim. I wonder what would have happened in our marriage if the first time he'd asked, I had said I didn't feel much.

Instead of rolling away, he snuggles up against me, his arm over my hip. It's the first time in eight years that he has done that.

The last thing I need now to confuse me even more, if that is possible, is the reappearance of the old David, the one who existed before he caught the scent of power and money. I feel sad when I think of the early days when he balanced his ambition against the needs of our marriage.

Our first year together we ate popcorn in bed and watched horror movies. We had snowball fights as we shoveled snow. Maybe the goofy memories are part of what kept me with him. Then again, being a success is not a recognized cause of divorce in Massachusetts, much less with my family. For a minute I picture Mother's face if I said, I'm leaving David because he's too successful.

At seven the next morning room service knocks, jarring me awake. With my eyes closed I hear David open the door. A squeaky cart rolls by my bed. I hide under the covers as he tips the waiter. I know he does because his change rattles, followed by the door closing.

When I open my eyes I see croissants filling a silver wire basket in an arm's reach of my pillow. There's a red rose in a vase on a pink linen cloth covering the cart. A silver coffeepot is matched by a silver sugar bowl and creamer.

I reach for a croissant and juice and pour myself a cup of coffee. Back in bed, I nibble on the croissant as I fight waves of nausea. Croissant crumbs aren't any more comfortable to lie on than cracker crumbs, although I'd expect them to be softer.

David looks up from where he's already tapping on his laptop. "I'll be in meetings the rest of the day. Why don't you go shopping on Peachtree Street? We can meet about six to grab a bite before you fly home and I go to California."

"I hate shopping," I say.

"But you haven't finished Christmas shopping. Usually you're done by now."

I don't tell him I haven't even started. This September when I was deluged with catalogs for every imaginable product, I put them aside instead of poring over them plotting how to get it all done without going to a store. David never asks how I accomplish our shopping for clients, colleagues and his sister's family. His idea of shopping is to give me X dollars. I work out the details.

"Do what you like. But if you do shop, don't forget Sylvia."

The inertia I feel toward shopping is based on the fact I don't care what David gives his partners or his secretary. This does not mean I'm unsympathetic to poor Sylvia. David has thought of replacing her with someone who doesn't drop her g's and wears business suits instead of skirts and sweaters. The only thing stopping him is that during the transition he wouldn't be able to locate anything.

He types another five minutes then, without turning to me, says, "Why don't you come with me for the weekend? Catch the red-eye out and go directly to your classes Monday?"

At one time I would have jumped at the chance. At first when I traveled with him, we would investigate wherever we were, but as he advanced in the firm, I would either poke on my own or sit in a hotel room and read as he worked. "I have lectures to prepare," I say.

"Fine. Thought I'd ask." He submerges all traces of the old David as he drinks coffee and makes two phone calls before arranging his papers in his briefcase. His body follows his mind out the door a few minutes later. Maybe he didn't say good-bye because my eyes are closed.

I stretch in bed and think of Scarlett O'Hara smiling the morning after Rhett carried her upstairs. Only this is different because I know that I don't love my husband. In fact,

I'm not sure I ever did.

Opening the drawer of the nightstand, I find *A Guide to Atlanta* that tells me about Stone Mountain's carving honoring southern generals. I debate hiring a car to look. Staying in bed sounds better. Using the television's remote control I discover *Moonlight Mile* is the pay movie. I half watch it, half doze. As always, Hoffman and Sarandon are incredible. The young actors who I don't know are rather vapid. I wish Peter were here so we could talk about things we would change.

About noon I call the airline. There are plenty of planes to Boston. There's notepaper in the drawer with the hotel's name and address. I dig my fountain pen out of my bag.

Dear David,
I decided to head home for the weekend because I've a lot to do. Good luck with the rest of the trip.

Me

An advantage of traveling light is that repacking takes seconds. The concierge orders a taxi.

On the way to the airport I see people playing tennis in shorts. Pansies flourish in the gardens as the taxi whishes by. It's so warm I carry my coat.

After landing in Boston I need not only my coat but my scarf, hat and gloves to protect me from the snow. My car, left in the outside parking lot, objects to being disturbed and coughs. After it condescends to turn over, I brush snow off my windshield.

I drive to Peter's wanting to be with him. He's not home. I let myself in. Whenever I do this, I worry he'll come in with another woman, which is dumb. He wouldn't have given me a key if he planned that.

The dog brushes past and rolls over in the snow. She tosses it in the air with her snout. When I call her back, she squats before coming. She looks frosted until she shakes the snow from her fur. The cold hits my bare legs.

"Did your master feed you?"

She gets her dish and drops it at my feet. I open a can of Alpo. She slurps her thanks.

At eight I take the miniature TV from the closet where Peter keeps it. We kid that he has a gay television. A woman showing the way to create a faux marble table fills the screen. I flip channels, settling on PBS's rerun of the *Story of English*, although I fall asleep during the American Negro's additions to my language.

Well after midnight, Peter stands at the bottom of my bed. "Hi!" His voice is very soft. "I was watching you sleep." Sitting down next to me he kisses my forehead. He smells of beer and musky aftershave.

When I wrinkle my nose, he says, "I worked for Mohammed tonight 'cause he thought he had a hot date, but she sent him home. He came back to commiserate and we went to Flan O'Brien's. I'm a little drunk."

I already knew that by how carefully he pronounced his words. "If both of you were out together, who's watching the stand?"

"A new kid I just hired. Since I haven't seen you much, I didn't get a chance to tell you." It's not said as an accusation. As he talks about the new kid, whom he doesn't think will work out, he pulls off his clothes then falls in bed in his shorts, T-shirt and one sock. We snuggle as he dozes off.

I've reached the stage where I've had enough sleep so I can't fall back. The nightstand clock reads three. Its hands shine in the moonlight. Peter found the clock in a Dumpster and took it to a watch smith who replaced the innards.

Boss creeps up on the bed. She's supposed to stay on the floor when I'm here. Instead she waits until she thinks we're asleep before joining us. I'm sure she considers me the intruder.

At five I slip into the bathroom to vomit then go to the kitchen to fix cinnamon toast and tea. I pour two glasses of tomato juice. Rummaging through a closet I find a copper bud vase. I open the door to cut a pine sprig for the vase. I scoop *The Boston Globe* off the doorstep. I put everything on a tray, add a dog biscuit, and carry it upstairs.

Boss has taken my place in the bed. "Wake up," I say. She slithers off.

Peter groans. "Let me sleep, woman. I'm dying."

"You have to be at work by six. So unless you're dead . . . wake up." I hand him his tomato juice.

"Mohammed's working all day." He takes his juice and grimaces before swallowing any. After pushing the tray to one side, he gets up to wash his face and brush his teeth. Wrapped in a quilt, I eat my toast, drink my juice and tea while sitting in the rocking chair in front of the window. Peter's clothes are strewn on the floor.

He crawls back in bed and holds the covers up so I can slip in beside him. I do. As soon as I'm in, he opens the front of my robe and licks my nipples, knowing how high I get when he does that. Long after we both come we hold each other, giggling about nothing. Lovemaking with Peter has nothing to do with orgasms. It has everything to do with sharing.

Showered and dressed, Peter makes me a cup of tea. I drink it at the kitchen table. Like so much of his furniture, he found it on the sidewalk where it had been chucked for the trash men. I'd helped him refinish it. I run my finger across the grain as he washes the dishes. "I was worried you wanted out of this," he says, his back to me. "Maybe that's why I drank too much last night."

"Excuses, excuses," I say.

"It's true, Liz. I got scared this will end." He turns to look at me.

"Where do you want us to go, Peter?" My stomach flip-flops. No matter what he says, it will mean some action on my part—a decision. The D-word. I know the baby growing in me has removed my procrastination option, but knowing it and acting are two separate things.

"I love you. I want us to live together."

"Just live?"

"You've a husband. I'm not sure how I feel about you jumping from one marriage to another. I'm not sure how I feel about marriage. It's one of those institutions that doesn't work like it should."

This is the first time I realized that he might have reservations about marrying me.

"What about children?"

"You said you can't have them. Although I always thought I'd be a father someday, it's not a driving urge." He dries a cup with a dish towel tattered on one end.

"And if you found out you were going to be a father?" I ask.

"You're getting off the subject. Whenever we talk about us you either change the subject, or bring up something less than real," he says.

I push out the words as fast as I can before losing my nerve. "I'm pregnant."

He sits down across from me, the dish towel still in his hand. He puts the clean cup on the table. "Holy shit! Am I the father?"

"I think so, but I can't be one hundred percent sure."

He blinks several times as if the movement of his eyes will clear up the issues hanging between us. "Wow!"

"Good wow? Bad wow?"

"I don't know. Have you told David?"

"No."

Peter is inches across the table from me, but it seems far. Our hands rest side by side, not touching. Usually, he covers my hand. Why did I tell him when I had planned to wait? I've no idea. I just did it. After making decisions not to act for so long, when I do act, it happens as if by accident.

"You must think it's mine if you told me and not him," he says.

The dog comes into the room and puts her head on Peter's lap.

We both look at her. It's safer to watch something neutral.

"I don't know if the baby is all right," I say.

"Why?" He frowns, something I almost never see him do.

"My age."

"I forget your age," he says.

"I need to have sonar done so we can figure out how far along I am. Then we'll do a test." The image of long needles through my stomach batters at my head.

"If it's defective?"

"I'll abort." The word catches in my throat.

"And if it's normal?"

"Oh, Peter. I want this baby so much."

He comes to me and pulls me from my chair. His kiss settles with the force of a feather on my lips. "That is the first decisive thing I've ever heard you say about what you want for yourself."

I hold him, feeling the heat of his body. This is one wonderful man.

"I'm coming with you when you have the sonar. This, my love, is my baby no matter who the father is."

CHAPTER SEVEN

Peter and I wait for the nurse to call me. The clickety-click of knitting needles echoes my nervousness as the receptionist works on a scarf. She has knitted "Harvard" in gray letters on a crimson background.

Only one other person, an older woman, is in the waiting room. She crochets, her hand moving back and forth, her lips silently counting out the pattern. It's too small to tell what it will become other than a white square.

"This isn't a waiting room. It's a sewing circle," Peter whispers. His smile mutates into a frown. "Are you worried someone will come in?"

"A little. All I need is my sister-in-law to walk through the door." I sneeze. My head hurts, and my throat is scratchy.

"I'll pretend I'm with the crochet lady." He shifts in his chair so his body leans toward his suddenly adopted parent. When he moves the red plastic covering of the chair squeaks.

In reality I'm more than a little worried I'll see someone I know. I'm petrified. Mother's oft-quoted words of what the neighbors might think beats in my brain. Even though my options are closing fast, I'm holding onto my indecision until the last possible nanosecond. Better to talk about a different topic. I sneeze again. Peter hands me his mega-handkerchief. I honk into it.

"I have to go to the bathroom," I say. Queen Mary allegedly said a woman should never pass up an opportunity to use the powder room. The last few weeks I've taken her philosophy as an eleventh commandment. My bladder feels like an overfilled water balloon. I concentrate on holding my sphincter muscle shut. Each sneeze tests its power to stop a flood.

"Check with the doctor about that cold." Peter raises his hand as if to pat mine, but then picks up a magazine. Its cover is ripped off. "If anyone sees you, they'll think I'm just another patient," he says. "Unless of course I throw you down on the awful plaid carpet and make love to you." Fortunately the knitter and the crocheter don't hear his whisper. Maybe both their hearing aids are off.

"Mrs. Adams?" The nurse looks at Peter, the crocheter and me. It should be obvious which one of us is going to have a sonogram to determine how far into a pregnancy she is. Peter mouths, "Good luck."

I move carefully, trying not to pee or sneeze. I cough and a little water seeps onto my panties. Inside the examining room the nurse hands me a green paper johnny.

"Designed by Gautier?" I ask.

The nurse's name tag reads Deidre Bronk. I try and figure out more about her to make me forget my full bladder, the neighbors who might say something, David, my cold and everything else happening to me. She may be in her forties. She has a slight moustache and a few chin hairs. I can tell she bleaches them because they have dark roots.

I ask from behind the screen, "May I go to the bathroom, just a little?"

"It's better to wait in case he finds you're further along than you think and does everything today." She helps me onto the table and adds, "Relax." Although the table is padded, relax is not one of the possibilities I have contemplated.

Looking every bit like an out-of-uniform Santa Claus, a man arrives. He's chubby with white hair, a beard, flashing blue eyes and cheeks like cherries. Since there are no reindeer hovering nearby with sleighs full of toys, I suspect this man is the doctor. Saint Nicholas, Father Christmas, Santa Claus, Kris Kringle or Pere Noel would never give a sonogram for Christmas, would they? Coal in my stocking maybe, but not medical tests.

"Mrs. Adams, I'm Dr. Charles."

I've seen him in the building when I visited my other doctor and dentist. However, the beard is new and he's put on considerable weight. He launches into an explanation of the procedure.

"Thank you, but I know most of it. I'm a professor of nursing."

"Still, it's a lot different telling people about it and having it done to you," he says.

"How about I tell your next three patients, and we'll forget about doing it to me."

When Dr. Charles laughs, his stomach shakes like a bowl full of jelly.

"This is just the first step. Once we figure out how pregnant you are, then we can determine if that baby of yours will be normal or not."

The doctor starts the sonogram. The room is overheated like my office. I feel hot, although the only thing I'm wearing is the johnny. The green paper crinkles whenever I move.

Deidre Bronk bustles around setting up this and that, and I wonder why she didn't do it earlier. Maybe she was getting ready to bleach her facial hairs. I realize I'm being bitchy, but it gives me mental distance since I can't have physical distance. I look out the window at the snow. It's soft, the kind that can fall for hours, without accumulating more than an inch.

The curtains are natural beige cotton with little brown balls like the ones advertised for years on the back cover of *Yankee Magazine*.

The doctor puts the sonar screen where we can all watch it. I sneeze and my baby moves then settles down. Its little hand seeks its mouth. After it's born, I'll help it.

Love washes over me in a high tide of emotion for my child. I cry silently. The salt from my tears stings my face where my skin is chapped.

Now I've seen my baby I could never give it up for any reason other than major deformity. I'm a foxhole agnostic. In tough situations I check in with God. "Dear God, let my baby be normal." I forget peeing, the neighbors, Deidre Bronk's hairs. Well, almost.

Dr. Charles clears his throat. "Ha. I'd say this little tyke is about three months old. That means we can do the amniocentesis about mid-January, February at the latest. I think I know the sex, do you want to know?"

"Can I think about it?" I ask.

"Of course," he says.

The nurse takes blood samples for other tests. I sneeze several times.

"That's a nasty cold," he says, shoving a thermometer in my mouth. "I want you to go to bed, but don't take any medicine."

I get dressed, but I'm trembling. It's a good thing Peter came. He takes my arm as we walk to my car and he deposits me on the passenger side.

The snow has changed. It's falling faster and heavier. I once read an article that said Eskimos have lots of different words for snow and couldn't understand why we only have one. I don't know the Eskimo word for snow that makes roads slushy. The car in front of us swerves until its tires grab the tarmac.

"I'm taking you home with me," Peter says. He doesn't ask me if I want to go. I do.

I'm in Peter's bed. He calls it our bed. The quilt is pulled up to my neck. The warmth from the electric warming sheet feels good. I sneeze.

Snow swirls outside the window, a real nor'easter with wind howling so hard that the window frames shake. According to the radio, this is a different storm than this morning's. The first has been driven out to sea by this one.

Peter brings me a tray. He has wrapped a small bottle with a green ribbon and put a candle in it. I sit up.

"Cocoa and French toast." He puts the tray in my lap. He has swirled cream through the cocoa, making a spiral. There is a small pitcher of warmed maple syrup. The candle flickers.

My lover blushes. He must have blushed like that when he was little. "I love you." He almost whispers it.

I feel as mushy as the toast I nibble. A big daub of butter with flakes of cinnamon near the top crust melts into the bread. I save it as the last bite.

I call Claire, my secretary, with a list of things for Tina Masters to do. Claire knows where to find the finals I've already prepared.

Peter takes care of me until I am ready to go back to school three days later.

When I do go back to school, it is the last day before the Christmas break. I still have two finals to give and tons of tests and papers to collect.

When I check the answering machine at home, Tina tells me she has graded all one-word and multiple choices on the exams she gave in my absence. All that is left for me to do are the essay questions.

Another message says, "I forgot to tell you. I've like separated the marginal students from the good ones." She did all this automatically. I call her answering machine and tell her she is the best teaching assistant I ever had and that I'll be back in the morning.

As I walk into the college, Tina stands at the entrance to The Caf, waiting to grab me. The Caf sells drinks, sandwiches and junk food. It is located in the middle of Lowell Hall where most of the science classrooms and labs are.

Tina is like a little child, hopping up and down. "I've got great gossip," she says. She tails me through the line as we get breakfast. As I put hot chocolate on my tray, I feel virtuous it's not coffee. More truthfully, drinking The Caf's coffee is like sucking coffee beans. There's not enough sugar or milk in all of Boston to cut the acidity.

One end of The Caf has lots of glass windows and greenery. Some of the trees have been decorated with silver balls. Faculty usually settles at the long tables nearby, but Tina indicates we should go elsewhere. We walk past my colleagues and groups of students drinking coffee from paper cups. Some talk. Others read from books or spiral notebooks. None pay any attention to us.

I follow Tina. Her hair has been newly cornrowed since I saw her last week. Each plait is fastened with a wooden bead and they swing back and forth making little clicks.

We choose a small round table in the remotest corner. The closest students, a group of four, shuffle cards. The Caf smells of coffee, onions and wet wool. Maybe the doctor is right about my being about three months along because the odors don't turn my stomach.

"First, I'll tell you like the unimportant stuff." She puts her cup on the table and shoves the empty tray on the free chair. "Claire's engaged." Tina spills some of her coffee and grabs a handful of napkins to wipe it up.

"Shit," I say, not about the spill but about Claire. I swear our young female staff develop a mental illness from the chemical reaction of a diamond ring on their skin. For months they can only discuss wedding plans with the same urgency of summit meetings. Shoes, the wrong shade of pink, bring the same trauma as terrorist bombings. When the wedding ring is added, the metal seeps through the skin reversing the earlier damage and their conversation becomes normal again.

"When's the wedding?" I calculate how long it will be before Claire's mind will be able to focus again on things like word processing and filing.

"June."

By then I will be on or getting ready for maternity leave if my baby is okay.

"And like all hell broke loose the day after the storm," Tina says. "I tried you at the house last night, but you weren't home, and I was like out when you called back."

"I felt so lousy that I stayed at a friend's. David's out of town."

Tina gulps her remaining coffee. On her interview she spilled her cup all over me. One fellow klutz to another. Probably that was the major reason I chose her. That and her spirit. Tina is feisty with a quick sense of humor and a "don't give me no shit" attitude. Those are her words, not mine.

As Tina bites into her donut, jelly oozes out. She catches it and then licks it off her fingers. This must be one of her junk food days. After the holidays she'll be back nibbling nuts and tofu. She never apologizes for falling off her health food wagon, claiming everyone needs some sins, and Big Macs, fries and donuts are really low on her sin scale.

I wait. Tina relishes being dramatic. She looks to both sides, then says in a penetrating whisper that the students playing cards could hear if they weren't concentrating on their game, "Melissa Greenbaum is like suing Henry Sumner and the college for sexual harassment."

"Son of a bitch," I say. I use the phrase as an expression of surprise.

"He is," Tina says. "He's hit on like half the women in the school. Of course, he denies it."

"What happened?"

"The morning of the storm the process servers showed up. This was supposed to be all hush-hush, but the grapevine . . ." She smiles.

I don't ask how much she had to do with fertilizing the grapevine. Tina has a network of sources that would make the FBI and CIA jealous. I'm convinced there's no bit of information she can't get her hands on. I'm also sure to maintain her sources she needs to give out stuff as well.

"Of course, President Baker defended Sumner," she says.

"What do you mean 'of course'? It's a women's college. We are supposed to protect our girls."

"Think about it. Baker like brought him here. He'd have to."

"But still . . ."

"Baker is like an idiot except as a fund-raiser."

I would never deny Baker is an idiot. He also is related to the chairman of the board of regents. The Old Boys Network operates even at women's colleges.

Tina wiggles in her chair, checks to see that no one can hear, and whispers so softly I can barely hear over the hum of The Caf noises. "I also found out that Melissa's father tried to get the president to get Sumner to issue an apology to Melissa and then like resign. Greenbaum wanted to handle it behind the scenes. He also wanted to make sure that Sumner didn't go after another student."

"Good for him. So what's the president doing about the lawsuit?"

"Probably for one crazy second the president thought he could keep the suit a secret, but like word's out," Tina says.

"How did the faculty react?"

"Split. Most of the men like agree with Sumner, the women with Melissa. Not totally. Yesterday there was a big fight in the faculty meeting about it. I didn't tell you that part yet. The president had to call like a faculty-staff meeting to discuss it. He was mega-bullshit."

"Were you there?" I ask.

"Yes and no. Like teaching assistants weren't included. Neither were secretaries, clerks and that sorta person. But I heard every word."

Do I want to know? Tina sees my dilemma.

"You want to ask how I like eavesdropped, but I'm not telling." She remembers her donut and washes it down with the last of her coffee. "The president wanted to tell like everyone that he was behind Sumner one hundred percent. Sumner himself got up and said he hadn't done anything out of line."

"You're kidding."

"Nope. Then like Judy Smentsky got involved. She said that she'd heard several complaints from students that he'd hit on them. Sumner turned scarlet and said she should name names. She said she couldn't break doctor-patient confidentiality. Then Sumner like said he was tired of being accused by innuendo from rich spoiled brats and stomped out."

"With all the sex scandals with the church, I'd think Baker would have responded differently."

Tina sent me a withering look. "When has he like ever acted sensibly except if he's sucking up to a donor? He mentioned the hysteria of the Salem witch trials, little girls needing amusement. He also claimed to have like investigated but found no cause for going further."

Having finished my hot chocolate, I place the cups and napkins on the tray to carry to the clean-up area. "Let's go to my office." There's lots of work to be done.

Opening my office door, I'm hit by a blast of heat. Too bad Tina can't use her magic sources to fix the heating system. Claire comes in, waving her left hand around.

"What's on your finger?" I ask.

She shows me the ring. "I'd never seen a canary diamond before," she says. "Look how it catches the light." She shoves her hand under my lamp. We discuss her wedding plans.

Claire places my copies of the finals I need to give today on my desk, except the quantities are wrong. She has mixed up the number of students in "Record Keeping" with the number in "Geriatric Nursing." The wedding disease has begun. I ask her to copy more and have them back by noon.

When Tina and Claire leave, I look at the stack of exam books as well as the pile of final papers that Tina has left for me. I will spend a good first part of Christmas break correcting them. I suppose that is retribution for all the work I assign to my students.

Before I start correcting the papers from the tests Tina

monitored, I spot-check to see what she has done. It's flaw-less.

Claire peeks in and says, "I'm sorry I forgot." She hands me six messages from David taken over the last two days. The last one came ten minutes earlier. He's in his office. He wasn't supposed to be back until the end of this week, at the earliest.

I call. Sylvia answers. "Hi, Mrs. A." She never calls me Ms., Doctor or Professor. The most formal or informal she gets is Mrs. A. "Your husband said to interrupt him if you called." She lowers her voice. "He's in a terrible mood."

He finally picks up his phone. In the interim I listen to *Bolero*. David's firm doesn't like to play Muzak while their clients are on hold. They think classical music gives more prestige.

"Where the hell have you been?"

"I've been staying in town because of the weather."

"Claire said you were out sick."

"I was."

"So why didn't you go home?"

"We had a nor'easter."

"I hate coming home and not finding my wife where she should be. The last time I saw you was in Atlanta. We were supposed to go to the airport together. But I get back to the hotel and you had disappeared. Then you disappear from home."

For years I've heard when attacked it's better to go on the offensive. For years I've backed down or made a few sarcastic remarks, but it's time to test a new method. I don't want my baby to have a wimpy mother.

"You weren't due home 'til next week. You usually don't call me from the road, so when you're gone I do as I please."

"That's no excuse. For all I know you were murdered."

"So call Judy Smentsky. If I'm not with her, she knows where I am."

"How should I know that? I don't know your friends."

I'm almost yelling. "Whose damned fault is that?" Since David or I didn't die when I yelled, I pushed again. "If you didn't refuse to have anything to do with people here, then you'd know whom to call." I didn't add anything about how many times before I'd told him to check with Judy. He has a great head for his work, but can't remember a loaf of bread unless he is the one who wants it.

"I hate those fake intellectuals. If they could do something more they'd be in the real world, instead of in that haven where you insist on working."

For David "real" is anything in his world. I've danced on cue for his friends enough to know what he and they consider "real." Real is a Mercedes, a good stock portfolio, a second home in a desirable location. That second home is usual grander than the homes of ninety-five percent of the people on this planet. "Real" is thinking that everything one says or does needs a commercial consideration.

"Educating the next generation has some socially redeemable value. Maybe you and your greedy clients should start thinking about giving back instead of taking all the time."

David sighs. "Let's not fight. I was worried. I didn't even know if you got back from Atlanta."

Anger shifts to guilt. Nice girls don't make people worry. I've no more energy to battle.

But before I can say more, David finishes the conversation. "I'm in the middle of something. I've got to go. I'll be home for dinner around eight. Try and drop in."

The phone clicks. I stare at the dead receiver. When I finally decide to fight back and state my case, my husband's work schedule intervenes. It's one thing not to fight out of choice. Not to fight by default annoys me.

On my way home I stop at Bread and Circus. Although they're a bit pretentious as a grocery store, they've a wonderful deli. David and I love their free-range chicken salad, which I buy as a peace offering. As I push the cart around the store, I try and find the normal jubilation I feel at being out of school. It's not there. What is there is a carton of stuff to grade, the fact I haven't done any Christmas shopping, and what I must tell David.

At the deli counter I see the chubby man who usually works there. "Please, can I have the chicken salad with lots of grapes? That's my husband's favorite."

"You know, it's really nice to see someone who cares about their husband's wants. Too many of you women only care about your careers," the man says. He's a real grump and always says negative things, which is totally out of character with the rest of the store. I don't bother to correct him.

"Happy holidays," I say to him in case he's Jewish.

At home I set the table. I put ten skinny candles in the ball-shaped candle holder and open a pinot noir wine that I know David likes with chicken salad. I heat French bread I bought at the bakery and put it in a napkin-covered basket.

David comes in, the portable phone to his ear, giving somebody instructions involving a contract, an address and a deadline. From his scowl I know that his mood hasn't improved much since our phone conversation.

He goes into the bedroom to change before coming to sit at the table. The salad doesn't help. "At least you could

117

have cooked something." These are his first words.

"I'm in the middle of finals. I'm still recovering from flu, if my being sick makes any difference to you."

"You can't keep disappearing, Liz. I don't know if you're dead or alive."

"The police would let you know if they find my body." I drop the sarcastic tone. "You're never here. You only call sporadically, and I refuse to hang around waiting for a call that may never come." I pause. I could learn to like taking the offensive. "You never tell me where you are."

"Sylvia has my schedule. All you have to do is call and ask her."

"Doesn't that strike you as a little strange between a husband and wife?"

"Liz, I'm a busy man. If I were one of your professor-type husbands I might be home more, but we couldn't live like this." He sweeps his arm around. "Look at this house. You never have to clean, do laundry or iron. Do you have any idea how many women would consider that heaven?"

"Did you ever ask me if that was what I wanted? You designed this house. You hired a housekeeper."

"Because you were always too tied up in your own career. You're a lousy housewife."

"Thank you. That's a compliment."

"You're impossible." He slams down his napkin as much as it is possible to slam cloth and storms off into his study. I can hear him talking on the telephone and see him pacing back and forth in front of the open door.

About ten minutes later he comes back. "You've done nothing for Christmas. Don't forget we're giving that open house for my office next week."

Oops. I'd totally forgotten. I wonder if there's a caterer still free in all of New England.

"I'll call Rick tomorrow to help you set up." Rick is our handyman. David goes back into his study, slamming the door. I scrape the food down the garbage disposal and load the dishwasher.

Sometime in the night David joins me in bed, being very careful not to touch me. When I wake the next morning, he's left for work.

CHAPTER EIGHT

Galen McEnroe mans the Boys Club Christmas tree sale. He's the Unitarian minister as well as the Boys Club advisor. In his spare time he coaches Pop Warner Football. He says kids from good families need attention just as much as kids from poor ones. Neglect happens at all socio-economic levels. A lot of kids' parents are too busy working to have much time for them. I can imagine if this were David's baby, his father would need to wear a name tag when he came home.

The kids adore Galen because he has a great sense of humor and treats them as people. Standing by a small fire, Galen drinks coffee from a Styrofoam cup. Ye Olde Muffin Shoppe is printed on the cup. Steam from the holes fogs his glasses whenever he drinks.

"Hi, Liz. We've got some really nice trees this year." Galen smiles a lot. They are sincere smiles, because he really looks at the person he's smiling at.

We go to the Episcopal church, but we know Galen from the country club. He's an avid golfer. Club membership is based on two things—family connections and length of time in town. David qualifies since his family has lived in town since the 1900s. His grandfather helped start the club. Galen takes kids out on the course. David uses it to entertain clients.

"I haven't seen you at the club for a while," Galen says.

"I've been out straight," I say, walking up and down the rows of trees. As I consider each one, Galen alternately stamps his right and left foot to keep warm. I find the largest, fullest tree I can, a large wreath for the door and a larger one, almost five feet in diameter, for over the fireplace.

Galen ties the tree to the roof of my car as I open the hatch. When I struggle with the catch holding the back seat upright, Galen comes to help me so we can lay the seat down flat.

"Do you want me to throw that box away for you?" he asks, referring to the carton of exams and papers I forgot to take out of the car last night.

"No, thanks."

He takes his time placing the wreaths in the car. "They won't get crushed this way," he says as he lays the little one in the center of the big one and rearranges the carton on the floor in front of the passenger seat. "Merry Christmas to you and David."

Our living room is hot from the sun. The sky is blue against the white snow. I don't want to block the view by closing the drapes. Rick, who'd been let in by the housekeeper, puts the tree up and starts stringing lights while I open the ornament boxes, which Rick has brought up from the basement storage area.

Each ornament is wrapped in tissue paper and placed in its own compartment of boxes that David ordered especially made to store them. Most are antiques he has collected. There's a special rider on our insurance policy to cover them.

Rick picks up one and holds it to the light. The ornament is a pink glass nest in gold netting. A small yellow bird perches on the edge.

"That's my favorite," I say.

"Certainly different," Rick says. "I like it."

While we work, the doorbell rings. The florist delivers two dozen perfect white poinsettias in matching white ceramic pots that Sylvia must have ordered.

The tree is done. Prisms, once part of a chandelier, hang from the branches, throwing rainbows around the room.

I remember when I was little we cut our Christmas tree from our own woods. Each year when we finished decorating it, one of us always said, "This is the most beautiful tree we've ever had."

"What a pretty tree," Rick says. Maybe it's part of human DNA that we have to say something when we finish decorating a tree. It's the same when one person yawns: everyone else yawns.

When Rick has gone, I take the Yellow Pages and look up caterers. I call five I used before. They decline politely, although I hear the "you've-got-to-be-kidding" tone in their voices. I start at the letter A and work down. Zitzow's Catering dashes my last hope. The alternative is that I prepare everything myself. Even if I wanted to I'm not sure I have the energy.

Then I get an idea. Florian! He's the Swiss-trained chef at the country club. The club is closed next week and won't open until New Year's Eve. Hopefully he won't have gone on holiday or have an unlisted home number. Miracle of miracles, I find the number and he answers. As I tell him my problem, he laughs. He has a deep laugh and a deep, very sexy voice. Maybe it's the French accent.

"No problem," he says. "What do you want to serve?"

"I really don't care. Anything to impress fifty very stuffy people."

"I'll draw up a menu and costs and get it over to you."

"You've saved my life, Florian. *Merci.*"

"*A votre service,* Madam Adams."

My hand isn't off the receiver before it rings. "Hi, cutey," Peter says. "How's the mother of my child, and can you talk?"

"Coast is clear," I say.

"Can you come in and see me?"

"David's home this week."

Silence.

"Are you there?" I ask.

"Yes. Move in with me now. Before we know if the baby is fine."

I look at the decorator-perfect tree, the perfect poinsettias and their perfect containers. Rick has carried the empty boxes back to the basement.

The house is perfect. The housekeeper has even won the battle against dust. I shiver in the sun. "When do you get out of work?"

"About an hour."

"I'll be there."

"Forever?"

"I don't know."

I leave a note that I've gone into the city. David will think I've gone shopping.

Leaving the car at Peter's, I notice the carton of exams in the back. I'd forgotten to ask Rick to carry it into the house. It takes only a few minutes to reach the stand. When I enter, my chickpea kisses me.

"Don't worry. We won't talk about anything important to upset the little mother," he says.

Mohammed comes in. "Hi, guys, what are you doing tonight?"

"Getting a tree. If it's all right with you, Liz?"

I tell him it's fine.

He puts on his Down East plaid jacket. Glove in glove we walk to Brookline Village.

"How 'bout that tree?" I point to a bonsai in the Japanese art store. "We can hang little balls and open little presents."

"Get real. I want a serious tree," he says.

After the crystal shop, Rocks R Us, Gourmet to Go, a take-out restaurant featuring cassoulet and foie gras, the bakery selling nonchemically grown wheat bread, is an old-fashioned Woolworth's, probably one of the last in the world. It was bought by a private person when the others went out of business. This one has the traditional mothball smell and sells parakeets, goldfish, yarn and practical bras just like the store in Concord where I bought my first Tangey lipstick, something from my mother's time. Going into it is like changing time zones.

However, we aren't there to buy anything. We cut through to the parking lot where a man sells Christmas trees. Needles litter the pavement. We discuss the merits of each tree. Peter grabs a blue spruce and a pine. He holds one in each hand. "Which one? Brand X? Brand Y? Think carefully before you choose or you won't appear in our commercial and earn all those residuals."

"Brand X." I point to the blue spruce. It's fat and stands about three feet high. The trunk is hidden by the dense branches, although it's a little lopsided.

Peter whips the price tag off. "Fifty-five dollars. There must be gold inside."

The man takes Peter's cash. He wears a glove without fingertips so he can count his money better.

When Peter hoists the tree over his shoulder, he looks like a lumberjack.

On the way back to Peter's we pass Mark and Judy's.

After an exchange of looks, Peter opens the gate leading to their front door.

Sable answers the bell. "Mom is in the kitchen," she says. From the good smells in the house, this is not a surprise.

As we enter the kitchen, Judy scoops a wooden spoon full of tomato sauce and gives it to Peter to taste. He blows on it before tasting, then makes a circle with his thumb and first finger.

"Wanta stay for dinner?" she asks. She's dressed in jeans and a Harvard sweatshirt. One shoulder where she spilled bleach is lighter than the other. Her hair is held back with a plastic band. She looks more like a teenager than a college doctor.

"Sure, if you come to our place for coffee and tree decorating after," Peter says. He takes the spoon from her to take a second taste. When I look at him he says, "When you taste-test, you have to be absolutely positive. One mouthful wasn't enough." He reaches for a third, but Judy grabs his hand and shakes her head.

"It's a deal if Mr. Taster leaves some sauce for dinner. Sable, add a couple of places, please," Judy says.

"Where's Sasha?" I ask.

"At a sleepover." Judy washes lettuce.

Mark comes in. He's carrying a couple of baguettes. "What a battle I had with Saul Mouse. I was walking down the street and this little mouse with a yarmulke jumped out. He wrestled me to the ground, but I saved the bread." He holds the loaves up for inspection. We can see that the heel has been nibbled. "I saved them except for the little bite on the end."

Sable sighs at Mark's story.

"Mark has this problem," Judy says. "Whenever he buys

bread he's attacked by mice who eat the crunchy heel. When we spent that summer in France it was Pierre Mouse. He claimed Pierre wore a beret. And in Harvard Square it's Biff Mouse that attacks, and in the North End it's Luigi Mouse."

"Sounds like a Mark Mouse," I say.

"I don't believe it," Judy says. "Mark is my bread defender." She puts her arms around his waist.

Sable sighs.

"Sable, stop sighing. She's grounded again. Sighing is her revenge."

Sable blushes. "Not true," she says. "Don't listen to her, Liz."

If there were a spaghetti hall of fame Judy would qualify as the first inductee. She makes a salad with simple oil and garlic dressing. The warmed bread is in a long basket. The crust is crisp, and butter melts into it. I reach for the wine, remember my baby, and say, "I'll stick to water."

Watching the action around me, I suddenly understand what is missing in my marriage. Play. Having fun over nothing. Enjoying things for what they are, not for what they cost. Enjoying each other as Mark and Judy do—as Peter and I do.

"You were out a couple of days. Have you heard what happened?" Judy asks.

"Do we have to discuss boring work stuff?" Sable asks.

"I know about Sumner and the suit. No, Sable, we can discuss other things. Your mother and I can talk later," I say.

Somewhere in Peter's genes there has to be a drill sergeant chromosome. He marshals us back to his place and

126

assigns us jobs. Mark is ordered to find a table in the storage shed for the tree and to set it up. Peter has decided the decorations will be edible this year, things like cookies, popcorn, etc.

"What about Boss?" I ask.

"That's why the tree is on a table," he says.

Judy and I are assigned to bake cookies. Peter gives us three recipes and arranges everything we need: cookie cutters, canned frosting, colored sugar and wire. As the cookies bake, we string cranberries and popcorn. He hands us needles. "Liz, don't you think it will be better to have separate strings of popcorn and cranberries? I know Judy and Mark mix theirs, but we want to be original."

"And you don't do them in advance as we do, either," Judy says.

The timer dings. I pull out the first batch of gingerbread angels.

"Pete, help me get the lights on." Mark wears a string around his neck. They are lit. He spreads his arms out. "I can be your tree, but I want some decorations in my mouth." Judy sticks half a star that has broken into his mouth. She eats the other.

When the tree is almost done, Peter remembers the CD he bought last year at the *Revels*. He digs it out and puts it on softly so the music is in the background until "The Lord of the Dance" begins. He turns up the volume. The four of us snake dance around the living room. Shutting my eyes I think of last year.

The music stops and Peter kisses me tenderly and long. A combination of horniness and tenderness comes over me so strong that I have to swallow several times before I can breathe. We break apart, frightened by the intensity, and look at and into each other. There's no more time for procrastination. "I'll stay," I say. "I know what I want. You."

Peter leads me to the phone. Dialing my number, he hands me the receiver. Judy and Mark move into the kitchen to remove the next batch of cookies from the oven.

"Hello." David sounds drowsy.

"It's Liz." No need to say hello.

"Where are you?"

"In town."

"The house looks great."

I inhale and spit out the words I have avoided so long. "David, I want a divorce."

"What did you say?"

I repeat the words slowly. They are easier the second time. Peter has his hand on my shoulder. I lean back into his body.

"Stop joking, Liz. You're not funny," David says.

"I'm not joking. I won't be home tonight. I'll pick up my things soon."

"This isn't a unilateral decision. If you're unhappy about something we can negotiate," he says.

"I don't want to talk about it now. I won't be home to-night but I didn't want you to worry. I'm going to hang up." My hands shake. Peter leads me to the couch where we sit. As he puts his arm around me, I start crying. He pulls my head into his shoulder and strokes my hair. Judy and Mark creep by on their way home.

The timer dings as another batch of sugar trees finish baking. Peter leaves me only long enough to pull them out, but not long enough to take them off the cookie sheet.

The tree is almost done without the last two batches of cookies. "I think it's the most beautiful tree I've ever had," Peter says.

I agree.

"And you're beautiful even when you're splotched from crying."

I don't agree, but I don't tell him that. I start to say lots of things, but his kiss interrupts me.

CHAPTER NINE

Saying "I want a divorce" wasn't hard after all, especially over the phone. Hanging up is a wonderful way to end a too-difficult conversation. Devout Cowardice is a religion I can understand.

Peter's patience borders on saint status. He needs it. I would be certifiable at any insane asylum in the country. For the entire weekend I cry, laugh, feel relieved or agonize over my guilt.

When I run out of Kleenex, I resort to toilet tissue to wipe my drippy nose. It really does serve the same purpose. In college I only used toilet tissue. At my uncle's funeral while Mother sniffed daintily into a white hanky embroidered with pink roses, I pulled out a strip of toilet paper. Later she declared herself mortified.

Thinking of Mother sends me into another spasm of tears. If toilet tissue mortified her, what will she say after I tell her this? I then indulge myself in feeling guilty that I haven't called her since she arrived in Arizona.

Peter listens to me, holds me, reassures me; in short, he does everything humanly possible to calm me. As I rave on, jumping from emotion to emotion, he brings me tea, plays devil's advocate, agrees or disagrees, depending on what seems right at the moment.

He keeps saying, "If you . . ." and gives me all sorts of possible options. I refuse all of them. He makes love to me. I don't refuse that.

He spends well over an hour massaging my body, from my head to my toes, trying to relax my muscles. In between his different therapies he goes to work, although Mohammed is working extra hours this weekend to give Peter more time with me.

Each time my lover comes back from the stand, I'm worried about something else. The worst part is that I know I'm not making any sense.

By Sunday evening I've pushed him over his limit. "Enough!" It's one of the few times I've ever heard him raise his voice. He holds up both his hands and walks to his telephone. It's shaped like Garfield.

Without saying another word he hands it to me. I look at him and the phone. He says, "If you want to go back, call David. He doesn't know you have a lover. I'm sure he'll think it was just your time of month or something."

I say nothing.

"Go on. Change your mind, if you want to."

Suddenly I start laughing. There is something humorous—no ludicrous—in the situation. The idea of groveling to my husband on a cartoon cat telephone, which I gave to my lover, is beyond what I can take seriously. Besides, the phone is defective and it's hard to hear. Besides, I don't want to go back. Besides, I want to live with the most probable father of my baby. I place Garfield's back on his body.

"I'm sorry, I've been acting like an idiot," I say.

"Apology accepted. I want us to be a family, but only if you want it, too."

"I want it," I say.

"Good. That's cleared up." Peter glances at his watch. "Now let's watch *Boston Cop*."

I don't believe what I'm hearing. In the middle of the biggest crisis of my life, my sensitive New Age guy, the candidate for sainthood, wants to watch TV? Well, why not?

I've had my turn all weekend to vent, let poor Peter relax. We snuggle on the couch watching the opening credits.

As the commercial comes on, I feel smug that I can be totally myself with Peter. There's never been anyone in my life before that I haven't had to put on some false face for. That honesty is more seductive than roses, candy, perfume or the most passionate sex in the world.

Even if I'm totally content with Peter, I still don't like this detective show. It's filmed in Boston. What bothers me most is that the hero always finds parking places even on Commonwealth Avenue where there's resident parking only. He doesn't even have to parallel park. This time he pulls into a three-car space. As I complain about him getting yet another parking place, I watch him get out of his car and walk to Peter's stand to buy coffee from my favorite chickpea. My lover was on television for at least forty-five seconds. I sit up straight. Peter grins.

"You didn't tell me," I say.

"I wanted to surprise you," he says. "Want my autograph?"

The phone rings, and Peter answers. I can tell from his remarks that Mark and Judy are congratulating him on his performance.

"Great publicity," he says. He speaks louder because he's using the Garfield phone.

I know they ask about me because he looks at me and says, "Better," before hanging up.

"Let's go to bed." He leads me upstairs. His lovemaking is tender. Pushing the hair from my face he kisses my eyelids. There's something sweet about having your eyelids kissed. We both come quickly, no bells, just a quiet slide of two people sharing.

"Have you calmed down?" he asks. His head is propped

on his hand as he lies on his side, watching me put on my nightgown. My legs are sticky, but I like this damp memory of our lovemaking.

"I guess so."

"When I met you, you were so super-cool and organized. Now you've turned into a featherbrain. Fortunately, I love both of you."

"Maybe I was so cool because I held so much of myself inside. If you want a cool lady, you may have to keep looking."

He grabs my left hand and kisses my wrist. It tickles, but not disagreeably. "I only want you," he says.

As we fall asleep I realize that we have never discussed the issue of our age differences. Instead of becoming phobic about it, I decide that if it had been important to him, he would have said something. Therefore, it isn't important to me either.

The next day Peter leaves before I wake. He is so quiet I don't hear him at all.

When I go downstairs, I wear a sweatshirt over my night-gown. I never brought over a housecoat. The house feels toasty. Peter made sure the wood-burning stove was well stoked before he left. A pile of logs is next to it. It wasn't there last night.

The Boston Globe is on the table and open to the death notices. Neither Peter nor I ever miss reading them. Although we've tried, we've never figured out why we enjoy them so much.

Next to the paper he has left a pot of coffee and a note saying, "Decaf for my baby." Feeling totally pampered for the first time in years, I toast a raisin cinnamon muffin and spread it with peanut butter and cream cheese as I nuke the cold coffee in the microwave. I eat slowly, trying to muster the force to make my calls..

Finally, with the paper read, the coffee drunk, the dishes washed, the bed made, the house dusted, myself showered and dressed, I can think of nothing else to delay what I should be doing. It does enter my mind to correct exams, but that's over the top even for a person of the Devout Coward sect.

After picking up and putting down the phone several times, I dial my house or former house as it is now. David doesn't answer. Part of me thinks, Good, but the other part knows how easy it would be to lose the little momentum I've gained.

I zap the messages on voice mail. One is from Mother. She says David told her that I've left him. At least I don't have to tell her or deal with her initial reaction, which is lost as the message ends. I would bet a million dollars it isn't "What wonderful news."

Before I call Mother, I phone my doctor. Nurse Bronk puts me through.

"I've decided I do want to know the sex," I say.

"I'm ninety-nine percent sure it's a girl. We'll know for certain after the amniocentesis."

I call Peter. "How do you like the name Chloe?" I ask.

"You know it's a girl?" His voice seems to have happy bubbles in it.

"The doctor's almost sure. We'll know definitely after the holidays."

"Why Chloe?" he asks.

"The first French movie I ever saw had that as the name of the heroine. It's the only thing I remember about the film. Can you think of another name?"

"We don't have to decide this minute, but I like it."

A customer interrupts our chat. Peter says he adores me before we hang up.

I put my hand on my stomach and touch where my daughter is growing. Having accepted long ago that this was something I would never experience, I feel myself incredibly lucky.

Instead of calling Mother, I call my brother. Next to Devout Cowardice the religion of Devout Procrastination has its place.

Janice answers, not Ben. "Where are you?"

"Brookline."

"Are you OK?"

"You've talked with Mother?"

"She called here. And David. What's going on?" Janice is the easiest person to talk to that I know. Even more than Judy. When my sister-in-law asks for information, it's neither to be nosy nor to criticize. She's good practice for me before talking to the rest of my family.

"I've asked David for a divorce."

"Do you mind if I ask why? No, I want to know even if you do mind," she says. I hear Sam in the background. "Hush. That's hush Sam, not hush you, Liz. Talk to me."

I pace as I talk. The phone is tucked between my shoulder and ear. I make more decaf and then pour it into the white ceramic mug with violets cut into it. What I tell her as I do this are generalities about no time together, business encroaching on everything, nothing in common. Blah, blah, blah, blah.

"Does David have someone else?" she asks.

I take a deep breath. "No. I do." Better get it out all at

once. "And I'm pregnant."

After a silence she says, "Whew! Let me call Ben." I hear her briefing my brother as she hands him the phone.

"Boy, Sis, you've got the family turning around. What are you doing?"

After I tell him he asks, "Are you happy?"

I wish I could hug him for asking me that question. "I don't know."

"You don't know?" His voice is shocked.

"I've so much to sort out. Like calling Mother." When I say that he draws his breath in. But I also tell him I know I'm really happy about the Peter and baby parts.

"Can we come see you?" he asks. He repeats the address and telephone number for Janice to write down.

"Don't tell David," I say as an afterthought.

"Whatever you want, Sis. Seriously, Janice and I are behind whatever you do. I've great faith in you." His last words are, "Good luck with Mother."

"There's never been a divorce in our family," Mother says as soon as I say hello to her. "What will people say, Elizabeth-Anne?" She only uses my full name when furious as in, "Elizabeth-Anne, I told you to clean your room."

Better not to answer questions about other people's opinions. "There's more. I left him for another man, and I'm going to have a baby girl. It's Peter's—not David's." No need to share the teeny-tiny percentage of doubt I feel.

Silence is followed by Mother crying. "I'm too upset to talk now, Elizabeth-Anne."

The phone goes dead. I put another log in the stove.

Before I can make the most dreaded call of all, the phone rings again. This time it's Auntie Anne.

"Don't get mad at Ben, but I told him if he didn't give me the number, I'd come north and beat him up," she says. "I was sure you'd call him before us."

"It's fine," I say.

"Don't worry, Lizzie," Auntie Anne says, just like she told me not to worry about not being asked to the junior prom or only making the alternate baton squad. "Everything will be fine. Are you happy?"

"He's wonderful," I say.

"That's all that matters," she says.

"Auntie Anne, did you watch *Boston Cop* last night?"

"You know I always do. All those scenes of Boston are better than a trip home. Cheaper, too. Your mother doesn't like it. Says it makes her homesick."

"Peter was on it."

"Whom did he play?" she asks.

"The chickpea who sold coffee," I say.

"Your new young man is an actor? He's cute. Thought so at the time."

They've had enough shocks so I decide not to mention how young my young man is. "He's not an actor. He really owns that stand. He wears the costume as part of his marketing."

"Fun. He must have a great imagination." My aunt pauses. I can almost hear her thinking. Then she says, "I shouldn't say this . . ."

". . . But that's never stopped you before," I say.

"You know me too well. I'll feel funny if you and David get back together, but I always thought that husband of yours was a cold fish. Lizzie girl, you do what is best for you and my new grandniece."

"Thank you," I say.

"I love you," she says. "And I'll get your mother on the

right track, don't worry."

Given a year or so my aunt might be able to pacify my mother. I hope so, but I have doubts.

Rather than tackle David, I call Jill, waking her. I'd not only forgotten the time difference but what a grump she is early in the morning.

"I need to tell you something before the rest of the family gets to you," I say, launching into essentials only. She is definitely not of the camp that wants to know if I'm happy.

"My sister is a forty-year-old unwed mother," she says.

"I won't be forty 'til next month and I'm wed. Only not to the father of my daughter."

"How can you be so glib?" she asks. We talk a little longer. Words like immoral, adultery, unfaithful, cheat swim through the telephone lines. We hang up coolly. Considering her own situation, I understand why she is upset with me.

The call to my sister is a good warm-up for David. My hand shakes as I dial his office. By Sylvia's chatter, I know he's said nothing to her. I listen to two Muzak songs, "One Less Bell to Answer" and "I'm Leaving on a Jet Plane," after she puts me on hold. I wonder what has happened to the classical music.

"We have to talk," I say when he answers. He doesn't notice my lack of greeting.

"Come home. We'll talk tonight," he says.

"I'm not coming home. Meet me for lunch."

He agrees without a counter-proposal.

"Legal Seafood?" I ask.

"Mirabelle's," he says. It is not a question. I give him

this round in our silent war. The restaurant is not important, only that it provides neutral territory. Mirabelle's is quieter than Legal anyway.

Mirabelle's is a French restaurant decorated in gray with pink accents. I'm the first customer, arriving a little after eleven-thirty. A waitress puts fresh holly in small bud vases on each of the tables as I hang up my coat. I choose a seat at the back, facing the door so I can see when David arrives.

He brings his coat to the table, folds it and drops it on one of the two spare seats. He is afraid someone will steal it if they see the label.

The waitress, now finished with the holly, immediately asks about cocktails. We decline. Looking over the menu is a farce. Eating is as unimportant as which restaurant we're in.

However, the waitress expects people to order. We live up to her expectations. I choose a salad and cassoulet. David orders a salad and veal.

Two blue-haired grandmother types come in. One wears a Geiger boiled wool jacket and the other is dressed in a tweed skirt and matching cardigan set. Both have strings of pearls.

The next person through the entrance is a young woman who carries a case. She sits at the opposite end of the room and moves a music stand in front of her. She's dressed in black pants and boots with a white flowing-sleeved blouse. She takes out a flute and plays "Silent Night" followed by "It Came Upon a Midnight Clear."

The ambiance would be lovely except for the topic that must be discussed. My procrastination habit allows David to begin.

"What are you doing, Liz?" He plays with his knife.

139

Looking at him, I think how handsome he is. His suit is perfectly tailored to his body. I want to muss his hair so it won't be so damned neat. I try to picture him dressed as a chickpea. I can't. I feel him staring at me.

"I want a divorce," I say.

"You already said that on the phone. Why?" His voice is calm.

"We don't have a relationship. You've your interests. I've mine. We share property, not our lives."

David laughs, but it carries no humor. Its dryness is all-knowing or at least all-knowing from his interpretation. "Is that what this silliness is all about? You want more attention. Quit your job and travel with me. I've told you that hundreds of times."

The waitress brings our salads and a two-foot pepper mill to give us the absolute freshest pepper possible.

"Where is that pepper from?" David asks.

Our marriage is coming apart and he terms my request for a divorce as "silliness" and worries about where the pepper was grown. He is making this much easier for me than I thought it would be.

"I have no idea," the waitress says.

He indicates he'll accept inferior pepper. She gives his salad a few turns.

"No, it's not," I say about my need for attention being the reason I want a divorce. I'm mad that two people as intelligent as David and me can live together for over a decade and can still totally misunderstand each other. I tell him this.

"I understand you better than you think." He reaches for a piece of bread. He looks at the gold foil–wrapped pats of butter and beckons the waitress. "Have you any sweet butter?" She brings a few silver foil–wrapped pats. He tears a bite-sized piece of bread and butters it methodically. He chews it ten times as he always does before selecting a piece of avocado from his salad.

"Your mother is upset," he says when his mouth is empty.

"I know. I've talked to her. Also Auntie Anne, Ben, Janice and Jill." I head him off at the pass in case he wants to manipulate me through my family.

"You certainly aired our dirty laundry with your relatives."

"You told Mother before I got to her. I didn't call your sister."

"You never liked my sister."

"Neither do you," I say.

He spears a cherry tomato. "That's one thing we share."

I have to smile at this unfortunate summary of our marriage. "David, can you please explain to me why you are so driven?"

He puts his fork down. "I don't think I'm driven. I work hard like my father, like my grandfather. We need money to support a certain quality of life."

"I could have been content with a lot fewer possessions if we'd shared what we had."

"We play golf and bridge together," he says.

"Mostly with business connections. Where are our friends of the heart?"

"You are so innocent. It's a dog-eat-dog world."

I think of David telling me how his father punished him if his marks dropped below A's, how he had to choose a sport and make captain. He only made assistant captain of his football team. His father refused to go to any games.

When David and I were first married, I remember thinking that I could soften his earlier life by offering warmth and humor. I did both of us a disservice. Although I should have put it together before, I didn't. I must have bark marks all over my face from pressing it against all the trees in the forest.

I shouldn't be surprised at his competitiveness. But somewhere, just maybe, he should have examined if that was for him. I ask, "Did you ever want another kind of life? One where you can relax? Just enjoy stuff for what it is, not for power or . . ."

He looks at me. This is the first theoretical discussion we have had in at least seven years. Then he stares off for a long time. Finally, he says, "About five or six years ago, I had a client. Built a huge business, a real shark he was. I brokered the sale of his company. Seven million dollars. Then he went off to Kentucky to become a gentleman farmer. I visited him there once, because there was a great opportunity for him. You know what he did?"

"What?" I think I could like that guy who changed his life.

"He took me for a horseback ride and kept pointing out rocks and trees. I asked how he stood the quiet after the excitement. He said the weirdest thing."

"What did he say?"

"He said that peace was his excitement. I thought about him for a while after, maybe a week or so. I wondered if I might be missing something."

"And . . ."

"I decided the guy was a wimp and couldn't hack it. The country was just an excuse to save face."

A memory works its way up to the front of my consciousness. When David and I were first married, we'd gone to the Topsfield Fair. He bought me a helium balloon that I tied to my wrist, but I hadn't knotted it tightly. It flew off into the sky.

I felt sad, because it had been such a nice moment when he'd gone up and picked a pink one without my asking, as if he'd known I'd been wishing for it. David had wanted to buy me another, but a replacement wouldn't have made up for the loss. He hadn't understood. After all my explanations, he had shaken his head. I think it was the last time I tried to tell him about my feelings.

From nowhere memories of hitchhiking through Italy flood over me. I'd had this overwhelming craving for a tuna salad sandwich and went into a little grocery store. It was so dark after the bright sun I had trouble seeing.

The store owner, a fat little man who looked as if he had died years ago but was too busy to be buried, greeted me in a tidal wave of words. I had left my dictionary with my backpack in a locker at the train station. The more confused I looked, the faster and louder he spoke, punctuating his speech with hand motions.

I tried asking for canned tuna, mayonnaise, a can opener and celery. I mimed fish swimming, opening cans, waving my hands. I tried talking faster and louder, too. Finally, I bought the sausage, cheese, olives, a packaged cake, and a can of juice the man had selected for me. I didn't get to drink the juice until the next day when I found a can opener. The grocery man never did respond to my pantomime of opening the can.

The waitress removes our salad dishes.

"Where are you staying?" he asks.

"With a friend."

"Does that mean you won't tell me?" He picks a berry from the holly, twirling it in his fingers before dropping it in the ashtray.

"Correct." I veer the subject in a slightly different way. "I'd like to think we can reach an agreement between us."

"If you're going to hold me up, it won't work. You're deserting me. You're the one changing the rules without giving me a chance."

I imagine the same dollar signs in his eyes that are in Scrooge McDuck's eyes in a Disney comic. "That statement just shows how very far apart we are," I say.

The waitress brings his veal and my cassoulet. She places his dish just out of position. He turns the plate until the veal is exactly in front of him.

We start to eat. David always finds something to complain about, with the exception of our recent meal in Atlanta. I wait.

"The sauce needs a little more wine," he says.

"My cassoulet is wonderful." In reality I can barely taste it. I want to throw up, more because of nerves than Chloe.

"Why don't we wait a few months to decide?" He sips his water. His ice cube has melted. "May I have your ice?"

I nod for the ice, not for the delay. "We're too far apart. I'll admit my failure in not trying to tell you how unhappy I was, but it took me a long time to realize it myself." This is true. It is also true that Chloe is growing.

"Maybe we should see a marriage counselor," he says.

A marriage counselor won't turn him into a person who likes to look at rocks and trees. Or me into a nonpregnant Aggie Lou–type wife. "Maybe we should talk to an attorney," I say, proud of my counter-proposal.

"If we were to do that, and I still think it's premature, we should save money by using the same one. Perhaps someone in my firm." Before I can answer he says, "You know that you don't have any grounds."

"Irreconcilable differences." I push my plate away with half the cassoulet uneaten. The waitress swoops in and takes our dishes. We decline an offer for coffee.

"Have you thought what you will live on?"

"I work. Remember?"

"Your pathetic little salary won't go far," he says.

He's negated my salary just as he's negated my work for years. I see clearly. It isn't disinterest in what I do; it's lack of respect for my accomplishments. And me. Even when it means the end of our marriage, he has to put down what I do.

Instead of anger I'm lost in a mist of sadness. I continue for reasons that make no sense. It's useless. "Lots of people live on less than what I make. Whole families live on it. I'm only one person." Actually I'm one and one-third persons.

"People don't live in the style you're used to on it," he says.

"It's your style not mine. I don't need a boat, country club membership, etc."

When the waitress brings the bill, I reach for it. It's terribly important that I pay for lunch, because I got more out of the conversation than David did: backbone and my physical freedom. I need to use money to prove money isn't important.

"You always go in for childish displays," he says, putting his credit card away.

"Yes, I do." I get up.

"I still haven't agreed to a divorce," he says. "And if you go ahead with it, you'll have nothing." Since I'm walking away from him, he has to raise his voice. The two blue heads swivel towards him as I put on my coat. I walk back to the table. The little old ladies eye me, hoping to get some more information, maybe.

"I forgot Florian is sending menus and prices for your open house. Call him to set up final details."

He won't. He'll ask Sylvia to do it.

I've done my last official wifely act.

CHAPTER TEN

During the afternoon I attempt to phone attorneys. Six times I can't get by the secretary. Two lawyers sound annoyed at being interrupted.

Another just doesn't feel right. Finally a woman, Carol Goss, who has a one-woman office in Coolidge Corner, answers the phone herself. She doesn't brush me off. We arrange an appointment for January sixteenth.

I make tacos and guacamole for Peter's dinner. The hamburger gurgles in the pan. The food processor doesn't work until I remember to push the top in all the way. The avocado smooths into green glop. When I test it, the taste is bland. I add some more lemon and Tabasco, and take a bite. It bites back.

Peter arrives about eight with a bouquet of mixed flowers and a present wrapped in paper covered with yellow ducklings. I open it to find a size three-month pink dress with matching ruffled rubber-lined panties.

He fingers the ruffles. "Aren't they incredible? They're so tiny. I got them at the Coop." The panties are the size of his hand. Watching him handle the material, I know I made the right decision.

The doorbell rings just as I bite into the last of my taco. Peter, who has finished, answers. Boss trots behind him. The dog never barks at humans, just other dogs.

As I clear the table, I hear, "I'm Ben, Liz's brother. You must be Peter. This is my wife, Janice."

They follow Peter into the living area. Ben sweeps me

into his arms, his flannel shirt soft against my cheek. It's a long hug ending in a double arm pat.

Peter offers them coffee as he takes the coats they've already shed.

Janice kisses me, the scent of her Shalimar perfume a familiar comfort. She scoops up the baby dress from the chair. "It's so cute. Reminds me of one Sammy had."

"Peter bought it today. Chloe's first outfit."

"Chloe?" Janice says. "You've named her already?"

"It's her name for the moment. Although it will probably stay," Peter says.

"You've always wanted a baby," Ben says.

Peter brings a tray lined with a cloth and four cups. The saucers all have spoons facing in the same direction, and there's a basket filled with cookies left from the tree trimming.

He points to my cup. "That's decaf," he says. Janice and Ben look at each other. Because I know them so well, I read their signal of approval. Still there is a strain, not an undercurrent, more like a whisper of air on a hot afternoon.

"What are your plans?" my brother asks.

"Stop playing father," I tell Ben, who says he's sorry.

Peter excuses himself, saying that he'll let us talk. Boss chooses to stay with me or maybe with the cookies. She places herself so there is a straight line between her nose and the basket.

"I like him," Ben says after Peter disappears upstairs. He breaks off an arm from one of the angels and looks at the dog and me. I tell him it's fine to share with her.

"He seems awfully sweet," Janice says. "I just hope you know what you're doing."

"I'm muddling through somehow. But he's wonderful." I tell them how I got from Point D to Point P, including my waffling back and forth. Janice, who is sitting on the hassock at Ben's feet, reaches across to pat my knee.

When I finish my tale, Ben suggests we recall Peter from his self-imposed exile. I run upstairs to find him watching *Alf* on the station that reruns series from before God was born.

"No problem," he says in his best imitation when I ask him to come downstairs. Then he puts his hand under my chin and tilts it up. "Are you OK?"

"Yes. My brother and sister-in-law accept us." I watch Peter's shoulders relax and he hugs me. We don't need words to share and understand.

Ben and Janice stay for a couple of hours after we go downstairs. We talk about music, the stand, Ben's apple orchard, Sammy, the latest political scandal.

"What are you guys doing for Christmas?" Janice asks.

"We haven't talked about it. We've been too busy adjusting," Peter says.

"Come for Christmas dinner. Or even Christmas Eve and stay over," Janice says.

"Since we're the only family we've got in this part of the world, we've got to stick together," my brother says.

"Yes, do," Janice says. "Our place is a shambles with the move and all, but if you can take the mess, we can take you."

Peter sweeps his arm around, calling our attention to his clutter. "It'll seem like home."

As they leave, Ben says, "I'll tell Mother we like him. It may help."

January is bitter cold, driving away the warmth of the holiday season. Two nor'easters sweep down on the city, back to back, canceling the start of second-semester classes.

The city stops for two days. Snow muffles all sounds. When the sun reappears, the low temperatures nullify any progress the sun might make melting the drifts. It is already the worst winter in a decade.

When school does reopen, I walk to the campus bundled up. A ski mask covers my face. It feels wonderful to be out after being cooped up. Because none of the sidewalks are shoveled, staying upright is a challenge.

I wear a huge sweater to hide my growing tummy and woolen tights under my slacks to keep my legs warm. Even if I weren't pregnant, I'd look fat because of all the layers protecting me from the cold.

I'm scheduled to teach three courses, all of which I've taught before. I'm not one of those professors who teach their courses exactly the same for years. I try to update and vary my material. I've two new committee assignments and an invitation to co-author an article for *The Professional Nursing Journal*. It will be a busy semester.

The thermometer in my office registers ninety degrees, which feels wonderful after being outdoors. For once I'm grateful that the heating system hasn't been fixed.

My fingers still feel numb from the outside cold as I pick up a brown interoffice envelope marked confidential. Someone must have shoved it under my door, because it is not in my official mailbox. The envelope has forty-four rows of lines so it can be recirculated, saving money and trees. Scotch tape seals the fastener and the tape is marked with a red slash to make sure no one has tampered with it. The sender's name has been crossed out with a thick black marker.

I open it gingerly. Usually this type of envelope comes from personnel who mark everything confidential. I once found an article on lawyers that our personnel director clipped from *The Wall Street Journal*. She'd put a post-it note on it and had written, "Maybe your husband will find this interesting." That envelope had been marked confidential. Maybe she didn't want to get caught doing anything nice.

A second reason that envelopes are marked confidential is that there's a problem inside. This one contains a problem.

The faculty women want to ask the president for Sumner's dismissal on moral grounds. There's a meeting next week to select strategy.

The image of our president flashes into my mind, and it is followed by the word jerk. I remind myself what a great fund-raiser he is. We've built a new research building because of his ability to get money. Our endowments have increased sixty-one percent, none of which translated into faculty salary increases.

The phone rings. After exchanging holiday news Judy asks, "Did you get the meeting notice?" I tell her I did and will be there. She asks me to check with several others. She suggests we talk before the meeting. "Come on over now and bring some coffee. Decaf for me," I say. She arrives in ten minutes with two Styrofoam cups, one with a D scratched on the lid.

"I don't remember you drinking decaf," she says, putting the cups on my desk then taking off her coat. She looks fantastic with a scarf over her turtleneck jersey.

"I started when I found out I was pregnant."

There is silence.

Judy sits down and leans toward me. She's in her counselor pose. I see her struggle between professional and friend modes.

"You want to ask me if it's Peter's?"

"Oh yes! I'm fighting between being polite and wanting to know all the dirt."

"I'm almost positive it is. I'm really happy. I bet that's the answer to your next question."

"Naturally it is." She pries the plastic lid off the cup.

"I don't even care anymore that he's younger than me," I say.

"I read in *The National Enquirer* about all the actresses dating younger men. Think of Sarandon, think of . . ."

"You read *The National Enquirer*?" Judy reading *The National Enquirer*? I would never have guessed it. *The Nation*, *The New Republic*, even *Martha Stewart Living*, but *The National Enquirer*—that's not anything I'd ever guess about her.

"I read everything, including ketchup labels. Let's get back to Sumner," she says. "I've counseled at least four girls he has had affairs with. Yet I couldn't break their confidence to do anything."

"I heard what you said in the meeting," I say.

Judy fiddles with her scarf. "That wasn't the best time for me to do it, I'll admit. I lost my cool when he stood up and lied to us." Her face becomes hard. "I want to nail that bastard. He's screwed up some of my kids." Judy's possessiveness towards the students is legendary. Being pro-student here can be a political kiss of death, but Judy has such community recognition that the president is afraid of her. Viva la fear!

There's a knock on the door. Before I can say, "Come in," Tina squeezes between Judy and my desk and reaches to switch on my radio. She tunes out WERS and flips on Jack Kane. He's a talk-show host who fought against and won repeal of several no-smoking laws. I didn't agree with him, but I admire those who buck the system and win.

Melissa Greenbaum is one of the guests. The show is about sexual harassment.

"Maybe you went to his office, your jeans might have been a little tight," he says.

"I went to his office because he flunked me on a perfectly acceptable paper. My jeans were the same I have on now, and you can see they're not too tight. He told me the way to get an A was to (bleep) him."

"Fuck," the three of us fill in together.

Melissa continues. "Your jeans are tight, Mr. Kane. Your shirt is unbuttoned; you've got a gold necklace entangled in your chest hair. Does that mean you want me and your other guests to grab your (bleep)?"

"Balls," the three of us chorus.

"Do you think she's jeopardizing her case by being on the radio?" I ask, still the lawyer's wife.

"She's out to get Sumner any way she can. I didn't think she was that strong a person," Judy says.

Kane goes into a commercial without answering Melissa's question. When he comes back, we listen to him talk to three other students from different universities around the city. All talk about the problems they've encountered. Jack asks people to call in.

"You're on the air," he says.

"I'm tired of pretty young women tempting perfectly nice husbands," a woman's voice says.

"Perfect husbands wouldn't be tempted," Jack says. The woman hangs up on him before he can hang up on her.

"You think President Baker will back down?" Tina asks.

"He's stubborn," Judy says. "Very."

After work I stop at the stand. It's crowded. Mohammed is already at work. Peter is interviewing a new employee.

My chickpea wants to cut back his working hours to ten a day. We've discussed money, and by combining salaries we'll be fine. I'm glad my pay is now viewed as a contribution instead of a "pathetic" nothing.

The candidate is a young woman and I feel a pang of jealousy. "Can I be a piece of celery?" she asks. There's some consolation that most employees last about three months. Mohammed is the exception.

Peter glances up as I come in. "Liz, meet Andrea. Andrea, my fiancee."

We examine each other as I reach to shake her hand. I never cared who worked for David. I hope it's hormonal on my part and not on his.

"What about security?" she asks.

"Truthfully, the stand has been robbed twice, but not since the hospital security guards have added it to their route," Peter says. He shows her the other security measures, the cameras, the sign saying no more than twenty dollars in change is available, and the emergency buttons that are tied into the police station.

"Cops stop a lot, too. They like the coffee," Mohammed says. He beckons me to help while Peter finishes the interview. The long line is surprising because of the cold.

"Someone is taking pictures of the stand." Mohammed points to a black VW bug across the street. When the man behind the wheel sees us looking, he puts down his camera and starts his car. A few minutes later he's gone.

Peter gets out of his chickpea suit and bundles up. We walk home, his arm around me, the snow crunching under our feet. As we wait for the crossing light, he kisses me.

"Careful! Our lips might freeze together," I say.

I prepare for my lecture in the corner of the loft I've appropriated for a workspace. I'd rather be downstairs with my head in Peter's lap watching the news.

Peter calls me to come fast. I run downstairs to see Fenway President Jonathan Baker saying, "Male faculty members are often approached by our young female students. Professor Henry Sumner is the victim of that old quote, 'Hell hath no fury like a woman scorned.' And although we take any charge seriously, because we need to protect our young women, we also need to protect our faculty."

Regina Hughes, a new anchorwoman—imported from New York in a career downgrade, but said by the station to want to come back to her native New England—asks, "Then you don't believe the charges against Professor Sumner are true?"

"We've done a full investigation. As a result he denies them and he has the backing of the faculty, me and the Board of Regents. We can't ruin careers because of hysterical young girls. Think of what happened during the Salem witch trials not so far from here. Innocent people died because some teenager . . ."

Baker's face fades and Hughes reappears. She holds a piece of paper in her hands. "I've just had a phone call from Dr. Judith Smentsky, the well-known authority on teenage eating disorders and head of the clinic at Fenway College. Dr. Smentsky has said that the entire faculty is not behind Professor Sumner."

"You've just seen the shit hit the fan," I tell Peter.

"I always wondered what it would be like," he says.

I never thought of myself as materialistic. When I lived in a house with every gadget imaginable, I dreamed of a simple life free of David's toys.

Peter's kitchen is well-equipped but not with gadgets. He doesn't need a special appliance for cooking hot dogs and another to make hamburgers perfectly round.

Had I gone into my own apartment, I might have missed more things because I'd have nothing, but I went from David's kingdom to Peter's sanctuary. Yet, I find I miss some possessions terribly. Not many. Some.

Emotionally, I want my grandmother's painting of Venice. I was in kindergarten when she painted it, about a year before she died. She was my mother's mother, and she lived with us. The painting is of a boatman standing in a gondola outside a small house.

Grammy had never been to Venice. She'd never been much farther north than Hampton Beach, New Hampshire or farther south than Providence, Rhode Island. She was a real New England Yankee who saw no need to venture far because she was already where she wanted to be.

She'd copied the Venetian scene from a stereo-optic card, and I remember watching her paint it. She kept picking up the stereoscope, looking into it, then putting it down before dabbing paint on the canvas.

I often wonder if she ever dreamed of being an artist at a time when there were so few choices for women. At fifteen she'd quit school to clerk in a store until she married. Then her mother, a widow, had moved in with the newlyweds.

Thinking about Grammy I wonder if Mother had expected one of her children to invite her to live with them. Maybe having Ben next door was the same thing to her.

The painting hangs in my old dressing room. David didn't feel it good enough to hang anywhere else, although an art critic who stayed with us asked about it. She'd said it was exceptional. After she'd left, David had said that she was being polite.

156

Every morning when I looked at the painting, I felt in touch with who I was and who I wasn't. I felt connected to my grandmother far beyond my simple memory, with so many of her memories passed on in stories told to me.

Although I was just starting school when she died, I remember her telling me how she rode the first bicycle in town. She'd been equally adventurous in learning to drive a car and was known in Concord as "the woman with the Ford" for two years before another woman began driving. The painting is the only thing I have of hers. I miss it.

I miss my flannel nightgowns. Much washing has softened them. It takes a long time to break in jeans, shoes and nightgowns. I miss my computer. Writing on Peter's electric Smith Corona after the joys of word processing is like going from a Corvette to an oxcart.

I decide to get the few things I want from the house while David is away. I remember my future ex-husband was scheduled to spend the middle two weeks of January in Europe.

My chance comes Tuesday morning when I have no lectures. I call the house to tell the housekeeper I'll be coming out, but there's no answer.

When I tell Peter what I plan, he offers to come with me. Andrea is still being trained but he feels he can leave her alone for a couple of hours.

At first I say no, but I dread the trip so much I agree as long as he's willing to wait at the coffee shop. There's something unfair about inviting my future husband into the territory of my old one. Peter agrees without argument. Without counter-suggestions.

I'm still unused to not sparring over every point. When Peter says he'd like to see where I lived, it's a statement anyone might make, like saying that they think it will snow or reporting how the Celtics beat the Lakers. There are no points to be gained or lost.

I drive. Sometimes Peter drives. He doesn't care. Both of us are neutral about driving, doing it to get places, with no real pleasure or dislike.

Some men hate riding with a woman. You see wives in the passenger seat while hubby parks and gets out. Wifey then slides behind the wheel and takes off. Even Mark and Judy are like that.

On Route 93 I worm my way into the middle lane. A huge truck barrels behind me. I hit the accelerator, praying the car will react. It does. Peter applauds.

Maybe it's dumb, but my stomach knots as I drive into town. The past encroaches on my present. I pull into the parking lot and point out where Peter should wait for me. There are only a few cars. The lunchtime sandwich crowd hasn't arrived and it's too late for morning coffee.

"One vanilla soda with chocolate ice cream coming up," Peter says. He always orders that. He varies his flavor of cones, picking the oddest ones like mango or pineapple chocolate chip. "Want anything for courage?"

I say no as he gets out and pecks me on the cheek. He has *The Boston Globe* tucked in his armpit.

The house is less than a half a mile away. As I drive by my soon-to-be-ex-sister-in-law's, I look for her car. Her garage is empty. So is David's.

I ring the bell. No answer. My key doesn't work. He's changed the locks. Damn! It's still half my house. I am locked out of my own house. I should have come when the housekeeper was there. I wonder if she's been told not to let me in.

I look for my phone. I must have left it home. Damn. Damn. Damn.

158

Chickpea Lover

Peter comes out of the coffee shop as soon as he sees me. "That was fast and . . ." Rather than let him finish I storm out of the car. He watches as I go to the pay phone at the other end of the parking lot. I dial David's office.

When Sylvia answers, I wonder whom David sent to buy her Christmas present. I can't imagine him doing it himself. I'm sure she was the one who bought my presents as well all these years. That's because before each gift-giving holiday she asked me what I wanted and it always turned up.

I tested it by asking for weird things like a set of acrylic paints and a child's coloring book. David had seemed surprised when I opened them.

"Long time no hear," she says. She sounds her old cheery self. She tells me David is flying back from Paris tomorrow.

"Do you know where I can reach him?" I ask. There's silence. "Am I putting you in a spot?" I stamp one foot then the other. It's cold.

"Well, I hate to say no to you, but . . ."

"Don't worry, Sylvia. Don't even mention I called. We'll pretend this conversation never took place." I hear her sigh, probably with relief, as we hang up.

I search my straw bag for more change. The bag's been out of style for years, it's the wrong season, but I still use it because it holds so much stuff—paperbacks, notebooks, pens, Lifesavers, change, sugar cubes, magazines, miscellaneous. Stuff! No change. No money at all. I try my phone card. The operator tells me it has been canceled.

Peter doesn't have a phone credit card. I'll phone my lawyer this afternoon or tomorrow. I walk back to the car and explain what happened.

"I'm sorry, I don't have any change either. Look." He

points to the maternity shop across the street. "While I waited for you to finish the call, I kept thinking how nice that dress in the window would look on you. Let's buy it so it won't be a wasted trip. We can get change as well."

We dash across Route 28 to look at that blue corduroy dress. Chloe is lucky that her parents didn't get squished by traffic.

As I try on the dress, I examine my tummy in the three-way mirror. It's definitely that of a pregnant woman. I glance at my cellulite. The doctors who say it doesn't exist never looked at my thighs. Cellulite reminds me of Jill, who has never had any. Maybe I got her share. I still haven't been able to talk to her. She leaves her voice mail on and hasn't returned my calls.

I slip the dress over my head, run a comb through my hair, and adjust the sailor collar. Opening the dressing-room curtain, I stroll out like a professional model.

Peter smiles. "You look beautiful. Let me buy it for you." I do.

We now have the change I need for the telephone, but I can wait to talk to my lawyer. Instead I want a new pair of boots to go with my dress.

We stop at the discount shoe store right before the Route 93 entrance. I find a perfect pair with a slight heel.

I hand my charge card to the clerk whose bald head shines with the reflection of the light directly overhead. He runs the card through the machine. It whistles. He runs it through a second time. It whistles again.

"Can you call?" I ask.

He does. "I'm sorry, your card's been rejected," he says.

"I'm up-to-date on my payments. I've over ten thousand left on my credit line."

The clerk looks embarrassed. "How many times have

you used it today? Most banks have limits on the number of daily uses in case the card is stolen. Good thieves know store limits and make lots of little purchases."

Peter and I look at each other. I wonder if the clerk thinks we're robbers. I take out my checkbook to write a check. It's a new account with my name only. I no longer have a right to use my joint account with David.

"I'm sorry," the clerk says. "The check has to be a number over three hundred and you need your name and address printed on it." These checks are part of my plain blue starter kit. My regular checks haven't arrived. The number is too low.

Tears run down my cheeks. How funny we must look, a pregnant woman crying with a younger man trying to console her and a bald clerk with a wishing-he-were-anywhere-else expression.

Peter writes out a check. He has the right number, the right credit card and license for identification.

Back in the car, anger replaces helplessness. I splutter all the way back to the city as Peter makes proper sympathy sounds. He parks in the college faculty lot and then walks to work. I storm into my office to call my lawyer.

She comes on the phone and listens as I rave on. I'm sure she's heard this same story so many times from so many people that it's boring. We make an appointment for that evening rather than wait for the sixteenth.

I call Sylvia again to give her Peter's number and to have her ask David to call me as soon as he can. A week goes by. Nothing from David. I call Sylvia daily. I call my old number. I call Carol Goss. I give up.

Peter takes me to my amniocentesis. It's as bad as I thought it would be. There is pain afterwards, and I stay

161

home from school. As I lounge around the house in a sweat suit I've bought to expand with me, I realize that I've missed the meeting about Sumner.

Saturday arrives and I feel better. We watch a PBS special about Native Canadians. They beat out an ancient rhythm as their breath crystallizes in the air. Calgary is as cold as Boston. The dog curls up at our feet. My head rests in Peter's lap.

He's covered me with an afghan. His mother made it with double yarn to guard against the New England cold when he came here to college.

The phone rings. Peter reaches behind him to grab Garfield's back.

"Hello." Pause. "Hold on." Covering the mouthpiece, he whispers, "David?"

On the TV the camera focuses on a little girl. I take the phone. "Hello."

"Hello, whore."

On the television, a little child in buckskins watches the elders of his tribe dance as Peter pushes the mute button so I can concentrate.

I think of crushed goose eggs. I think of a dropped vase. However, David doesn't usually resort to vulgarity in his attempts to get even. Like handling angry students, I decide not to react. This isn't being a wimp, this is energy-saving strategy. "I need some things from the house: my computer, my grandmother's painting, some clothes."

"Tough. Is it his brat you're carrying?"

"How did you know?"

"I ran into Dr. French. He congratulated me on becoming a father. Only I'm not the father. Your brat's father is some weirdo."

"He's not a weirdo."

"I've had you watched. I've a photo of you serving junk food and another of you kissing him. For God's sakes, Liz, he's ten years younger than you. He's a dropout."

"David, please." My hands shake.

"You'll get nothing from me." The phone goes dead.

Peter guides me to the kitchen and makes me hot chocolate.

"What's the worst your husband can do?" he asks. We both sit at the table with the untouched cups in front of us.

I think about it. "Not give me a divorce. Chloe will be illegitimate."

"So we might not be married before Chloe is born. That's not terrible these days. Nothing will change between us whether we're married or not married."

The hot chocolate is too hot to drink so I blow on it. "I guess not, but I'm conventional enough to prefer being married if I have a baby." Living with a man not my husband is no problem.

"So am I, but we'll make a family in any form."

He prepares supper—beans, franks and brown bread. As I set the table the phone and doorbell ring, one almost drowning out the other.

Peter goes for the phone, in case it's David. I hear Peter talking with Mohammed who can't find something at the stand. Andrea has her own system, and the two men constantly play Guess-Where-She-Left-It-Now. Peter is torn between letting her go and having more free time.

When I open the door, a blast of cold air comes in. A cab driver hands me a manila envelope. He waits for a tip. I've a dollar stuffed in my jeans pocket.

There's no return address. After closing the door, I open it. It's my grandmother's painting cut in at least thirty pieces, not even squares but like a jigsaw puzzle.

As I burst into tears, Peter hangs up. I don't have to tell him what it is, because he picks up the boatman, still in the gondola, which is cut out as a single piece. I've described the painting to him before.

"That bastard," he says. His stroking my hair and holding my hand doesn't make the feeling of loss go away.

CHAPTER ELEVEN

Fenway students circle the parking lot. They carry signs saying, "Stop Sexual Abuse," "Good Grades for Good Work Not Good Sex," and "Just Say No."

A Channel Five photographer, his Minicam balanced on his shoulder, shoots what a young woman directs him to. She waves to me. She graduated from our communication department four years ago, but I can't remember her name. Like the cameraman she's dressed in jeans. The students' coats are opened, revealing sweatshirts with the message "No Sex for Grades." Michael Lucci, the station's newest reporter, gets ready to interview Amanda Silver. She's taller than he is. He is beautiful with bleached blond hair perfectly cut, not at all like the scruffy cameraman and director.

"Stand a stair above her," the director says, pointing them to the main building with its Greek columns. Amanda and he are eye to eye. Amanda wets her lips as the camera begins to roll.

"This is Michael Lucci at Fenway College. Students are protesting administration cover-up for a professor accused of propositioning student Melissa Greenbaum. I'm talking to the leader of the demonstration, actress Amanda Silver. You may remember her as Elsbeth on *Heavenly Hospital.*"

Amanda speaks slowly, letting her hair blow away from her face. "I was an actress. Now I'm a nursing student." She stands so her sweatshirt can be easily read. I truly respect her ability to work this scene.

"We've all heard about the casting couch. Is this any different?" Lucci asks.

"It's exactly the same thing, and they're both wrong," she says.

"Have you ever been approached by Dr. Sumner?" he asks.

"No, but my roommate left school last year because of her affair with him."

"Cut," Michael says. He turns to the director. "Do we have a libel problem?"

"Use alleged in your wrap-up," the ex–Fenway student turned director says.

Michael keeps stumbling over his words. They reshoot twice before he can finish the sentence. "Dr. Henry Sumner, a renowned chemist who served on the Presidential Commission for the Responsible Use of Chemicals in the Environment, is accused of attacking Melissa Greenbaum. Ms. Greenbaum is the daughter of Dr. Saul Greenbaum, President of Masterson Pharmaceuticals. The attack had . . ."

"Cut," the director says. "Use alleged attack."

Michael picks up: "The alleged attack and the resulting lawsuit have torn this small upper-class girls' school apart. Amanda Silver, well-known child star and daughter of Hollywood actor Christopher Silver, has said she knows of sexual indiscretions by the professor with other students. The alleged acts are the reason for this demonstration."

"Cut. We can edit what we need, Mike." The director points to me. "Interview Dr. Adams."

I protest, but the students clamor. I know they are right. "Dr. Elizabeth Adams, head of the nursing department," I say into the mike. I forget to wet my lips.

"Do you believe the charges against Dr. Sumner?" As Michael hovers over me, I realize he must haven eaten garlic. I hope the camera didn't catch that I wrinkled my nose.

"I know sexual intimidation by those in power is not new. I believe it exists here and at most colleges and universities."

"Do you support the students?"

"Yes," I say, grateful for my tenure status. This will drive Baker ape-shit.

"Way to go, Doc Adams," a voice calls out.

Judy waits outside my office. "The next meeting of the Get Sumner Committee is at six tonight. I've reserved a room at the old HoJo's in Kenmore Square." She lowers her voice. "Fred's been denied tenure and so has Laurie Jawolski."

Fred teaches computer science. The kids love his courses. Laurie teaches women's studies, a program that the administration wants to discontinue. Both support Melissa and have gone directly to Baker, asking him to rethink his position. Although a committee handles tenure, the members are in Baker's camp.

Fenway is, like all schools, heavy with politics. Sucking up to some people is a good career move. I can't understand how Baker can take this stance with all the sex scandals, especially those in the papers about the Catholic church. He seems to be acting like the bishops. I wonder if he reads the newspapers. I wouldn't dare ask him. Maybe I don't suck up to Baker, but I never have attacked him until today.

The Get Sumner Committee has met a few times, but the president has issued a new directive. All meetings must have his permission. A representative of his office must be present at all times. The only way to meet is to do it off-campus and after-hours.

The floral print of the wallpaper at HoJo's looks funny

against the snow on the window ledge. An orange butterfly clashes with the foot-high pink flower where it poses for eternity or at least until the management changes the wallpaper.

Fred is the only other person there when I arrive. I wonder if the president's power is cutting resistance. My fears disappear within ten minutes as others straggle into the room. We are ten women and two men. Bob, the other man, has tenure, but we're the only two of the group. The twelve of us represent about twenty-five percent of the faculty.

A waitress, about thirty pounds overweight with a too-tight uniform, comes in to take our drink order. I choose apple juice and dream of a wine spritzer. We all talk at once until Judy takes over.

"Tough luck, Fred," she says.

Fred leans back in his chair and shrugs. "Shit happens. I'll find something else."

"OK, you dirty dozen, let's get this show on the road," Judy says. There are twitters.

I'm curious about something before we decide how we're going to fight Baker. "How many of you have been approached by a professor in college?"

Six women raise their hands.

"A man came onto me my senior year, and a woman prof also. I didn't like it either," Fred says. He looks and acts like Alan Alda from the *M*A*S*H* reruns, not like Alda looks today. If Fred's wife tires of him, there's a waiting list of women who'll offer to take her place.

"I changed grad schools because of it," Marcy says. "I thought I was the only one, until I found out I was the student of the semester. Like playmate of the month." She looks at her fingers. "The bastard was my first love."

A busboy rolls in a television that rests on a raised table. We switch on the Channel Five news. Anchor Natalie Jacobson looks at the camera and says, "Students at Fenway College protested the administration's support of Dr. Henry Sumner. Michael Lucci was on the scene."

The camera pans the iron fence and zooms to the sign, a gift of the class of 1951. We see the students' signs and Amanda, followed by me.

Lucci's closing comments are far smoother-sounding than they were at the taping.

"I look so fat," I say.

"Everyone looks fatter on television," Bob says. He teaches TV production.

The next news story is about a possible toll hike on the Mass Pike. Marcy shuts off the set.

Tina dashes in, late as usual, and slams her books on the table. She's wearing a scarf so long it could double as an afghan. "I just heard from one of my spies. Like Whittier and Baker had a screaming fight this afternoon over contract renewals."

"What else do you know?" Bob asks.

"Well, they like threw everyone in listening distance out of the office so my source couldn't get all the dirt. I think the upshot is anyone supporting Melissa is out."

Everyone talks at once. I can pick up some comments.

"They can't do it."

"Thank God for the teacher shortage."

"McDonald's is paying over minimum wage."

"That's more than I make lecturing."

Everything they say except "They can't do it" is correct. Massachusetts has a real shortage of unskilled employees. Unfortunately, Ph.D.s are plentiful. The administration will fill the posts without difficulty. I feel guilty because I'm protected by my tenure.

"We need to up the pressure. Let's call *Dateline*," Judy says.

"Do we have to do that to the college? It will hurt enrollment," Bob says, again followed by people talking at once.

"Fuck enrollment."

"The administration is doing it to itself."

"It'll be our jobs."

"Our jobs are probably gone already."

"How can they do that?"

Judy bangs the table. "Quiet. One at a time. Let's vote. All in favor of calling *Dateline*?"

Before she can finish, Dean Whittier blows in. She's dressed in boots, jeans and an Irish knit sweater. Her white hair is tucked into a blue knitted cap. Snowflakes melt into the wool.

We all freeze. She's administration, and despite Tina's gossip, we don't really know which side she's on.

"That's what I like to see—terror. Relax, group. I'm not a spy." Dean Whittier takes off her woolen cap. I have never heard of her telling a lie.

"Then why are you here?" Laurie asks.

"First, to tell you although President Baker doesn't know I'm here, he does know about this meeting."

"How did he find out?" Judy asks.

"I have no idea," Dean Whittier says. "I'm with you in principle but, and it's a big but, you need to know that he's determined to stamp out every bit of opposition to Sumner."

In the middle of her explanation the waitress comes in and asks if we want anything else. Another order goes around the room.

"There has to be something we can do," Tina says.

"I've been trying to talk some sense into Jonathan, but he's convinced that Melissa is a little bitch who made up the entire story, Amanda's a publicity-seeking actress, and Dr. Greenbaum is just another annoying parent who believes his spoiled brat." To our collective groan she says, "He believes, really believes, he has to take a stand to protect all male professors against preying women."

Judy says, "I remember him telling me once how when we educate a woman, we educate a family. He thinks a woman's place is ultimately in the home."

"Male chauvinist pig," Marcy says.

Dean Whittier says, "It's not that simple. Sumner and he were friends from sandbox days. Jonathan will never admit he was wrong bringing him here."

We nod, suspecting that Jonathan Baker has never admitted being wrong in his life. We fall silent.

"Where do you stand?" Bob asks her.

"With you, but that's limited help. He threw me out of the office when I suggested that Melissa might be right." Dean Whittier looks awful. She's pale and I never remember seeing such deep circles under her eyes. Her hands are shaking a little. When she smiles, the tiredness in her face disappears. "This old lady still has some fight left in her. However, unlike any of you, I can activate my pension anytime. I don't need this job." She puts both hands on the table and leans toward us. "I refuse to compromise myself at the end of my career."

Respect is such an old-fashioned word, yet I respect this woman. Where does she find her courage? Where did my colleagues find the power inside themselves to risk their jobs? Did they know they had so much at stake?

Judy says, "We were just talking about getting *Dateline* to do a segment on us when you came in."

"Before voting, why don't you discuss your motives?" Whittier says. "Then when you vote, you'll know why. I'm for it. I don't think pressure from within will work."

Marcy says, "I'd like to think the good guys will win and we'll save your jobs. But it doesn't affect me, since I'm taking a post in Seattle next year."

"It's too late to save your jobs unless the regents vote in a whole new administration," Dean Whittier says.

"For me I'm going to have to go to Baker and grovel for my job," Terry says. We all know she's the sole support of three kids. "I'll still work underground for you."

"I hate misuse of power," Laurie says. "Ignoring it makes it worse."

We ramble on about power. "Maybe if we make it enough of an issue, a professor will think twice in the future before he feels up a student," Tina says.

"Let's vote," Judy says.

One by one hands go up except for Terry. Then she, too, raises her hand. "Shit! I teach a course in ethics."

Judy and Marcy hug her in turn. Judy says, "We'll pretend you're not with us. We can even stage a mock fight, or when you sit down with us in The Caf, we can get up and leave. Something like that."

"Do you want me to make the call?" Marcy asks.

"I'll do it," Dean Whittier says. "I have more protection than the rest of you. But what do we do if they won't cover it?"

"Demand the regents meet," Bob says.

"No go," Dean Whittier says. "They gave him a vote of confidence the other day. He called each of them. He has them bamboozled."

"Shit," Fred says. "He's a clever old devil."

Bob gets up to pace. "Donors. That's the other key. If

172

we write them, they'll pressure the regents. But how can we get our hands on the list?"

"It may take some time, but like I'll find a way," Tina says.

Dean Whittier looks at her. "You know Tina dear, I think you know more about the college than the rest of us put together. And I know you'll go far, but I don't want you stealing mailing lists." She reaches into her large backpack and pulls out several long rolls of labels. "Goodness gracious me. How did this happen to fall in my bag? Bob, I trust you to throw it away for me."

Two people volunteer to write the letter and bring it to the next meeting. We vote to adjourn and meet next week.

Everyone but Fred and I decided to eat dinner.

I head home. I'm tired. The phone is ringing as I walk in.

"What a hypocrite you are. You talk about sexual morality on television and you've got a bastard in your belly." David's voice is slurred.

"You're drunk."

"I've had a couple, but I'm far from drunk, bitch."

I don't want to deal with this. Then I realize I don't have to deal with it. "David, if you want to talk about something constructive, fine. If not, I'm hanging up."

"I'll never give you a divorce. I'm going to make your brat stay illegitimate," he says.

I hang up without listening to the rest of his words. I know he fights hard at work, but I didn't expect him to fight me this hard.

CHAPTER TWELVE

In my office with the heat pumping full force, I try correcting the first essays of the term. They are short, two pages.

Even though morning sickness is no longer a problem, I find if I let myself, I could sleep twenty hours a day. I know pregnancy produces a surplus of hormones like the ones released after making love. Those little devils make sleep compelling. Losing the battle to my hormones and the heat, I rest my head on my arms and drift off to sleep. I dream about a little girl running through a field.

Since my head is next to the phone, when it rings I jump, throwing myself back. The only reason I don't fall over is the walls stop me. For a minute I wonder if there's a long phone cord to the field, but as I focus on my office around me, I realize what happened. I pick up the phone.

"Hello."

"Dr. Adams, please come to the president's office." The crisp voice belongs to Norma, Baker's personal assistant. In another era she would have been called a spinster. Tina once said that after work Norma hopped between the pages of a Barbara Pym novel to talk to vicars and to run jumble sales.

"I'll be down in about twenty minutes," I say. Baker probably wants to tear me up one side and down the other for the newscast last week. I'm sure he would have done it earlier had he not been away raising money.

"Cluck," she says. There's something more disapproving about a cluck than a disparaging remark. The cluck tells me racing was expected.

Gathering some books, I drop them off at the library, which is in the same building as my office. Outside, I avoid the puddles that have formed in the parking lot. The weather has turned mild, melting the snow and giving false hopes of an early end to winter. Every year at this time it warms up for a few days. Then we're plunged back into winter. Global warming or not, New England has always had an irrational climate.

Two concrete planters, which hold tulips in the spring, geraniums in the summer and petunias in the fall, are mud-filled. They flank the double carved-oak doors that open into the main hall of the administration building. They should belong to a European cathedral.

Half the administration building is classrooms, the other half is offices. Although no money has been spent on decor, the building is cheery. Large windows run from the floor to the high ceilings, letting in tons of light. In most offices the staff have hung posters and photos, making a hodgepodge but one with personal ambiance.

The president's office is at the end of the hall on the third floor, totally removed from activity areas. It's even necessary to go up three little stairs to get to the door, like climbing up to heaven. Unlike the other offices, which are painted institutional white, the president's suite is oak-paneled.

As soon as I cross the threshold into the outer sanctum of the inner sanctum, the linoleum gives way to a parquet floor protected by Oriental rugs. Norma's desk, which is directly in front of the entrance, is antique. Hers is a rolltop, popular in New England during the Civil War. Even her computer, sitting on her left side, is on an antique table.

The president's door is open a crack. I can see the newspaper he sits behind. At least I assume he is sitting there, and the newspaper is not suspended, or that someone else has sneaked in to take his place.

Norma points to a seat. She doesn't offer me tea or coffee, which she did the last few times I came in. The president really must be angry and have given her a "no niceties" order.

Picking up *The Chronicle of Higher Education*, I see plenty of university jobs, which makes me feel really good for my co-workers who are losing theirs. At least they've places to apply to.

Jimmy, head of security, comes in puffing. His forehead is sweaty. I smile at him. A former policeman from a small town, he considers the safety of everyone at Fenway his personal mission. For example, he set up a shuttle from the library to the dorms to make sure the girls don't have to walk alone after dark. Another one of his ideas was to give street-smart lessons to all incoming freshmen as part of the orientation.

Normally Jimmy and I chat freely. This time he doesn't make eye contact.

President Baker is tall and thin except for a tiny potbelly. He has a full head of slate gray hair, and an Abraham Lincoln beard. He looks like a college president should look. For such a big man he has a very high voice. I read somewhere that Lincoln also had a very high voice. That's where the similarity between the two men ends.

Instead of greeting me Baker just stands at his door. I read his signal and walk into his office. He seats himself at his Louis XVI table, which he uses as a desk. I notice a small chip in the inlaid wood around the leather center. It wasn't there last time I was in here. The desk is empty except for a telephone and Mrs. Baker's photo. She's a nervous little woman who never looks directly at anyone.

The president, on the other hand, uses his eyes to bore through his opponents. He treats everyone as a potential opponent. He always stands so close that I feel the need to move away. Then he moves in. I move away ad nauseam. If there were a doctorate given in intimidation, he'd have two.

His method of domination this time is to leave me standing. I'm not invited to sit in either of the embroidered and gilded Louis XVI chairs across from him.

He clears his throat. "Professor Adams, you are terminated immediately."

At first the words don't make any sense. Then I realize he's fired me. I've never been fired. Even when I worked at odd jobs as I went through school, I was always considered a good-to-excellent employee. Maybe I misheard. "What did you say?"

He repeated the same sentence.

"I've tenure. You can't fire me."

His elbows are on his desk. He makes a steeple of his hands. "Yes, I can. I just did. For two reasons: The first is based on the morals clause in your contract. You're pregnant. It's come to my attention your husband is not the father of your child and you're living with another man. That is not a role model we want for our girls."

I put both my hands on his desk and lean towards him. "I suppose Henry Sumner's propositioning them is a good role model?" As I hear myself say those words, I think, My God, I've never mouthed off at a boss like that before. I've never been fired before.

"Dr. Sumner is not the issue, Dr. Adams, you are."

"Pregnancy isn't a legal reason to fire me."

He taps his first two fingers together. "We might have a problem making the morals clause stand in a court of law.

But we won't have any hassles with my second reason. You're incompetent." He clears his throat. His face is totally impassive.

I sit down without being asked because I don't trust my legs to hold me. Incompetent? That's not a word I'd ever use to describe myself. Wishy-washy, naive, cowardly, too eager to please, are things I would include in my character fault list, but incompetent? Never.

"I've read the student reviews from last semester. It's absolutely clear from some of them that you are not doing your job. We can't have a bad teacher on campus and that is legal reason to remove you, not only from tenure status, but from the college."

"You can't do that."

"You know I can. You sat on the Teachers' Union Committee that approved the procedure. Surely you remember? It was only last year."

He's correct. Last year, the union, concerned that we had one professor with Alzheimer's and another having a nervous breakdown, agreed that if incompetence could be proven, tenure could be revoked. But in both those cases, the revoking of tenure involved disability.

I sat on the committee that had hammered out the agreement, and all of us had been careful to make sure the right balance was struck between fairness to the students and fairness to the professor under threat. Student reviews were selected as a major measurement tool.

"That wasn't the way it was intended to be used," I say.

He smiles. "It doesn't matter how it was intended. I used it. We are removing you because you're not a good teacher. According to what I read in those student reviews, I have no choice but to take action." He unfolds his hands and propels himself upward, hovering over me. I imagine him saying, "Gotcha."

"I would like to see those reviews."

"They are confidential."

"And what about the hearing I am entitled to?"

"I don't see that you are entitled to a hearing. It's recommended, but not guaranteed in the procedure that you yourself approved. I have the right to terminate at my discretion with sufficient proof. I have that proof."

He walks to the door. "Jimmy, please see that Dr. Adams clears out her office and is off-campus today."

I'm still seated, almost in shock. I have turned towards the door where the security officer waits.

The president comes and stands next to my chair. "If she doesn't move, carry her," he says.

Jimmy's face turns deep crimson as he stands in the door, shifting his weight between his feet. The poor man.

"Jimmy." The president's voice commands the security officer to action.

As he takes only half a step towards me, I hold up my hands. "Don't worry, Jimmy, you won't have to do anything." I muster all the dignity possible. Moving my body to avoid touching air that touched the president, I sweep from the office.

"And, Jimmy, see that Dr. Adams doesn't take any college property when she packs," the president calls after us.

I stop, my back to the president. When I open my mouth to say something, no words come out. I respond to Jimmy's gentle pressure on my elbow.

I feel so sorry for Jimmy. We've always gotten along so well, drinking coffee together in The Caf, chatting about life in general or his daughters in particular. He walks next to me, his blush a little subsided.

"I don't blame you. I'll do everything possible to

make this easier for you."

"Thanks. You don't know how bad I feel about this," he says.

We arrive at my office to find empty cartons stacked in front of my door. The administration is certainly efficient. As I unlock the door I'm hit by a blast of heat. "Well, at least I won't be cooking myself each day," I say, trying to joke.

Jimmy moves his mouth and head in something that isn't really a grin or a nod. We look around at the ten years of materials I've accumulated. I'm frozen in place unsure of where to start.

"What can I do to help?" he asks.

"I think I'll need more boxes."

He phones the janitor to bring more. "I'm sorry, but I can't leave you."

"We wouldn't want me to go on a rampage and destroy the school, would we?"

"Something like that, I guess. I can't imagine you doing that," he says.

We've filled about six boxes when Jimmy holds up a wood plaque I'd shoved into a drawer after graduation last year. There is a parchment certificate pasted on the wood with a band of gold leaf around it. The kids in my "Dealing with Parents of Sick Children" seminar had presented it to me. Written in calligraphy are the words, "To the most caring prof we've ever had." Each one of them had signed it.

"I sure must have slipped in a single semester," I say.

He raises one eyebrow and puts his finger to his lips. I frown. Picking up a pencil he looks for a blank piece of paper, which is hard to find.

Whenever I sit at a desk, I doodle. All my papers have

flowers, letters, buildings and stick figures on them. They're not just plain doodles. I color them with a variety of felt-tip pens.

Turning over a sheet he finds space. "Your office may be bugged," he writes.

"It's illegal," I write back.

He claps and nods. While he looks for wires, he chats about inconsequential things. When he unscrews my phone, I see the bug. He puts his finger to his lips and picks up the pen.

"It may pick up conversation, too," he writes.

I've already packed the digital camera I keep for special occasions such as the day Claire made a cake for Tina when she went to Florida. It was shaped like a torso in a bikini with cupcakes standing tall for boobs. A cherry was in the middle of each one. She even had matched Tina's skin in the mocha frosting. That was the last time I'd used it. I rummage through boxes until I find it. The batteries are still good.

"That won't prove anything," he writes about the pictures.

I snap another.

"You could have installed it yourself."

I write, "Would you testify for me?"

He shrugs and writes, "My kids." His daughters get free tuition, a staff perk. Jimmy needs his job, this job especially.

I write, "Can I take this for my lawyer, or is it school property?" He covers his eyes and I slip the bug into one of the boxes.

As he puts the phone back together, the janitor arrives with more cartons. "I'm really sorry you're leaving, I don't understand it," the janitor says.

"It happens," I tell him.

The three of us finish a little before lunch. The janitor loads the college's station wagon after putting the back seats down flat. The car is filled with my boxes from the hatch to the front seat. The janitor puts a box on my lap and a second between my feet. We still need another trip.

Jimmy drives me home, helps me unload the stuff, and offers to do the next trip for me so I won't have to go back on campus.

When he returns with the second load, I offer him coffee or hot chocolate and a tuna sandwich. He accepts coffee with the sandwich.

He sits at the table as the coffee perks. "Liz, there's so much going on at Fenway that isn't right. I'll tell you this, when the president asked me about bugging offices, I refused. He must have gotten a private company to do it." He stirs his coffee to the point he almost makes a hole in the bottom of the cup. "I don't feel very proud of myself at this moment," he says.

I want to make it better for him, but I also know we can't prove the bugging attempt without him. Even with him it would be doubtful. Baker could say he'd been joking or that he knew nothing about it.

"The thing is, Liz, I know you're a great teacher. Ellen loved your classes." Ellen is his oldest kid. "I don't understand how you could get bad reviews."

"Thanks for that." There's scum on my hot chocolate and I skim it off and drop it onto the saucer. "You've heard about the pregnant part."

"Yup. I did. There's been rumors around campus about your sudden love of Mideastern food, but that's your affair." He looks at me. "The older I get, the less desire I have to judge people. How's that for an Irish Catholic?"

"Not bad." We've discussed the pros and cons of religion enough, often prompted by student activists for pro-choice or gay rights.

Jimmy leaves and I sit there, not knowing what to do. Because of the bugging, I can't call anyone at the office without putting them in more danger. I don't want to tell Peter yet.

The phone rings. I'm beginning to hate telephones. They keep bringing disaster. This call comes from Nurse Bronk. "Your health insurance claim has been rejected."

I realize that David must have had my name removed from it.

What a shitty day. I call my lawyer.

Carol as always, picks up the phone immediately, listens then asks, "Did you sign any documents?"

"At the college or with David?"

"Either. Both?"

"No."

"Good. Under the COBRA laws, David can't take you off his insurance. Give me your policy number and I'll call his attorney and the claims division."

We talk about an unlawful termination suit. "I'm a rebel lawyer. There are a lot of stupid suits that should never be brought to court. This isn't one of them," she says. "Don't worry" is the last thing she says before hanging up.

"Don't worry" is one of those phrases that if you weren't worrying before someone says it, you certainly worry after. Don't I have every right to worry? I'm pregnant by a chickpea who isn't my husband, out of work for alleged in-competence, with no health insurance and no hope of a di-vorce.

Boss, who had been watching me from the time I got home, comes up and puts her head in my lap. I pat her and I wait, only I don't know what I'm waiting for.

★ ★ ★ ★ ★

Judy stands at my front door. It's getting dark and colder. The puddles on the sidewalk are ice-crusted. The dog skids in her rush to see who else might be in Judy's Beetle.

"Come in," I say.

"I've been calling your office all afternoon. Did you forget our lunch meeting?"

"Totally. I'm sorry."

"What happened? Forgetting a date isn't like you. I was getting worried."

I tell her. Then I show her the bug.

"Holy shit!" Going to the sofa she pulls the Fenway directory from her briefcase. It includes home phone numbers of the staff. She starts dialing.

Within two hours everyone who was at HoJo's for our last meeting, except for Dean Whittier and Tina, is in my living room. Judy left messages on their answering machines.

Peter comes in as the meeting is getting underway. He looks tired. He has fired Andrea and is working fourteen-hour days.

"Liz, wanta talk to Peter in private?" Judy asks.

We go up to our loft. I tell him.

"You poor thing," he says.

"We'll have a money problem," I say.

"I can support us."

"What if they won't reinstate the insurance?" Being without health insurance has always been my family's greatest fear. Forget what the job is. Does it carry medical protection? Ben almost didn't go into business for himself until he found a trade association where he could buy the insurance. Peter to this point has relied on luck.

"Then we'll have a big debt when the baby's born. I'm more worried about you." He brushes a strand of my hair from my cheek. "You love that job and the kids. You're going to miss that more than we'll miss the money."

"You're rapidly turning into the best friend I've never had," I say.

"You bet your sweet ass," he says. "Go downstairs and see what you can accomplish in the way of truth, justice and the American way."

When I turn to leave he whacks me on the bottom. As I turn he blows me a kiss.

Each person at the meeting had stopped at his or her office on the way to my place. Returning to campus between the time she visited me and the start of the meeting, Judy had found Jimmy. She'd asked him to help find more of the bugging devices. He told her he couldn't do it himself, but he could tell her how to do it. She waited in the parking lot and repeated his instructions over and over as each of us came in.

"This is out of control," Judy starts to say as the doorbell rings.

Tina comes in with her coat askew and her eyes red. "I knew like everyone was here by the cars. I'm sorry, Liz. Have you heard about Dean Whittier?"

"What about her?" Bob asks.

"About six tonight she came back from the meeting she had with the deans of the local universities. The one at like Copley Place. The president called her into the office and told her about you, Liz." Tina takes her coat off and throws it over the banister. "Anyway, Dean Whittier blew her stack. She started like screaming at him and . . ."

"I can't imagine her screaming," Bob says. "Although I can guess how mad she was."

185

"She passed out. They rushed her to Brigham and Women's Hospital, but I don't know what happened next." Tina says it all in one breath. She inhales and sits down.

"I saw an ambulance leave the parking lot as I was pulling out," Marcy says. "Since it didn't have any siren, I figured it wasn't too serious."

Everyone talks at once then Tina asks to use my phone. When patient information at Brigham and Women's refuses to give any news, Tina gets put through to the emergency room. Where doesn't that girl have sources? "May I speak with Farah, please . . . Hi, it's me, like sorry to bother you at work. There was an older woman brought in a little while ago. After six, before seven . . . Whittier . . . I want to know how she is . . ." There's a long wait. "Oh no!" She goes down on her knees, Garfield's back in her hand.

"What is it?" we all ask.

"She had a cerebral hemorrhage. She was dead on arrival."

Everyone is too stunned to say anything. Slowly they get their coats and leave.

Judy stays behind. "I can't believe she's gone. She was such a lady," Judy says.

Peter comes down from the loft and sits between us. We exchange Dean Whittier stories. He tells us about the day last week when there was a long line. "She came in the stand and made her own breakfast, wrapped it up and put the exact change on the cash register. Then with a twinkle she said, 'You don't mind if I don't give myself a tip?' She winked at me and was off."

The three of us sit on the couch. Peter has his arms around both of us and we snuggle into him.

Peter and I go to Dean Whittier's memorial service at

the Arlington Street Church. It's old-fashioned with boxes holding the individual pews. We open the white-painted door and sit down on red cushions.

Although we arrived early, the place is almost filled. Not only are current faculty and students here, but former professors and tons of alumnae varying in age from last year's graduates to some in their late forties. The Board of Regents, President Baker and his wife file in without indicating they know anyone.

A pretty blond with her hair in a bun stands up. She is wearing a slim blue skirt slit on both sides to the knee. She has a black jacket, and a scarf shot with gold picks up the blue and black. She looks classy.

"Thank you for coming. I am Diana Chambers, Alicia Whittier's oldest daughter. My sister Rita and my brother Harrison want you all to know this is not a day of mourning, but a celebration of the things she loved and believed in. We've asked some people to share with us their memories of her."

Dean Whittier's granddaughter gets up to play a flute medley of Beatles songs. She's blond, maybe sixteen at most. When she finishes she says, "No one knew that Granny loved the Beatles. When she baby-sat for me we'd mime to their music. She'd pretend she was Ringo and drum like crazy on an imaginary drum."

A former student recounts how Dean Whittier refused to let her quit school because of lack of money. "There's a special scholarship program for children of Czech descent that she found for me," she says. Her voice catches and then she sits down.

A friend, Dean Whittier's neighbor, stands at the podium. "When our kids were small, Alicia and I made a pact. Whenever one of us wanted to kill one of our children, we'd call the other, who would come instantly. Alicia often said that every parent has the potential to be abusive. The difference is some know how to find relief. She was right. I'll miss her, although neither of us have had to activate our pact for over three decades."

Bits and pieces of Dean Whittier's favorite writings are read. Rita recites Amy Lowell's "Patterns," Harrison picks a selection where Colette writes about her mother not coming to visit because she's waiting for a rare flower to bloom.

After Diana reads Alice Walker's "These Days," she says, "Mother believed in making the world a better place. She knew she couldn't save everyone and everything, but she contributed a little here and there. The poem I just read was open on her night table when I went into her room after we got the news. The people Alice Walker describes remind me of you here today. My mother isn't gone because she lives in our memories. Thank you all for coming to this celebration of a woman we loved dearly."

The organ breaks out into "Amazing Grace." No one says anything as we file out of the church. Peter and I share silence as we walk up Commonwealth Avenue.

CHAPTER THIRTEEN

The toilet flushes. Jane Pauley flushes my toilet. I never even thought about her going to the bathroom. Some women look like they never go. When I was a child I saw a photo of Trisha Nixon in a pink puffed-sleeve dress. She looks as if her body never grazed a toilet seat or needed a tampon. Jane Pauley is not as tall as I thought she'd be. And she's thinner.

There's an element of chaos, yet in another way everyone seems to know what they are doing. The three-man camera crew strings lights all over our living room as they eat the meal Peter sent over from the stand.

"This looks good," Jane says, picking up a brique. She holds the plate to her mouth as she bites into the filo dough. Egg squishes out the side. "Mmm, really good. I haven't had this since I was in Tunisia six months ago. Lots of onion. Good thing the camera can't pick up our bad breath."

She uses her little finger to wipe a trace of egg from the corner of her mouth.

"There's a reflection from the window," JR, the director, says. He's wearing a red flannel shirt, jeans, cowboy boots, red suspenders and talks with a Bronx accent. "Twist the light. Jane, sit on the sofa with Liz so I can get a reading."

Placing herself on my left she stops Phil, the youngest cameraman, from clearing the books off the coffee table by reaching out her hand as he tries to sweep them away. "She's a professor. There should be books around. I want the dog in the shot," she says. "In fact, let's try and get the dog to put her head on Liz's lap and she can stroke it as she talks to me. It'll make her look nice."

I am nice, I think.

"Jane, we want the table for the bugging devices," JR says. My colleagues and I have collected close to ten.

"There's room for both," Jane says, arranging them.

JR checks the monitor. "It works. Your makeup needs a touch-up, Jane."

She reaches for her bag and dabs her face here and there. As she does she asks me questions about Sumner, my students, my background. I can tell by the questions that she's done her homework.

I feel ugly next to her even though I had my hair styled at Paris Dreams and my face done at Filene's makeup counter. For luck I'm wearing the blue maternity dress Peter bought me.

Jane records some lines that the crew will splice in later. "President Baker refused to be interviewed, but he read a statement comparing sexual harassment claims by young female students to the Salem witch trial."

This reasoning is getting boring, I think.

"Let's try some test questions," she says. This is exactly what Tina and Judy said she did with them. Maybe it is to put us at ease.

She turns to me and the camera lights come on. "We have yet to find any student who thinks you do anything less than walk on water, which doesn't match with someone fired for bad evaluations. Did you ever get the names of the students who signed them?"

"My lawyer is working on it," I say. I wonder how my part of their story will fit in with what they've already done. I know that the *Dateline* crew, banned from campus, shot footage through the iron fence before coming to my place.

Amanda Silver, Judy, Tina, Melissa and her father have all been interviewed.

They found Henry Sumner in D.C. where he'd escaped to a conference. When she first arrived Jane showed me the footage of Henry turning his back and rushing away from the camera.

It's been eight days since Dean Whittier's memorial service, two weeks since I was fired, but I've been busier than ever in my life. The house has become campaign headquarters. I might as well have a phone surgically embedded in my ear as messages and strategies fly back and forth.

The reaction to my firing sent a bevy of students to my door. They hooted at the bad-evaluation idea. Tina has been trying to find out who wrote them. "Locked up tight," came the answer. "No way."

Jane pats the dog. "Phil, call Peter and get him over here. We'll shoot part of this with Liz alone, and we'll do the end with Peter and her together."

We chat with the camera running and with it off. I feel as relaxed as possible with a television crew in my living room. Peter comes in about ten minutes later, still in his chickpea costume.

"That's wonderful," Jane says. "Leave it on."

"No," he says. "It makes Liz look dumb getting pregnant by a vegetable."

Although Jane and JR wheedle, Peter remains adamant.

"We can mention it," Jane says.

"Fine," Peter says. "I was in costume when you shot this afternoon."

"This is for real now. No more horsing around," JR says. We go over the same ground as we did earlier.

Each time the camera goes on Jane wets her lips. I wet my lips too. And it's said that old dogs can't learn new tricks. "Woof"—wet—"woof."

Jane's good. I almost forget the camera's running. I talk about my students, my books, my frustrations. Peter sits next to me, his hand over mine. Jane goes for the kill and asks about my marriage.

"I didn't have a marriage, but a non-marriage. He had his interests and career. I had mine." I can imagine David's reaction to that statement, and it isn't pretty. I look at Peter's hand covering mine and I can see on the monitor how they've zoomed in to it. "Peter and I became friends because I was lonely."

"And then lovers," Jane says.

"And eventually lovers."

"Was that why you were fired?"

"Liz was fired because she opposed the administration. All the teachers who thought Melissa was right lost their contracts," Peter says.

"But I had tenure. Morals are a tricky issue to fire someone on. Bad evaluations are easier."

"How do you feel about the college now?" she asks.

"Terrible. I love teaching. I think Fenway gives my kids a great education, but the politics are tearing it apart."

"It's a women's college," Jane says. When the camera goes to me, she wets her lips again. "Who holds the power at Fenway?"

"Men. Ninety percent of the tenured positions are held by men. Eighty-five percent of the women who go for tenure are denied it. Less than one percent of the men are turned down."

"This sounds like a discussion we might have had thirty years ago," she says. "Do you consider yourself a feminist?"

"I'm not anti-male, but I am anti-injustice," I say. "We've come a long way baby only in cigarette commercials."

"Cut," JR says. "Have we got enough, Jane?"

"No. Let's talk about the bugging." We do. I pick up the various pieces, being careful to say we have no proof that Baker put them there directly or indirectly. That was Carol's advice and she thought, although the show could hurt our court case, we might be able to win with public opinion. She told me to go for it.

Finally Jane asks, "Are you ashamed of anything you've done?"

Without hesitation I say, "No."

JR calls cut again.

"You're good, "Jane tells me. "Really relaxed."

Relaxed wouldn't have been the word I'd have used to describe a conversation with a famous television reporter while cameramen shoot me from different angles. I have had the fifteen minutes of fame promised me. I no longer have to wonder when it will arrive. It has come and gone.

After the *Dateline* crew leaves, I call Mother to warn her of my impending national exposure. She's out. Glory hallelujah. Instead I tell my aunt.

She's excited. "I'll tape it. What did you wear?"

I describe my blue sailor maternity dress.

"I'm sure you looked wonderful. I forgot to tell you. I'm making a baby quilt. In cross-stitch. With the alphabet and teddy bears. From a kit, of course."

As I chat with Auntie Anne, Peter kisses me on the cheek, puts a note written on the back of a bill in my hand. He writes on whatever is handy, forgetting we have a notepad by Garfield. "I'm going back to work," it says as Auntie Anne says she is still working on my mother to get her to lighten up.

Feeling good from talking with my aunt, I dial Jill's number. She answers. "Caught you," I say.

"I've felt funny about talking with you," she says.

"Which is why you've been avoiding me." The silence tells me I'm right. "What bothers you most?" I ask.

"My baby sister broke her marriage vows."

Good for Jill, I think. She's always had a problem telling others what she really thinks. Like me. As adult sisters we've reverted to the patterns set in diaper days. She still recovers from grudges slowly, releasing her hurt a little bit at a time. Sometimes she takes so long that I get mad all over again.

Maybe it's time to move on. If Mother, who makes the Rock of Gibraltar look crumbly, can try, then Jill and I should be able. "Do you think," I ask, "that the secret behind our problems is resentment?"

"Why would I resent you?" she asks, but her voice is lower.

"Maybe you envy my independence. I'm jealous of your looks."

"You are?" Her surprise makes me realize even more how much we are caught up in our old roles, as well as our choices. Except I changed my choices.

"It's worth thinking about," she says. Our conversation is less strained than when I began.

I ask her about Harry.

"Better, I think," she says. "He's home more. A good sign things are winding down, but I can't be sure yet." She whispers, "If he doesn't leave me for this one, maybe he will for another."

"Maybe you can prepare for it," I say. "Be proactive instead of reactive." It's a new concept for both of us.

I warn her about *Dateline*.

She groans.

"Don't worry. I don't have your picture in the background. No one will ever know we're related," I say.

We hang up after one of the few significant conversations we have ever had in our lives. The communication channels are no longer locked with a missing key.

We hold a *Dateline* party catered by Peter's stand for the students and faculty involved. Judy brings sangria. Tina arrives with a cheesecake dripping with cherries. She talks about a pumpkin cheesecake her neighbor makes and says she would have preferred that, but the woman misunderstood her order. To my knowledge Tina doesn't cook herself. I'm not sure she even knows what a stove is.

Judy passes pita bread. As much as I love Peter I'm getting really sick of Mideastern food, but I'm not the least bit tired of the chef.

When Judy hugs me, the eighth hug I've had tonight, I suddenly realize that most of the people here, my fired and non-fired friends, are touchy-feely types. For the first time in my life it has become natural for me to hug people.

Even the men touch. Peter is the only non-Fenway person, but he's welcomed with pats from the men and hugs from the women. Tina gives him a pat. "Any lover of Liz is someone I love," she says.

"Keep your paws off," I say.

I hear parts of conversations. Marcy talks with Bob about the click sounds of an African language made by placing the tongue to one side and forcing air through. Bob and Judy were the only ones not fired, but he had been counseled by the president and given a last chance. The explanation that he is male is too simple.

Judy is safe because of the amount of grant money she currently brings into the college. Her community reputation is too high for Baker to risk letting her go. "I bet Sumner never thought touching Melissa's breasts would lead to him being featured on *Dateline*," she says.

Amanda Silver arrives late. "Guess who I found at the airport?"

Melissa steps into the living room. Everyone greets them with hugs and kisses until Bob asks, "This isn't sexual harassment, is it?"

"Not if it's with friends and it's your choice," Melissa says.

Peter has rented a giant television for tonight. I turn it on. The talk subsides quickly as Stone Phillips, every hair in place, previews the evening's three segments. Fenway is first. It's a balanced story, considering how uncooperative the other side was. The quiet continues into the commercial.

"What's next?" Marcy asks when it's over.

No one knows.

CHAPTER FOURTEEN

Shit! The correcting ribbon on the Smith Corona portable is useless. It's half-white, half-black. Because I make lots of typos, I've used up the white part.

I know wrong keys don't jump in front of my fingers when I depress keys. However, at some subliminal level, I've always suspected inanimate objects have feelings. As a child I'd sit in different chairs so none would feel neglected.

"I'm sorry I hate you," I say to Peter's typewriter, hoping it will forgive me. The keys refuse my apology.

Of all the firings mine was the only one to take effect immediately. I was the one on the news. The rest of the people are working out their contracts, which leaves me as coordinator for all underground activities.

My friends' contracts say the school has a right to terminate at will, making their cases shaky. They don't feel they can afford to go ahead with a court case they will likely lose. Still they want to make some statement.

As for me, under the union agreement I couldn't be terminated because of my tenure. In extreme cases the president must hold a hearing. This was denied me. However, the special committee dealing with incompetent teachers hadn't specified a hearing, a mistake. Carol tells me we have an uphill fight. She hopes we can negotiate.

I'm trying to bring pressure on them. Thus we need to know everything possible about these successful businessmen who appear to be totally behind the president. Somehow he has convinced them that they need to take a stand against false charges of sexual harassment.

We know this because Tina's network is still in operating order. I suspect her spies are the young women clerks in the president's office. They're probably frustrated by the power structure. Maybe they think this is one way they can help.

I need to go to the Internet center near the house to look up all I can on each regent. I have to answer the letters pouring in from the alumnae. They are running nine to one in favor of us.

The dog lies at my feet, stretching out each time I swear when the corrections frustrate me. I miss my computer. I miss my edit keys. Crumpling a page I've pulled out of the typewriter, I start to redo it. Two paragraphs need to be reversed.

It's not that my PC was the best on the market, but it was like an old friend. I'd bought it used. I remember the day. The temperature had soared into the nineties. I'd been floating on the rubber raft in the pool reading *Wanta Advertise?*, a publication listing all kinds of things including personals such as "SWM seeks SWF to walk beaches, eat out. Must be a nonsmoker." Among the Compaqs, HPs, Toshibas and Dells someone wanted to sell an old Apple.

"Listen to this," I'd said to David, who was working on a brief under the sun umbrella. He had his own computer and laptop but wouldn't share them for fear I'd mess up a file.

David had sneered. "Too old. Not state-of-the-art."

For $400 I didn't care. He had refused to go on what he called a wild goose chase, but after the woman showed it to me, I bought the goose. When I carried it and the manuals into the house, all he said was, "It looks beaten up."

The Apple and I became partners. Lectures, letters, articles became fun to write instead of a chore. I bemoaned the fact that I hadn't had it when I wrote my thesis. Although David offered me a new one, I had made a pact with the

Apple: I'll comfort you and keep you as long as we both shall live.

Thinking about it only increases my desire to get it back. Since David returned my grandmother's painting, I haven't wanted to say anything about the computer. I can just picture it arriving in a cardboard box in thousands of little circuit boards.

Although we can't afford it, Peter has offered to get us a computer. This is a problem of living on Peter's money alone. Poor Peter. When we met, he had no debts. Now I represent one financial drain after another.

At least we've sorted out insurance questions so we won't have to pay for the baby. Carol says that is the simplest thing that she has to do for me.

I want my word processor. I pace around Peter's typewriter, glaring at it. Inanimate objects don't react.

Surges of anger at David flush my body. The raw pain that he cut up my grandmother's painting surfaces anew. I feel a desire to tie Baker to a chair and stick pins in his eyeballs for firing me. As for Sumner I'd hand him over to Melissa with a book about the best torture techniques. All these people are playing with my life and others' lives. Why can't they just leave us alone?

I remember Melissa sitting in my office the day we couldn't finish our conversation. What she said was that she'd work it out or something like that. Well, she had. That slip of a twenty-year-old had refused to let Sumner victimize her. With *Dateline* and writing to alumnae, the professors are fighting back, too.

A few weeks ago I counseled my sister to be proactive in her marriage. A bit hypocritical considering the way I acted in my marriage.

Why should I allow David to keep my Apple? Since I

can't come up with a reason, I decide to go get it. First I have to make sure he's not home. He isn't.

I dial Judy's number. She answers on the third ring. "Cooking & Baking, Inc.," she says. It's Easter break, and I know she has had a surge of domesticity these past few days. She says it's a relief after the tension at school. Baker is trying to cut her clinic's budget. She says when he talks with her, she could catch advanced frostbite.

Even when school is in session I don't call anyone at their offices. Every day the faculty checks for bugging devices. When no one is looking even Jimmy helps search. He says he's part of the underground resistance like the French freedom fighters in World War II.

"It's Liz. Want to help me?" When she agrees I ask her to call David's office, pretend she's a secretary to Attorney Spillane in Buffalo to see if David's in town.

A few minutes pass before she calls back. "He's gone until Tuesday. What's up?"

"I'm going to get my word processor. I wanted to make sure he wasn't home."

"I'll go with you."

"We might be arrested for breaking and entering."

"It's more exciting than making cookies for Sasha's Brownies bake sale." Judy hates to cook anything she can't eat.

I rush around to get jacket and keys.

Judy is sitting on her front stairs when I pull up. She's dressed in blue jeans, a blue thick turtleneck sweater and black boots. "I looked in my etiquette book to find out what one wears to a burglary in the suburbs of a soon-to-be ex-husband of a good friend. But they didn't have any suggestions. I worked it out for myself. How do you like my cat burglar clothes?"

During the drive, which takes about a half-hour, we chat about the support we've gained from the alumnae group, NOW and Nine to Five. Judy also points out how none of it seems to make a whit of difference to the president or regents.

I pull into my old street. No one is around, but it is one of those neighborhoods where you never see anyone. The automatic garage door opener is still in my glove compartment. I'd forgotten I had it until I was planning this caper. Even as Judy and I chatter, I've been thinking how I'll accomplish this crime.

At one time David and I had talked about alarming the house, but we kept delaying it. He wanted three price quotes and was out of town whenever we were to meet with the salespeople. I hope he hasn't had time since I left him.

"No one driving by can see us," Judy says. "What's next?"

We get out of the car. The kitchen door is locked when I try it. We look around. The light from the window at the back of the garage reflects off the saws on David's workbench, which occupies half the wall. Most of the tools have never been used because David hires people to do things like that. He wants them to use their own. Everything is in perfect order including hammers of several sizes. One is sufficient to break the windowpane. The tinkle is melodic.

After wrapping my arm in a cloth that I had in the car to wipe moisture from the inside of my windows when they're frosty, I reach through the shattered glass to open the door from the inside.

"Are you sure you've never done this before?" Judy asks.

"Shut up!" We both know I'm joking.

Inside I shiver. Did I really ever live here? No, I existed.

I feel more as if I read about this place instead of occupying these rooms.

Judy follows me. "This place looks like it belongs on a program about fabulous homes of the rich and famous." I show her around and she oohs and aahs. "I knew you were well-off, but I had no idea. You really had to love Peter to give all this up."

"It's the other way. I'd really have had to love money to give Peter up." Over the last few months I have woken five times around three in the morning wondering how I could have been so stupid as to almost lose Peter for fear what other people might think. I forgive myself because it was the way I was raised, but I forgive my mother, too, for the same reason. If she can try to become more mellow at her age, I should try and follow the good examples she set as well as try and shake off the bad ones.

When Judy picks up a small Colombian statue, I realize she's wearing gloves. "Fingerprints," she says. "Don't worry about yours. The house is still legally yours. You've a right to be here."

"You sound certain," I say.

"I checked with Carol." My lawyer is a friend of Judy's, although I didn't know that when I hired her. "I didn't tell her we were going to do this . . . I asked a what-if question."

My office door is shut. David and I fought so often about the mess in my office, I can't look at it without getting annoyed. He thought the office destroyed the serenity of the house. I liked to see out when working.

When I open the door, I find a book I'd left open on my desk in exactly the same position. Running my hand over my computer leaves a dust trail. The housekeeper hasn't attempted to clean in here, although the rest of the house is pristine. I had never allowed her in here anyway.

Unplugging the machine we carry the box, screen, printer and keyboard to my car. I come back for disks, a few files and some books.

"Wanta get some clothes while you're here?" Judy asks.

"Why not? My nightgowns. A sweater or two." When I enter my dressing room it is empty. Checking the bedroom, I find David has removed every trace of me. I don't understand why he didn't clean out my office as well.

Judy picks up a lace nightgown hanging over a chair.

"It's not mine," I say as I take it. Good for him. Maybe with someone else in his life, he'll stop caring what I do. The idea of another woman doesn't bother me at all. Instead I feel relief. It's over.

"How's the divorce coming?" Judy no longer apologizes before her nosy questions.

"Carol says his lawyer won't even return calls. When she sees him in court, he'll discuss any other thing but my divorce."

"Any reason?" Judy follows me to the kitchen.

"Only they aren't ready to negotiate. Oops." Glass cracks under my feet. "We better fix this and get out of here."

I pick up the kitchen phone. It's white, sterile, cold. ABC Glass Company tells me they can have a man there in about ten minutes. They tell the truth. He is sandy-haired and in his early twenties.

"Was I stupid to lock myself out," I say.

"Happens all the time, ma'am," he says with a smile. "Keeps me employed." His accent is definitely not New England. Neither is the "ma'am."

"Where you from?"

"Bluefield, West Virginia, ma'am. Moved up here when I married my wife. She's from Wakefield."

"Don't worry. I'll clean up," I tell him when he asks for dustpan and brush. They are where they always were. The owner of the lacy nightgown has changed nothing. I put the shards in a paper bag to take with me.

I pay him in cash, although it flashes through my mind to have the bill sent to David. That would be proof, however, I'd been in the house. As it is now, it could be any burglar who loves antique Apples more than televisions, radios, VCRs, CD players, Dells, fax machines, Rolex watches and silver.

Before we leave, I take one last look. I doubt if I'll ever see this place again.

Now I have everything I want, even my painting. Peter, sweetheart that he is, took it to a restorer, who told him it was beyond redemption, which I had known anyway. Peter had looked him directly in the eye and said, "That's the wrong answer."

When he presented me with the final attempt at restoration, it looked like a jigsaw puzzle someone had glued and framed. Although it looks terrible, I love it all the more for now it carries not only memories of my grandmother, but the memory of Peter who had to do something to make my loss lighter.

"Maybe I should have destroyed something of David's," I say as we drive past the common with its typical white church.

"Don't sink to his level," Judy says.

All my life I've been told not to sink to someone's level. Sinking might be fun. However, it is not worth it to go back.

"I wonder how long before David notices the computer is gone?" Judy asks.

"I don't care."

"You're changing, Liz. I can't picture you doing this a year ago."

Maybe I'm learning to risk. And act. Maybe I'm finally growing up after the longest adolescence in history. Maybe I can get into the *Guinness Book of Records*.

I hum as I work on my Apple in the loft. I've finished all the write-ups of each regent. None are under sixty. All run their own companies. None have women in upper management. None have working wives. I'm not sure what this proves. I'm so busy trying to correlate data, I jump when Peter asks, "Where did you get that?"

"B&E." I know by his face, he's trying to think of a computer store by that name. "Breaking and entering?"

It takes him a minute to process what I mean. "I can't believe you did that."

"Believe." I repeat each step of my crime, including Judy's cat burglar clothes.

"How long do you think before he notices, my adorable not-so-little thief?" He rests his hand on my belly and Chloe kicks him.

"Don't know, care less," I say as my daughter kicks her father and me again.

April slips into May, May into June. The only thing happening is I'm getting fatter.

The sexual harassment story is yesterday's news. Reporters and cameras have disappeared to cover the next event. Our meetings fall away because of lack of progress. My friends job hunt rather than fight dead causes. I wonder if I should do the same.

"Do both," Peter says when I discuss it with him. "Fight but send out your curriculum vitae."

"Who'll hire me pregnant and officially a bad teacher?"

"You've a good reputation except for that. Work your contacts."

He makes it sound easy, but lethargy has taken over. I won't be ready to work in September because I'm not sure when Chloe will arrive, although my due date is estimated for mid- to late June. When I point this out to Peter, he says, "If you want to stay home with our daughter for a while, that's fine with me." That wasn't what I was asking, but I'm not sure what I wanted from him.

Ben and Janice are wonderful, especially Janice who listens to each of my fears in minute detail. Once a week, sometimes more, Boss and I go to Concord for lunch or she comes into the city. Boss prefers Concord where she can gallop through the orchard.

Tina and Judy stop by regularly. Tina hasn't given up trying to get her hands on my file. She's convinced there are two. One in case of a subpoena and one for their own use. She won't tell me why she is so sure.

"It's funny. I felt so confident when I broke into my house," I say when they are both sitting at my table with the refuse of lunch in front of us. All the windows are open. The lilac trees in the garden perfume the house.

"You did like what?" Tina asks. She pours herself a cup of hot water. Her latest diet fad is drinking six cups of it a day.

Judy pours herself a cup and drops an apple cinnamon tea bag in. "I want real flavor," she says. As she waits for it to brew, she tells Tina about our foray into crime.

"My God, Liz. You? I'd never have guessed. You seemed too goody-goody. But then I never imagined you'd have a baby by like someone other than your . . ."

She's too dark for me to see her blush.

"Don't worry about that foot sticking out of your mouth," I say.

Tina is very quiet. I thought it was embarrassment. As it turned out, she is thinking.

Three days later at seven-thirty in the morning, Tina knocks at my door. I'm not even out of bed.

"I'm hungry. Good morning," she says, heading toward the kitchen.

I put out juice, milk, strawberries, jam and butter. In the closet she finds Rice Krispies and puts the jam and butter in the refrigerator. We find bowls.

She half fills hers with the fruit before adding the cereal on top and pours a measured tablespoon of milk carefully down the side so it doesn't touch the Rice Krispies. "I hate soggy cereal. I hate snap, crackle, pop. See how like the fruit on the bottom keeps it dry. Where's your napkins?"

"Top drawer on the left."

She eats in gulps. Between mouthfuls she delves into her pocketbook and pulls out copies of the evaluations. "This is all I could find. I'm sure there's more."

"How did you get these?"

"Same way you got your Apple." She talks with her mouth full.

Her still nameless spy refused to risk getting caught rummaging in files where she had no reason to be. However, she was more than willing to take impression of file keys and the key to the president's office. She had told Tina exactly where the files were at the same time that she gave her the key impressions.

At this point, Tina helps herself to seconds and puts on

the teakettle. "Want some tea?" she asks me.

"No, I want the rest of the story. Now." I finger the evaluations, afraid to look at them.

Tina shrugs. "So, like I had the keys made. I hid in the administration building ladies' room like until after the building was locked. Then I waited until midnight. That's when the guards go over to the dorms for the rest of the night, although sometimes they do a quick patrol."

"Do you know what would have happened if you were caught?"

"Nothing. I'd have said I'd fallen asleep and was like waiting for morning."

"In the president's office?"

"That would be a little harder to explain. But nothing went wrong. Anyway, it didn't take me that long to like copy the stuff. I went back to the ladies' room until the first student needed to pee and I was outta there and over here."

Speechless is an overworked word. Not in this case. This girl had actually arranged a burglary, not of just any place but the president's office.

"Any good ghetto kid knows if people don't give you what you want, you go get it. Any chance I can take like a nap? Then maybe call your lawyer to see what she wants to do with these?"

I make a place for Tina on the couch in the loft. I leave a message on Carol's voice mail.

I read the evaluations. I can't believe the kids who gave me the bad reports. With one exception, I had had a great relationship with all. The most unbelievable is Mary O'Brien.

"She did what?" Carol demands, with the emphasis on the "what." She agreed to see Tina and me that morning.

Tina was still groggy on the ride over, but after chugalugging two cups of Carol's coffee she revived.

My lawyer's office is small with two desks, one for her and one for her secretary. One wall is covered with law books. The other has a table for the fax, photocopier and postage meter.

The more I get to know Carol the more I like her. With David's associates I began to have a great deal of belief in Shakespeare's line, "First kill all the lawyers." Carol should be spared slaughter. She practices women's law and takes a number of *pro bono* cases. From time to time I see her name in the paper because she has defended some welfare mother from getting evicted. Her most famous case led to a judge getting thrown off the bench after he refused to issue a restraining order. Only after the husband crippled the woman did the court act.

Carol sits with her mouth open, looking at both of us. When we start to repeat the story, she holds up her hands to stop us. "I'm afraid I heard the first time. I just didn't believe it. Do you have any idea of the risk you took? And for no reason. I could have subpoenaed them."

Tina slumps in her chair. "Oh shit."

Carol gets up and sits on her desktop. She is wearing a sweat suit. We caught her as she came back from a run and she hasn't had time to shower. Her apartment is behind her office. "As your lawyer I can't support what you did, but as a woman, you are terrific."

She gets down from her perch and walks over to the window. Since the office is in the basement, I assume she is watching people's feet as they walk by. After several minutes she comes back to her desk. "Liz, you need to make some decisions."

No more decisions, I think. "What ones?" I ask. Until

now we have only been dealing with ifs and what ifs as far as a civil suit is concerned. Carol has been trying to negotiate a hearing with the Board of Regents.

"If you want to file a civil suit against the school. It may increase the regents' desire for a hearing and out-of-court settlement."

"How much?" I ask.

"I can name two rates, one if you lose, one if you win. If you lose, I bill at twenty dollars an hour. If you win ten times that or fifteen percent of the settlement. Either way there'll be lots of hours on the case. I can keep you posted so there won't be any nasty surprises."

There's no doubt of the fairness. David's firm bills at twenty times that. "I need to check with Peter."

"Do you think it's worth it?" I ask Peter later that night. We have just finished dinner. The dog licks the last of the spaghetti from our plates. My lover calls Boss our pre-wash cycle.

"Worth it how? In trying to get your job back? In preventing other attacks on tenured faculty? In seeing those bastards get what they deserve? Yeah, I think it's worth it for all of the above."

"I meant the money."

He wipes his mouth after his last swallow of coffee. He puts his napkin down, and it falls on the floor. Boss checks it out.

"Money isn't the issue if Carol will take partial payments. We can sell your car or the antique table or think of something," he says. "We'll never be rich, but we've a roof over our heads and food in our stomachs. And we've other stuff, too." He starts to clear the table, but then stops to pat my tummy. Chloe must be asleep. She doesn't kick him.

He runs water into the sink and holds the detergent bottle under the faucet for a long time. Suds come to the top of the sink, a dish bubble bath. Peter loves suds. He submerges the dishes and the spaghetti pot, turning the bubbles pink.

"When I met you, you had no debts."

"And your point is . . ." he asks.

"I'm a bad investment."

"And your point is . . ."

I don't have one. Money is not a power tool in our couple.

CHAPTER FIFTEEN

Chloe and I go to war the day Israel attacks Palestine with heavy mortar. Only in our war, the casualties are my nerves. My body is our battlefield. I whine so much that if Olympic medals were given in bitching, I'd take the gold. Gone, totally gone, is my earlier thrill of feeling the flutter of life.

July's oppressive heat destroys me. Me, the person who curses winter and fantasizes about baking in the sun at Wingarsheek Beach.

Every day I'm overdue I worry the baby might be David's, not Peter's. That is a thought I try to ignore. My doctor, my training and *Our Bodies Ourselves* all tell me gestation time varies.

Chloe has become a monster inhabiting my body, a resident alien from a horror movie. B is not for Baby but for Bitch. I prefer to think the creature or the heat is responsible for my ugly disposition rather than admit a major character flaw.

Flaw, heat, creature, it matters not. I chant my litany of wants like the rosary.

I want my body back.

I want not to pee every five minutes.

I want to be thin.

Having always been proud of my flat stomach, the gods extract their vengeance for my smugness. I watch *Wheel of Fortune*. I'm so busy analyzing Vanna's stomach I can't guess any of the answers. I used to be good. Mother loves *Wheel of Fortune*. Before she moved to Arizona, we'd watch it together. I'd guess the answers before she did and she'd say, "Oh, Liz, you're so smart."

Does prepartum depression exist? Maybe I can write a new book on the subject. I picture myself talking to Oprah Winfrey about the phenomenon that all the GYNs in the entire world have missed. In my fantasy I'm thin, thin, thin—just right of anorexic.

Judy brings me her Jane Fonda exercise tape made not only before her divorce from Ted Turner but before her marriage to him. "This will give you hope."

We watch Jane demonstrate how to drag her feet across her face. "How about ripping out her jugular and using it to tie up her hair?"

"Nothing is happening at school. Everyone is gone," Judy says. "What have you heard?"

I know she wants to divert me because I've watched her do the same thing to Sasha and Sable. "Carol has talked to Melissa's attorneys who have talked to the school's lawyers. She's about ready to hit them with the suit and subpoena. Then we can interview the girls who wrote the evaluations."

"What if Baker destroys them?" Judy asks.

"He'll have nothing to back up why I was fired."

Judy shakes her head, and I know she is wondering why Mary wrote and signed the evaluation. We've discussed it too many times to go over it again.

I wonder why the regents refuse to budge, why they continue to feel they're protecting their cohorts from unjust accusations of sexual harassment. They continue to deny the firings are related to the professors defending Melissa. They stand firm despite bad press, reduced alumnae contributions, and the smallest enrollment in history. Two of the sheiks have pulled their daughters and their promises of endowments from the school. Tina's spy circle has reported all this.

When Judy leaves, the mid-afternoon heat boils my already bad, self-pitying mood to a new high—or is it a new low?

My breasts leak. As a nurse, I should have expected it, but I'd forgotten. "I want dry nipples," is added to my litany of wants.

I've been ignoring my doctor's recommendations to buy bras. I've changed to a local doctor. Had he looked carefully he'd have discovered that even at nine months my breasts barely fill an A cup. Despite the heat, I decide to go on a bra-buying safari.

Peter arrives home from work and says, "I don't think it's a good idea for you to drive."

"You . . . you . . . you male chauvinistic manipulative controlling pig," I screech.

For a second he stares at me then hands me the keys. I flounce out the door as best a whale can flounce. Trying to wedge myself behind the wheel for the first time in three weeks, I realize it's unsafe to drive. After prying myself out of the car, I stomp back into the house, slam the door and throw the keys at him.

He catches them as he would pluck a baseball from the air. Saying nothing, not a "good-bye," not a "I'll see you later," not a "I'll be back in an hour," he leaves for who knows where, quietly shutting the door behind him, a more effective rebuke to my tantrum than any words. I sweat half from anger, half from the 103-degree temperature. It is only nine a.m.

Judy rescues me by offering to drive me. When her salmon-pink Beetle chugs into the driveway, I squeeze in, my stomach against the dash. If she slammed on her brakes, Chloe would be a pancake squished between my backbone and the dashboard.

The odometer on her bug has turned over three times. It has no gas gauge. When we run out of gas, she kicks a lever on the floor letting in one last gallon. We make the gas station saving two-point-nine humans from becoming cannibal-pleasing roasts.

At the store I try a white cotton bra. I think of the lacy camisoles I have bought since I started sleeping with Peter. I console myself that I won't stain them, a moot point since none fit over the resident alien anyway.

Looking in the three-way dressing-room mirror, I see a brown stripe from my pubic hair to my navel. Something else to hate—being a mismarked skunk.

Riding back, Judy asks how long have we been friends? I say a long time.

"Then you know I mean this as a friend. Have you noticed how the word 'hate' peppers your sentences the last few weeks? It's so unlike you."

I tell her she's right. I hate my leaking, the heat, my shape. I hate waiting for my daughter. I hate waiting for my divorce. What I hate most is the feeling I've no control over anything. That the feeling is based on reality makes it worse.

Peter and I go to a party two nights after I buy bras. It's a potluck attended by medical students who frequent Peter's Mideastern food stand.

Although I don't feel like going, when Peter says the magic phrase, "It's in an air-conditioned apart . . . ," I heave myself out of the chair, before he adds "ment."

Because of the heat, I've eaten little. I've only gained fourteen of the eighteen pounds the doctor allotted me. In the cool apartment all the food tastes wonderful. Strate-

215

gically arranging my plate, I pile on scalloped corn and grab slabs of roast beef.

"Take some tabbouleh. It's great," someone says. I turn to see a woman. She's tall and blond. She's THIN!!!!!!!!!!!! Earlier I'd heard her talking about being born again.

"Maybe later," I say.

"It'll be gone," she says. "We should accept Christ's gifts."

"This doesn't come from Christ. My lover made it so I can have it anytime. My husband can't make a decent tabbouleh at all."

She looks at my stomach and backs away.

Totally shocked at my bad manners, I search for Peter. He's talking to a group of men. Hearing what he says makes me feel terrible.

Even at midnight the temperature is in the nineties. As Peter walks and I waddle home, I say, "You didn't have to complain about me."

"I wasn't."

"Saying you wish we were married so you could have the pleasure of divorcing me isn't exactly a compliment." I start to cry. I wish I could cry daintily into a lacy handkerchief like movie heroines. They always look pretty. I blotch.

Peter puts his arm about me and turns me toward him. He kisses me on the forehead and sighs, "Smell." He refers to the rosebushes we're passing. I'm in no mood to stop and smell the roses. I ignore the one he just picked for me. He throws it in the gutter.

At home I change into my nightgown in the bathroom where he can't witness my deformity. I flop on the bed, a whale landing on a sea of green sheets. I decide to hate whales and green sheets. Sleep is impossible as the resident alien tap dances on my bladder.

When I get back from the bathroom, Peter holds out his arms. Cuddling beats sulking. When I wake again to pee, his hand holds mine. This man is a saint.

My lover wears nothing. The moonlight on his face makes him look angelic. With him being so much younger, I'm once again afraid at some point he will say, "Get out, old woman."

He wakes. "Pregnancy makes you beautiful." He looks at me through sleep-filled eyes. "You glow."

With having to pee again desperately, with my breasts leaking, and with my stripe undoubtedly growing darker by the minute, I feel anything but beautiful. Gone is the tenderness of our cuddle.

"Pregnancy makes me fat and ugly. Glow is a word invented by men to keep women wanting to be pregnant." As the words fall over my tongue I want to push them back down my throat.

His body stiffens, and he lets go of my hand. "Liz, you got pregnant because every time we looked at each other we felt horny. Think about it."

I think about it. Until I met him my sex life was dull even by married couple standards. Pregnancy did many wonderful things for my sex life, including driving me from David's house into Peter's.

Pregnancy made me a semi-unwed mother of forty. There's nothing like carrying your lover's child to clarify which man—lover or husband—you want. Better to live with the man I love and father of my child than the person with whom I shared a house, but not a life, for years.

Advanced pregnancy changed the type of sex I enjoy. Until the heat wave began, our lovemaking was long hours of oral sex. Peter claims I taste different since my body was taken over. I'd let him lick me into multiple orgasms. When the heat wave started, the idea of anything as warm as his tongue became unbearable.

He turns his back to me. I worry he regrets our relationship. Certainly he doesn't need me adding to his problems.

The heat has made him abandon his chickpea costume, the symbol of his food stand. The material gives my vegetable lover prickly heat. His work problems go beyond costumes. Since Mohammed went back to Lebanon, Peter has tried many replacements. He's lost three chickpea suits to new staff who didn't show up for work after wearing their costumes home. He did recover one because he went to the person's apartment for it.

As Peter sleeps next to me I promise myself I will be nicer to this man. I will go back to being the good girl I almost always was until before the heat wave.

On the twenty-fourth straight day of the heat wave, Peter works back-to-back shifts because his latest trainee never showed up. The sun has set, but the thermometer reads 102 degrees. I don't ask what the humidity is. My skin could be sold as Super Glue guaranteed to stick to anything it touches.

My brother Ben and his wife Janice keep me company. Sam is asleep in the house on the couch. We sit in the garden, a brick patio surrounded by drooping marigolds, geraniums and petunias. A wooden fence hides the garden from our neighbors. A breeze blowing through the oak tree ripples the air too gently for relief. We've kicked off our sandals.

Ben sprawls on the lounge chair while Janice and I sit at the table. My brother has stripped to his shorts. I'm amazed how trim he is. Before he began the apple orchard he had a potbelly. Too much directing other people what to do, while in the orchard he does most of the work himself.

The gate creaks opens. Boss ambles instead of bounds to greet her master. With her long golden fur, she must suffer more than we do.

"Man, you look terrible," Ben says. He stands up so Peter can drop on the lounge.

"The fan died. It was one hundred twenty degrees or more. Two candidates showed up, said, 'No way,' or maybe they melted like Little Black Sambo."

"Little Black Sambo is out. Too racial," Janice says, getting up to refill the lemonade pitcher. It's shaped like a corncob with a husk for the handle. We found it at the Beth Israel Deaconess Hospital Thrift Shop. Peter said it was identical to one his grandmother had. I think it's ugly but refuse to knock childhood memories.

Realizing Peter doesn't have a glass, Janice goes back inside to get one. It doesn't match the others. With David everything had to match. Unmatched for me is a statement of freedom as strong as, "Give me liberty or give me death." Ah ha! A positive thought. Maybe my prepartum depression won't last forever.

After tossing back three glasses of lemonade as an alcoholic would whiskey, Peter explains his problems to Ben and Janice.

"Let me help," Ben says. "The apples don't need me to watch them grow. When the baby comes home, I'll run the stand." Peter makes a few obligatory refusals before accepting.

My brother and sister-in-law talk about Mother's adjustment to Arizona. Peter's snores punctuate our conversation. He has such a cute snore, more like a pop, pop, wheeze, pop, pop, wheeze. Hm. A second pleasant thought.

I'll have to be careful, or this could become a habit.

The alarm rings at five a.m. Peter rolls over and touches my face with his fingertips. "Stay in bed, sweetheart," he whispers, a small ritual bringing comfort in its familiarity.

Usually I kiss him and fall back to sleep. This morning I'm wide awake.

"I'll make breakfast." I propel myself and the resident alien out of bed.

The kitchen is cool. I smell roses from the bush outside the window. It rained during the night. Wet earth smells mingle with the roses.

Boss scratches to be let out. When I open the door, she lopes around the garden for the first time in over three weeks. Throwing herself on her back on the grass with her feet in the air, she gives herself a back rub. The thermometer outside the kitchen reads seventy-five degrees.

After starting the coffee, I reach for pancake mix and a can of pumpkin. Peter loves pumpkin pancakes.

My vegetable lover—dressed as a carrot, a cooler costume than the chickpea one—comes into the kitchen. Two small pieces of toilet paper, pasted with blood, stick to his face. I look up.

"My God. You smiled. You must be feeling better." He walks around me, staring as if I were a zoo animal.

"Cute, very cute," I say. As I pour Peter's coffee into the mug with Larry Bird's picture, the door opens. Boss walks in followed by Ben.

"I'm starting today. No telling how long before my niece shows up."

"Things are looking up all over," Peter says. "Your sister is acting human this morning."

Ben kisses my cheek, and puts his finger in the pancake

batter and licks it. "Be nice to Peter. I know what a bitch you can be. Remember eating my last cupcake?" He drags up a thirty-year-old memory that gets retold regularly to annoy me.

"Mother used to make a special hot chocolate sauce to eat over vanilla cupcakes. We were allotted three from the dozen she made. Jill and Liz always ate theirs the first day, but I saved mine so I could have one each day after school," he says.

I take over. If Ben tells this story, I want my two cents in there. "My school bus arrived ten minutes before his. I could see the pantry from the kitchen door. In the pantry I spied his last cupcake on a willow plate, the kind Woolworth's sold with all the Chinese scenes in blue. The sauce was next to the cupcake in an old Skippy peanut butter jar. I couldn't resist . . ."

"You didn't try," Ben breaks in. "As I walked in the door I saw her pick up a fork. I screamed 'Mother!' "

He yells like he did that day. Boss jumps, legs askew, ready to attack if needed. When she isn't, she lays her head on her paws, but she watches just in case.

"Mother was upstairs." Ben's voice is laden with melodrama.

"She refused to believe I'd stoop so low," I say.

"And I got so frustrated I bit her, Mother not Liz, although I wish I'd bitten Liz."

"By the time Mother finished punishing Ben for biting her, I'd cleaned up all the evidence."

After my lover and brother leave, visions of cupcakes dance in my head. As fast as the alien and I can move, we find the recipe. Smelling the vanilla, tasting creamed eggs and sugar, creates sensations even possessed pregnant ladies enjoy. I scrape the bowl with a spoon, then use my

221

finger to get every molecule of batter. The bowl looks washed. As baking aromas fill the kitchen, I melt chocolate for the sauce.

The first cupcake tastes fantastic in its own right, but it also tastes of childhood, of after-skating parties and jigsaw puzzles in front of the fire when school was canceled for snow. I chuckle thinking of Ben, his eleven-year-old face frozen in shock, as I mumpfed his cupcake.

As I scrub baked-on crumbs off the cupcake tins, I notice the window over the sink is dirty. After I wash it, the curtains look gray. A clean window shows up dirty shelves. I wash everything on the shelves. I wash the shelves themselves.

During *Wheel of Fortune*, Vanna's thinness isn't as important as the dust under the chair. I hear the contestant guess "Michael Douglas" just as I notice the mantel needs polishing.

The fireplace has a soot-encrusted chimney, but I can't get it clean enough. I climb inside the chimney. Soot tumbles down on me.

Peter comes in. Through the bricks I hear him call, "Liz? Where are you?"

Startled, I jump, wedging myself in. I hear his footsteps stop in front of the fireplace.

"Santa Claus is either six months late or six months early," he says. "Want to tell me why you're standing in the fireplace?"

"It was dirty," I say. Light filters down from the opening.

"Most chimneys are," he says. "Are you staying there all day?"

"Maybe." I don't want to admit I'm stuck.

"Maybe?"

As I twist to free myself, soot comes pouring down around me. It gets as far as my waist. Soot stinks. I sneeze. What if he goes back to work, leaving me? "I'm stuck."

His hands pull on my leg. Nothing happens. "Turn."

"I can't."

"Where are your arms?" he asks.

"One is straight down, the other is resting on my stomach." I try not to panic. I sneeze, dislodging another soot shower.

"Can you pull your dress up?" he asks.

I grab the fabric at my breast. It moves up. "Why?"

"Try pulling it up and sliding down at the same time."

I pull and dip. I come loose. Soot and I tumble out. He stares, his mouth open. Then he laughs, not a quiet laugh, but great rolling uncontrollable guffaws. He leads me to the mirror.

I glance at myself. I'm a reverse Michael Jackson.

Footprints mark my path from the fireplace to the hall mirror. My slippers are ruined. Peter picks them up with the broom handle and drops them in a wastebasket.

"Take a shower. I'll wait in case you slip," he says. Residual giggles escape him as he helps me climb into the tub.

My huge stomach doesn't embarrass me this time. Peter's hands are black. When he scratches his face, a black streak scars his cheek. He strips and follows me under the shower. Black rivulets flow between my breasts parallel to my brown stripe.

I watch, fascinated. Never, ever, even as a child, have I been so filthy.

He soaps his hands into a lather to wash me down. I do the same to him. The suds are dark gray with soot.

His penis responds. I take our hand-held nozzle and rinse his penis, then kneel with his help. I take his organ into my mouth. He comes fast. I pull off as he spurts. He helps me to my feet.

Soaping his hands again, with suds now almost white, he takes the nozzle to rinse me. His turn to kneel. His tongue probes nerves I never knew I had. Water cascades over us. I come and come and come.

"That's a sexual experience we'll never forget," he says, wrapping me in a Coca-Cola bath sheet.

"Or duplicate," I say.

"Especially the chimney part."

Ben told Peter he didn't want to see him at the stand for at least two hours. I serve him coffee and cupcakes.

We chat as we did in the early days when I stopped at the stand to talk and eat salad in pita bread. "I'm so sorry I've been so awful lately," I say.

"If you were just an affair, I'd have left," he says. His hair is still wet. "Or rather I'd have asked you to leave, since this is my house. But this is just a glitch we need to get through." He takes the last bite of cupcake and scrapes his fork across the plate to pick up the last of the sauce. "Or it had better be."

"I hear you," I say. There's something I need to tell him, an idea that floats in bits and pieces around my head but I can't formulate it coherently. It comes out scrambled.

"What you mean is you trust me enough to be yourself," he says.

I nod. The truth engulfs me in sadness and happiness. For the past. For the present.

When he leaves for work I give him two cupcakes and a jar of sauce for Ben. I put the sauce in a Skippy peanut butter jar, an overdue apology for childhood misbehavior.

The phone rings.

"Your bastard born yet?"

"Hello, David. No, she isn't."

"Someday your brat will hate you. She'll know her mother is a whore." If venom oozed from the phone, I wouldn't have been the least surprised.

"David, you're sick." I hang up on my husband. If he'd lost an adored person instead of a function when I left, I might feel guilt. David's motto of "not getting mad but getting even" backfired because I don't care about his weapons—money and property.

Not wanting to deal with David or callers asking, "Have you had the baby yet?" I click on our voice mail. Peter has recorded "Climb Every Mountain" before the usual speech of no one being able to come to the phone.

"Hello, Elizabeth, this is your mother."

I argue with myself for a moment about picking up the phone. The good-girl part of my personality wins. "Hello."

"You're screening your calls. How will I ever know if you're listening and making fun of me?"

Heavy-duty guilt sweeps over me. If guilt would trigger labor pains, then it might be of some use. All it triggers is anger. However, I hold my tongue. "I was screening David out."

"Poor boy. He's lost so much." She must hear me sucking in air as my adrenaline surges. "Still, he shouldn't upset you," she adds.

"Thank you. For just a second I wondered whose side you were on."

Mother threatens to come east to help with the baby. All her friends pop back home to help their children with new babies, and Mother always tries to do the proper thing.

"That's sweet but we've got it under control. Ben's helping with the stand so Peter can spend time with me and Chloe."

"You still are going ahead with that stupid name? Ow!"

"Leave her alone." I hear Auntie Anne in the background.

"Your aunt just hit me."

Nice-girl Liz, who hates rocking a boat, who hopes if she's nice to others they'll love her, has decided to do some serious boat-rocking. Maybe it is the resident alien, but I am continuing to grow up after having had the longest childhood in history. I realize that I think of myself in the third person when I don't act nice. I'm like Ollie North or Bob Dole who kept referring to themselves as "this lieutenant wouldn't" or "Robert Dole thinks." At least it didn't become a national trend, but if it had I would have an excuse.

Being nice to David didn't make him love me. I hadn't been nice to Peter, and he still loves me. And Mother, although we love each other, has gone beyond all accepted limits of criticizing me. Granted, she's better, but she still has a long way to go.

"Good for Auntie Anne. You upset me, too. In less than five minutes you've told me everything you don't like. You've sided with a man who considered me an appendage. If you want to talk, let's make it pleasant."

She coughs the cough that says, "Go ahead, do what you want, just as long as you know you're killing me."

Whether it's the resident alien or just my new backbone telling me to take control of my own life, I feel good. I'm learning to act. It's a new habit. Habits need repetition. "I'm sorry you're displeased. We'll talk again when you feel more positive. I love you."

She manages to gasp, "I love you, too."

My moment of control passes as a cramp tugs at my insides. The desire to clean is gone. I opt to watch "Oprah."

Her program is on women who love younger men. Now if she ever does one on women loved by younger men who cross-dress as vegetables, I'd offer myself as a guest.

I go to the bathroom just as another cramp hits, but my water hasn't broken. I'm just dribbling.

The phone rings again and the voice mail picks up.

"Hi, Liz, it's Judy. I hope the message means you're doing something constructive like writhing in labor."

I grab the phone. "I'm having cramps."

Within twenty minutes her Beetle thumps into my driveway. "I thought you might like some company," she says.

"The pains aren't that bad," I say.

I'm rocked by a pain that says, "Resident Alien here. Don't get cocky, Mummy."

Judy dials Peter and the doctor. She drives me to Brigham and Women's. Peter waits at the entrance as the Beetle pulls up.

Peter goes to do the paperwork as an orderly puts me into a wheelchair. A nurse waits for me at the elevator on the fifth floor. "I'm Karen Petricone."

When Peter joins us, she shows him where and how to scrub up and then introduces me to the room, which will be my haven for the next few hours. She never mentions he is dressed as a vegetable. She probably has seen him at the stand.

My room is air-conditioned. Maybe they use it as a meat locker when no one is in labor, but I don't see any meat hooks. I ask for a third blanket. Karen tucks me in. Peter, who looks adorable in his green hospital gown, appears at the door. He's adorable anyway, whether he's dressed up as a doctor, a chickpea or stark naked.

Mine is the only bed in the room, although I hear another woman screaming down the hall. "This is not a good omen," I say.

A lounge made of green Naugahyde is in the corner. Peter tells the old joke about naugas being an endangered species. I groan. He thinks it's a pain, not an editorial comment on his humor.

A television is suspended in front of my bed. The hands of the clock next to the TV tell me it's eight at night.

My doctor is a Hungarian with huge black eyes and eyelashes that look as if he bought them at a makeup counter. Dr. Lazlo checks to see if his orders for a half-shave and an enema have been carried out.

"Thanks for not messing up my office hours. Trust a nurse to do it right." He peeks under the covers, letting in cold air. My sexual organ is of great interest to everyone. "Your little girl should arrive about midnight."

He lied. Midnight comes and goes as do one, two, three and four. Peter naps in the chair. His green gown clashes with the Naugahyde.

I sleep between pains. One bad one comes. I scream. Mistake. Big, big, big mistake. Screaming makes it hurt more. Peter starts. He switches off the TV. I'd lost interest in the test pattern anyway. He coaches my breathing.

Karen enters. "You're almost ready," she says. I don't tell her I've been ready for weeks. The resident alien and I are about to separate. How will I take other separations from her? When I find a job and go back to work? When she starts school? When she leaves for college? Will I cry when she walks down the aisle? My God, I haven't even seen her face-to-face, and I just married her off.

I tell Peter what I'm thinking and he squeezes my hand. I cry as another pain hits.

He says, "I'm sorry," mistaking a labor pain for a hand-squeeze pain.

Karen goes behind my bed to push it out through the door, down the corridor to the delivery room. Peter never lets go of me as we roll along.

The doors open. I see green gowns, masks, caps and eyes. The walls of the delivery room are green. The ceiling is green. I'm trapped in a green nightmare. I spot my doctor's eyelashes.

Pain after pain comes. "I want a spinal," I say. The bed is pushed next to the gurney where my daughter will be born. Hands grab and shift me, swinging me like two kids swinging a third into a pool. Someone puts socks on my feet. My legs are lifted.

"No time," Dr. Lazlo says. "She's crowning, Liz," Dr. Lazlo says. He points to a mirror directed at my vagina. "Look!" Not a pretty sight. Chloe's head, dark and wet, appears between my legs.

"Push!" Lazlo says.

"Pull her out," I direct him.

"Is she always this bossy?" he asks Peter.

"Almost," Peter says.

Chloe is free. And silent. The silence seems to last for hours. Then she mews. Tears run down Peter's face. And mine.

The doctor holds her up for our inspection. Wow! Is she ugly, with her pointed head, her fat cheeks. Wow! Is she lovely. They rest her on my stomach before cutting the cord then take her away.

"You'll have her back in a few minutes, Liz," Dr. Lazlo says.

"Looking good," the pediatrician says from the corner of the room. "We've got another healthy one." Besides the normal tests he will do a DNA test to determine the father.

By now Chloe is screaming. My ex–resident alien. Someone brings her to me, wrapped papoose-like in pink flannel. A pink bead bracelet on her wrist spells Andrews, one letter per bead, my name, a social comment on my marital status.

My chickpea. He reaches for her hand. "Hi, kid," he says.

CHAPTER SIXTEEN

We settle in. Within a week, I can't imagine life without Chloe. She is one of those lovely babies who eats well, sleeps well. Except for a half an hour a day when nothing pleases her and she howls nonstop, she's a perfect baby.

Nights when Peter's home, he feeds her, saying he's letting me stay in bed. I know it's just another excuse to hold her. He was like that even before we got the results of the blood tests, which prove he is the father. David has a rare blood type. Twice in his life the Red Cross has called him on behalf of someone who desperately needed a match. One was in Kansas, the other in Wyoming. We don't have to wait for the DNA.

I have to admit my daughter really isn't pretty. She has stuffed cheeks and her dark hair has fallen out. Baldness never hurt Charles Blakely or Kevin Eubanks.

Other than soreness as my stitches heal, I'm a normal person again—for a has-been. My friends, Judy, Tina, everyone comes to see the baby. It's like when Jack Kennedy said, "I'm the man who accompanied Jacqueline Kennedy to Paris." Well, I'm the woman who brought Chloe into the world. But I revel in their words on what an adorable, pretty baby she is, even if they lie about the pretty part.

Peter, who hasn't spoken to his parents for years, although he writes his mother at a neighbor's address, decides to call and tell them about Chloe. He has never said much about his parents. His father hangs up on him as soon as he says, "This is Peter." Peter looks at the disconnected phone. Ignoring me, he leaves the house.

While he is gone the phone rings. A woman's voice says, "I'm really embarrassed to be calling. I'm Peter's mother. Are you Elizabeth?"

I tell her I am. "But how did you know my name?"

"I saw you on *Dateline*. Have you had the baby yet?"

"Last week. A little girl. We've named her Chloe."

Peter's mother lets out a long sigh. "I guessed that was Peter and he was calling to tell us. I can't believe it. I'm a grandmother."

We talk about babies. She tells me how stubborn Peter was. "He always fought with his father who is even more stubborn. He can't accept our son as he is," she says. "I was always in the middle."

"How long has it been since you've talked to Peter?"

"Too long. I want my son back. And his family. But his father is a proud man."

There is a pause because I have no idea what to say. As angry as I get at my sister or Mother, I can't imagine not talking to them for years.

"I'm not even sure either of them remembers what set their final battle off. Peter just moved out," she says.

Unforgiveness seems so unlike the Peter that I know. I guess my chickpea does have limits, but I only know him as a man patient to the point of sainthood. I wonder what I could do to make him turn against me. It doesn't shake my security in his love.

"Would you like to come see the baby? You're welcome here."

"I can't."

"We can e-mail you photos."

"I'm afraid I'm a technophobe."

I hear the sadness in her voice. I promise to send her normal photos.

When Peter comes back some three hours later, we talk about his mother's call. Mostly we talk about how we don't want to make the same mistakes with Chloe that our parents made with us. Probably all parents have said the same things. I imagine Cain telling his wife how his parents always ignored him and favored Abel.

For the first time, I imagine how Mother must have felt for me exactly what I feel for Chloe—strange being on the other side.

Over the weekend we borrow Ben's video camera to film the baby. We make two cassettes, one for Peter's mother and one for my mother and Auntie Anne. My mother calls us when she receives it. For once she doesn't say a bad word.

"Would you and Auntie Anne come to visit us in the fall?" I ask. I really mean the invitation.

"Liz has invited us, Annie," I hear Mother say.

"We'll make reservations," my aunt's voice filters through.

"Let's do it at Thanksgiving," Mother says.

"Great idea," I say. I really think it is.

August melts into September. For the first time since I was four I don't begin a new school year. It's strange not buying new pens and notebooks and getting out my winter clothes. January first never seems new to me, merely a continuation of the year that began in September.

Judy sits in my kitchen when the postman brings me a registered letter. She's popped in for salmon salad and

233

baby-admiring during her lunch hour. She finds me chopping celery and takes over as I go to answer the postman's ring. The letter is from the Fenway Board of Regents, announcing I've a hearing date on October first.

Carol has been requesting it since the week after I was fired. Maybe it was the lawsuit she filed last week that made them change their minds.

Judy prepares the table as I rinse my hands to get rid of the fish smell.

The phone rings. Before answering I dry my hands on a towel and, because I don't get it by the third ring, I can hear the recording from voice mail. The new message is Chloe's music box playing "Twinkle, Twinkle, Little Star." We wait for it to finish before we can start talking.

"Hi, Liz. It's Carol. I've sent a second subpoena for all your personnel records and evaluations." She had me write a registered letter asking for a copy of my file three weeks ago. Of course they didn't send them. "We are on the way at last," she says before saying good-bye.

"I'm still glad we tried the non-lawsuit route first," I say to Judy as she stirs mayonnaise into the salmon salad.

"Dealing with most people can be done nicely enough, but not with this group. You have to resort to being a bitch or they'll destroy you," she says.

"Self-protection is not being a bitch," I say.

"Not from our point of view. And what is wrong with being one?" She takes a spoon and tastes the salad. "Needs a little more curry."

The letter is the first big event since Chloe was born. For several weeks big events have been a smile from my daughter, not anything related to my career or my divorce. I can't believe how involved I've been with her.

As Judy cuts lemons for more iced tea after lunch, I

234

bathe Chloe in the kitchen sink. She jerks her little arms. She wasn't too sure about all this bath stuff the first few times, but now she loves it. I wrap her in her hooded towel before carrying her upstairs.

We didn't buy a lot of baby stuff, just a crib and a portable seat I can plunk anywhere. However, I'm beginning to see the merits of a dressing table. I wonder if the kind that doubles as a bathtub is still made. Mother had one in the attic for years with a cloth top and a band across the middle to anchor the baby. The canvas back had pockets for whatever and could be used to stick pins. Maybe it's still there. I'll ask Janice when I see her next week.

While I'm dressing the baby, Judy picks up the next phone call. She hollers upstairs, "It's Carol again. I'll come up to finish the baby." She takes over pinning diapers. We don't use paper, but it was hard finding a place to buy cloth diapers.

"I've got the evaluations," Carol says. She's bubbling. "They're exactly the same as Tina stole. The process server said they called their lawyer before giving them up, so I'm convinced there aren't any more."

"What does the rest of my file look like?" I ask.

"I'll send a copy over to you, but the way your good ones read they should have paid you more, not fired you," she says. "Check it carefully. Now about the three bad evaluations, we need to get to work."

"How so?" I ask.

"Do you happen to have any old test papers Mary might have written? I want to send both to a graphologist."

I think. "I may have thrown out everything."

"Ever think of just calling and asking her?" Carol asks. "She should be back home, shouldn't she?" She has been told about Mary's problems and what we did to help her.

The information was treated as lawyer-client confidentiality, so I didn't feel guilty about revealing Mary's private life. Even though I could wring her neck, ethics win.

"I'm too angry at her," I say.

"Let me think about the best way to deal with this. I'll get back," Carol says.

Judy has come down with the baby in her arms and she sits, listening. After I hang up she says, "The more I think about this, the less sense it makes. Mary adores you. It has to be a phony."

As we talk I pour canned formula into a bottle and give it to Judy to give to the baby. Chloe falls asleep with her bottle in her mouth. Occasionally a reflex causes a couple of sucks. Formula oozes out around the nipple.

Suddenly I remember a thank-you note Mary wrote me in her freshman year. I go to a box from my office that I never bothered to unpack. About halfway down among my papers I pull out the note. "Can you stay with Baby while I run this over to Carol?"

Judy agrees.

Three days later Carol telephones. "Bad news, the graphologist says without doubt the handwriting is the same."

"Shit," I say.

"Not only that, I called her and asked if she'd appear at the hearing and she said under no circumstances. She hung up on me. We can force her to testify in court as a hostile witness, but we can't make her appear at the regents' hearing."

"Her testimony could be damaging," I say as I think why, why, why?

"Exactly. With two bad evaluations and one fake, they might be able to explain that it was a student joke and they didn't check this."

"Let me digest this. Judy is here and says hi."

Judy comes for lunch almost daily. She says it's for lunch. I think it's to play with Chloe. We are sitting in my kitchen, the new center of my universe.

"Something's wrong here. If Mary knows you were instrumental in saving her, why then in God's name would she give you a bad evaluation?" Judy asks.

I put water on for tea. My hurt has clouded my ability to think.

"What's the point? Maybe the fighting isn't worth it. Maybe I should look for another job."

"And let those bastards railroad someone else?" Judy the cheerleader bolsters my courage. Give me an L! Give me an I! Give me a Z! What have you got? Chicken Shit Liz!

I need to actively make sense of these past few months, professionally that is. I've no problem with the personal side of my life. It has fallen in place. Now I have to beat the career part into shape.

Jumping off the stool, Judy dials Tina's number. "Get your buns over to Liz's . . . I don't care if it is your only day off." Tina has been working at the Au Bon Pain in Copley Square. She's exhausted from putting in eight hours on her feet followed by two-hour cleanup sessions.

She'll start next week as a teaching assistant at Simmons College. She's landed firmly on her feet. I'm thrilled for her. Most of the other people whose contracts weren't renewed are still job-hunting.

Tina saunters in within a half-hour. She's wearing cutoff jeans. "I like rode my bike." She pinches the skin of her thigh to see how much cellulite she's taken off by her few minutes of exercise. "What's up?" She flops on the couch.

Judy tells her. Of course Judy doesn't say anything about Mary's baby.

"That little bitch. I'll break her face. I really thought that evaluation was like a forgery."

"Don't jump to conclusions," Judy says.

"I like conclusions. I've concluded that I want to strangle her." Tina jumps up. "I'm going to go talk with her. Now!"

"Not yet. We need a plan. Liz, check the phone book," Judy says. I don't have to, because Tina grabs the Boston directory and starts looking through it.

"I think she lives on Mission Hill," I say. Mary once told me her father bought a triple-decker and lives in two apartments with his litter while renting out the third. I say nothing about the large family because Judy might start on her overpopulation-of-the-world tirade.

"There's an O'Brien on Calumet and another on Delle," I say.

"Delle, that's it," Tina says. "I heard her tell Amanda when they were going to do something together. I'd forgotten."

Tina picks up the phone, but Judy takes it out of her hand.

"Don't call her."

"I'm not." Tina takes the phone back. She dials then says, "Hi, how are ya? Real busy. If I ever see another loaf of French bread it'll be too soon . . . Can I meet you for lunch . . . ten minutes . . . very funny, no Au Bon Pain . . . like how 'bout the chickpea place . . . see ya."

On her way out she calls over her shoulder, "Don't go anywhere, guys."

Chloe dozes in her chair. Once asleep nothing wakes her. I rummage in the fridge for something for lunch.

Boss greets Tina when she returns. She pulls out a biscuit. The dog disappears with it.

"Boy, have I a scoop." She sits down, her elbows on her knees, and leans into us. Lowering her voice in case a Fenway spy could be hiding under my couch, she says, "President Baker like threatened Mary. He said that if she didn't cooperate he'd not only cut off her scholarship, he'd tell her father about the baby. How come you guys didn't tell me about the baby?"

"Shit!" I say. Chloe does.

"The president should keep confidential information confidential," Judy says.

"Anita's evaluation is a forgery," Tina adds. "Because she quit school, they figured they could get away with it. Although the brat didn't like you, Liz, she might be willing to show up at the hearing." She pulls a slip of paper from her back pocket. "Like anyone want her phone number?" Tina takes Chloe's finger. "You're adorable, but you stink, kid." She kisses Judy and me on the cheek and leaves, waving good-bye over her shoulder.

As I get ready to change my daughter, Judy says, "Tomorrow we'll go see Mary together. Early."

"Why not now?"

"I need to do some background work."

Peter comes home late or early, depending on the point of view. I glance at the clock when he lands in bed. It's 3:38 a.m. Mohammed is still in the Middle East, but the latest girl is working out well. I reach for him.

"Go to sleep," he says.

I am awake now, and I tell him what we've found out. He is half-asleep but struggles to stay awake and listen to me.

"You're going to come out of this," he mumbles and snuggles up to me.

I don't need an alarm clock. I've a baby that goes off at seven. Grabbing her out of her crib so she won't wake her father, I go downstairs and stick a bottle in her mouth as fast as I can. As I hold her, I let the dog out.

Judy arrives with Sable before Chloe finishes. The teenager takes my daughter and the bottle and sits down. "Mom said she was adorable, and for once she was right," she says.

When Judy rolls her eyes, Sable says, "Teenagers roll their eyes. Don't do a role reversal."

Judy ignores her daughter. "I thought Peter might be asleep so I brought my brat to baby-sit your brat. Won't kill her to be late for school for a good cause." She pours two cups of coffee, one for her and one for Sable. As I dress I can hear Sable baiting her mother about using too much sugar.

CHAPTER SEVENTEEN

Without traffic the drive to Mary's house might take five minutes, but it's rush hour. That should have added ten minutes more at most, but construction work at Children's Hospital—which seems to have lasted longer than the building of the pyramids—the redoing of the T tracks, and a new building on Tremont have traffic backed up.

A flatbed truck bearing a crane ambles down the road, leaving no room.

Pedestrians scatter as a Cadillac drives up on the sidewalk to pass. From the look on the driver's face, I think he realizes one more coat of paint on his car, and he'd be heading for an auto body shop.

Mission Hill is one of the few neighborhoods in the area to escape gentrification, partially because it was never totally run-down. The wooden triple-deckers have not caught yuppie imaginations. These buildings have always been owned by working-class people who have taken good care of them.

A wire fence surrounds the postage-stamp yard in front of the gray O'Brien house. Despite its size, it is full of marigolds and petunias. A sign reads "wet paint." A can of red paint, matching the shutters on the first two floors, sits on a newspaper on the front porch. A ladder is propped up against the house ready for the last part of the project.

Two girls, no more than ten, in matching plaid skirts and knee socks, come out the front door. They have on navy blazers with the St. Cecilia School emblem, and they carry green cloth book bags. They are identical.

"My God, miniature Marys," Judy says. A woman opens the door. Her full-length housecoat buttons up the side, not the middle. Her gray-streaked red hair is piled on top of her head. A few strands fall around her neck. Although she is frowning, she is pretty in a faded way.

"Katie Louise, you forgot your lunch." She waves a paper bag. One turns and runs up the stairs. "Franny, close the gate," the woman calls before shutting the door. The one who didn't forget her lunch closes the gate. How she tells them apart is beyond me.

We ring the bell and the same woman answers. "What did you forget this time . . . Oh, I'm sorry." Her hand goes up to her neck. "I thought you were one of the kids."

When Judy introduces us, Mrs. O'Brien says, "Mary Alice has told me so much about you. She's still in bed. Late classes today."

We know that because Judy checked Mary's schedule.

"My daughter's not in any trouble, is she? My husband has told all our kids if they get in trouble in school, it'll be twice as bad when they get home."

Judy assures Mrs. O'Brien that Mary is definitely not in trouble. She explains how she follows up on her students regularly to make sure the student is content. "Unfortunately, it took me a while to get around to Mary. Then today we found ourselves in the neighborhood and took a chance without calling first. We hope you don't mind."

Mrs. O'Brien leads us to the parlor. The house is spotless. The mantel holds eighteen trophies. She sees us looking at them. "My sons and husband are very athletic. Everyone is involved in Little League, Pop Warner, bowling."

On a piano there are dozens of photos of different baptisms, birthdays, weddings, Christmases. All the children are a variation of Mary, who is a variation of her mother.

"Can I get you some tea?" she asks.

I start to say no as Judy says, "That would be so kind."

Mrs. O'Brien goes into the kitchen. From my chair, I can see a large kitchen table still covered with breakfast dishes, an open loaf of bread, a jam pot and toaster.

She returns with a tray. A paper lace doily is under the pot. There are four cups, a sugar bowl and creamer. "I've called Mary Alice," she says. "She'll be down in a minute." She lowers her voice to a whisper. "She seemed really surprised you were here."

Before we've drunk half a cup, Mary enters, dressed in a Fenway sweatshirt, jeans and a frown. She greets us politely. Her hands shake as her mother hands her a cup of tea.

"Should I leave you alone?" Mrs. O'Brien asks. She sits very straight in her chair as does Mary. I find myself adjusting my posture.

"Please stay. I like to get to know my girls' families," Judy says as Mary rubs her thumb over a bitten nail. Judy talks about the nursing course, the importance of good grades and how proud Mrs. O'Brien should be of her daughter. She says Mary is good enough to get a scholarship at any school. "Did you consider other colleges for her?"

Mrs. O'Brien says no. "Mary Alice was the only one of my children to ever show any interest in college at all. Her father wasn't too sure that it was a good idea." She launches into a listing of her children's activities. Two sons have entered their father's carpentry business, another has joined the Marines. A married daughter has given her two grandchildren. She shows photos, which we admire. I don't mention her third unknown grandchild.

"Mary said you have a new baby?"

I tell Mrs. O'Brien a few things about my daughter. She gives me oodles of advice. Mary squirms.

"Listen, Mary," Judy says, "we're on our way to school. Want a ride?"

"How nice," Mrs. O'Brien says. "Run and get your things, dear."

Mary's face shows she doesn't think it's nice at all.

Once in Judy's Beetle with Mary in the back, Judy turns toward her, peeking through the two front seats. "You can relax, Mary. I wouldn't have said anything in front of your mother. But we need to know if it's true that you've been threatened if you say anything to the Fenway Board of Regents about being forced to make a bad evaluation of Dr. Adams."

Mary covers her face. Her mews turn into cries then into big heart-wrenching sobs.

"Let's go to Liz's house, because we want to talk to you without putting you at risk by being seen with us," Judy says.

Mary nods. Judy starts the engine and puts the car in first gear. The return trip is fast. Morning rush hour is over. The flatbed truck has installed itself off the street. Mary is under control, but her nose and eyes are red.

We pull into my drive. Sable opens the door. Chloe is nowhere around, and I bet Judy told her to keep the baby out of sight. Peter has left for work. Judy ushers Mary to my couch.

She looks so fragile. As I watch her I know I can't ask her to sacrifice her family and future for me. However, Judy can. And does. But not heartlessly. She brings out a letter from Boston College, offering a full and immediate scholarship to their school of nursing including housing.

"How did you do that since yesterday?" I ask.

"I pulled in every chip I had," she says. I will never again underestimate this woman's power in university circles.

Mary starts to whimper. She reminds me of a frightened animal. Judy goes into my bathroom. As usual I'm out of Kleenex. She returns with a roll of toilet tissue. Mary blows her nose.

"If they go to your father, I'll deny the whole thing. After all, I did examine you for flu. There are no records anywhere in the school of where you went and why," Judy says.

"I'm so scared," Mary says.

Judy puts a hand on her knee. "Of course you are. But don't you think it's important for Fenway to be run by ethical people who keep good professors like Liz? Think of the people who lost their jobs."

Mary looks around the room. Her eyes are swollen, her freckles joined by red splotches.

"All Dr. Sumner got was a sabbatical. Tuition will probably go up because of the cost of fighting the lawsuit Melissa Greenbaum has filed. Things stay wrong because people lack the courage to make them right," Judy says.

Mary thinks about it, but not for long. She turns to me, her eyes brimming. "You understand, don't you, Dr. Adams, why I did it? Don't you?" Her sentence is punctuated with a long snuffle.

She looks so young, so vulnerable. I can picture her in the same plaid skirt, knee socks and blazer as her sisters. This kid has been through a nightmare, starting with the guy who raped her.

"I'm not sure I wouldn't have done the same thing in your place," I tell her. Liz, the nurturer, the one who wants people always to feel better, can't help herself. But this time I'm doing it for the right reasons.

CHAPTER EIGHTEEN

"Are you pregnant or nervous?" Peter asks as I come out of the bathroom. I'm pale from vomiting.

"Nerves. I have my period."

He looks relieved. We've agreed to be a one-baby family. Neither of us slept much last night. He would have had I not kept tossing and waking him. He'd rubbed my back until I relaxed enough to drop off.

Today is the day of my hearing. Janice took Chloe last night and will keep her all day. Mohammed is back and working at the stand so Peter can come with me.

I hem and haw about what to wear. I settle on a simple gray business suit that I hope says professionally wronged woman.

Before we leave Peter insists I eat some dry toast. "To settle your stomach," he says.

"Settle my stomach, settle my life," I say.

"Why not?" He straightens his tie. It's the first time I've seen him wear one. He won't be in the hearing room but waiting outside. "Image," he says when he sees me watching him. He opens the front door and lets me walk ahead of him into the glare of the sun.

Carol's waiting for us in the campus parking lot. The walk to the conference room takes longer than anyone thought it would as students stop to greet me. Carol keeps pointing to her watch and pushing me along. Staff give me good-luck signs, winks, raised fists. It's sad they need to look around before they do it.

★ ★ ★ ★ ★

The conference room is part of the presidential suite and is oak-paneled like the office. Norma nods at me. Her face is without expression as she ushers us in.

The president is at one end of the conference table, which almost fills the room. The chairman, James Robinson, is at the other end. Six other regents, four on one side, two on the other, flank the two college officers.

A man I've never seen before is at the sideboard pouring coffee from a silver urn into a blue china cup. He uses tongs to take two sugar cubes. He must be Matthew Scott, the college's attorney. After introductions, I learn I was right.

We're invited to sit. Carol and I take our places at the table to the left of the president. The door is shut so I can no longer see Peter waiting in the outer sanctum.

Norma bustles around the room setting up a tape recorder. I expect Carol to object, but she says nothing. She ignores my raised eyebrows and takes out her own recorder. "Where may I plug this in?" she asks. Norma shows her, but the cord is too short. We wait for the janitor to bring an extension.

"You have been rather insistent on this hearing," Dr. Baker begins after Norma starts the machine.

Carol pushes the button to start her recorder then clears her throat. "I'm sure you will be glad we were, because it gives you one last chance to make things right before we go into court."

"Are you threatening us, Ms. Goss?" Scott asks. He takes a place opposite Carol.

"I prefer to think that I'm offering you a chance to avoid more negative publicity." She turns to President Baker. "Would you please tell me all the reasons you terminated Dr. Adams, a tenured faculty member?" There is a great deal of stress on her word "all."

Baker uses his eye-boring technique on Carol. She stares back and moves her chair, so she is closer to him. She pushes a few of her papers into his space.

He looks away. "Dr. Adams was not performing at the level at which we wish a tenured faculty member to perform. She herself helped work on a procedure that allowed us to take action in such a case."

"Did you work on that?" Carol looks at me. I had expected the hearing to be a bit more like a court case. I had expected Baker to keep control as a judge.

"For extreme cases of disability, yes, I did help establish a procedure for dismissal," I say.

"Have each of you seen the negative reviews?" Carol asks the regents. She holds the copies in her hand.

They all say they have. Carol asks if they could be read aloud. The president glowers at her. "I don't see why that's necessary. We all know they accuse her of not being able to present information clearly, playing favorites, erratic mood swings, mumbling as if she were not in total control of her faculties, although they say nothing directly about drug or alcohol abuse." Baker leaves the implication of a chemical problem hanging.

"Fine," my lawyer says. She'd warned me as we rode over that she would give in on some points that were unimportant. "Were there other reasons that you wanted Dr. Adams off the faculty?"

"Her teaching ability was why she was terminated," Dr. Baker says.

That was the best possible answer Carol was hoping for. He won't be able to backtrack later on the morality issue. She opens her briefcase. It's maroon leather and neatly arranged with legal-sized envelopes all marked with typed labels. She brings out four and removes the papers inside, making a pile approximately five inches high.

Baker shifts in his chair. He opens his mouth, but Scott signals him to be quiet.

"Perhaps, Dr. Baker, you wanted to ask what these are?"

"No," he says.

"I'll tell you anyway. These are the positive evaluations that Dr. Adams has received." She starts reading phrases haphazardly, like "best teacher I ever had," "tutored me in her own time for nothing," "knows her stuff," "makes it interesting even when it's not."

"That doesn't negate the newer negative ones," Baker says. "Excellent teachers can go bad because of illness, alcoholism, family problems." He stares at me as if to say he knows all about me.

"Not so fast, Jonathan," Robinson says. "Let's look at these."

Carol hands them over, dividing them between the regents. She says, "Maybe you want to read Dr. Adams's job reviews as well, all signed by the dean of faculty and President Baker. Or the articles about her textbooks?" She hands everyone a copy.

Baker is pale except for two red spots. He looks like a Kewpie doll.

"I can't prove that my client's firing was related to her approval of Melissa Greenbaum's accusations against Dr. Sumner, but I do find it peculiar that she was let go along with all other faculty that supported Melissa."

"That's old news," Baker says.

"That's a separate issue," Scott says. "If this were a court of law . . ."

"It isn't," Carol snaps.

Baker uses his gavel. "We are meeting to determine if

Dr. Adams was treated fairly. I think the negative evaluations speak for themselves."

"Do you?" Carol says sweetly. "Actually, I'd like the writers of those evaluations to speak for themselves, also."

"Out of the question," Baker says. "Students are entitled to their privacy." He runs his hand through his hair. "If students knew they'd be grilled for their evaluations, we'd never get anything but praise for our faculty."

I thank all the gods and goddesses in all the universities that Tina had stolen the originals. The subpoenaed ones in my file were nameless. I don't understand why Baker was so stupid to keep them, but often arrogant people do stupid things.

"I can see that," Regent Carl DeMar says. He's the one who operates a chain of women's clothing stores.

Carol turns to him. "Mr. DeMar, it depends on whether you believe in truth or not. These evaluations are a fraud. Excuse me." She goes to the door and Mary O'Brien and Anita Kryznowek walk in. Carol introduces them.

"I object," Baker says.

"So do I," Scott says.

"Mr. Scott, this isn't a court of law as I pointed out to you a few minutes ago." Carol smiles and turns toward Robinson. "Would you please let the girls speak? They are here voluntarily and wish to make a statement to the board."

Robinson has been going over the good evaluations. I watch as his expression changes from aloofness to a frown. Or at least that's how I read it. He motions to Norma to add two more chairs, which the girls take.

Anita has her elbows on the chair arms and is looking at her hands when Robinson speaks to her. "Miss Kryznowek, what do you think of Dr. Adams as a teacher?"

Anita is just five feet and probably weighs less than a hundred pounds. Her black hair is cut in a geometric way that reminds me of the Sassoon style of the sixties. Her voice is hoarse. "When I left Fenway, it is safe to say I hated Dr. Adams."

I see Baker smirk and sit back in his seat.

Robinson cocks his head. "Is that why you gave her this review?" the chairman asks. He has a copy in his hand, which he gives to her.

Anita takes the paper and looks at it. "I didn't write this review." Everyone, except for Baker, talks at once. Robinson finally hollers for silence. Scott puts his hand on Robinson's arm and the chairman nods.

"Are you saying this isn't your signature?" Scott asks.

"I am saying it is a good representation of my signature. I am also saying that I never said any of those things. Dr. Adams and I had a lot of disagreements. She tried to help me, although I didn't realize that at the time. I left school because of her, and it was the best thing that ever happened to me."

"You did not write or sign that review, correct?" Carol asks, just in case the regents missed the point.

Baker walks over to Mary. He hovers over her. "Are you going to tell us, Miss O'Brien, that you didn't write your evaluation of Dr. Adams? And I suggest you think very carefully of the consequences."

Mary moves away from him as much as she can without leaving her chair. Her eyes are huge. She shivers.

"Mr. Robinson, President Baker is threatening the student," Carol says.

"Let's not jump to conclusions," Scott says.

"I wrote the evaluation," Mary says. Everyone seems to relax a little.

Baker returns to his seat. "Thank you, Mary. Why don't you return to class?"

"No," she says.

"It's time. Go on," Baker repeats. He waves his hand several times as if telling a child to scoot and leave the grown-ups in peace.

"No, I haven't finished," Mary says. "I wrote the evaluation because you, President Baker, told me if I didn't you'd take away my scholarship."

"Jonathan, is that true?" Robinson asks.

"She isn't telling the truth," Baker says.

"Yes, I am." Mary's voice quivers. "Dr. Adams is a wonderful teacher and a wonderful woman." She takes the evaluation and tears it up.

"For the record, I think if you try and find a real student by the name on the third evaluation, you will have to look a long time," Carol says.

"I think we need to talk among ourselves," Robinson says. "I'm going to ask you all to go to The Caf and wait. Norma will get you when we're ready."

Carol, the girls and I leave.

Peter stands up as soon as he sees us.

Carol shrugs.

We tell him detail by detail what happened as we drink the coffee in The Caf. It has not improved. Students and colleagues surround me. The grapevine has spread the word about the hearing. What happened is the most common question.

"We can't say anything yet," Carol keeps saying.

"What can I do? She's my lawyer," I say. We talk about the baby and I show pictures. More comments about how adorable she is. No one talks about fat cheeks and baldness.

After my third cup of coffee, I see Norma totter in. Although she wears relatively low, practical heels, her straight skirt inhibits her movements. It's not sexy because it's covered with a baggy sweater falling below her hips. "They are ready for you, just you and your attorney, Dr. Adams."

"We'll be right up," I say.

She harrumphs and goes back without us.

"This is it," I say. Peter kisses me on the cheek.

President Baker pulls Carol's chair out for her and Robinson does the same for me. We wait as they shuffle papers around.

"Dr. Adams," Baker says, "there has been a mistake and, as a result, we will reinstate you at the first of next semester." He sees Robinson signaling at him. "With all your back pay, of course."

Carol starts to speak, but I put my hand on her arm.

"No," I say. Carol's head goes back. Her eyes open wide.

"I thought that is what you wanted, Dr. Adams? Reinstatement?" Scott says.

"That is part of what I want. As you know, we've a wrongful firing suit filed against the college. I don't want to go to court, even though I'm sure, especially after today, that we'd have a good chance of winning. Don't you agree, Mr. Scott?"

"I can't comment on that, but . . ."

"But nothing. I don't want to work for a man who intimidates students into committing unethical actions. I'll withdraw my suit if you terminate Baker and give me all my back pay, including paying my legal costs. I also would like to see a new Board of Regents, which reflects a more diverse cultural background—women, people of color and of different ages. I want a formal apology. With that I will return to work."

"And if we don't agree?"

"Although it would be a shame to have to go into endowments to pay for a court case, there is another issue. Who would want to come here after Baker's actions became known? After people realize that the regents have condoned such actions? I wonder Fenway could continue to exist." I recite the facts Tina dug out about how donations are down seventy percent.

"Donations are down everywhere. There are fewer potential students graduating from high school," Baker says.

Carol hands out a sheet of statistics on enrollments and donations from all the other major universities in the area. Fenway is at the bottom. She has a second sheet for the previous year where Fenway was in the top five colleges in receipt of donations.

"Fenway had a lot of bad publicity this year. For the first time in fifty years, three out of every four girls accepted decided to go elsewhere. Usually it is one out of six. Doesn't that tell you something?" she asks.

Robinson brings out a folder. He compares Carol's sheet with other papers. "These don't match with our monthly reports from your office, Baker."

I stand up. "Gentlemen, I loved working at Fenway. If you can restore a sense of integrity by doing as I ask, including reviewing the cases of other members of the faculty who were fired, I will gladly drop my case and return. If not, the courts will decide. I cannot work for any college or university that I am ashamed of." I cannot believe that I am doing this.

Carol puts her papers back in her briefcase. "I also know that Melissa's lawyers have four women who will testify that

Dr. Sumner behaved improperly with them. They're gradu-ates—one of whom is now a lawyer. I doubt if she would perjure herself." She starts to leave, but turns at the door. "Oh yes, another is a doctor. It may be hard to convince anyone these are hysterical teenagers."

We walk out. As soon as we are away from the office, she grabs me by the arm. "Jesus H. Christ! Why didn't you warn me you were going to do that?"

"Because I didn't know I was going to," I say. It's true. The words had fallen out of my mouth because they had to be said.

As we enter The Caf, Peter, Anita and Mary are waiting for us.

"You won't believe this," Carol says to them.

They do.

EPILOGUE

I won. In January I return to school. When I walk into my first class, my students give me a standing ovation. I stand there, tears flowing, trying not to blotch.

The Board of Regents has made many changes.

There is now a required course for faculty and staff members on sexual harassment and a review process for people accused. This is not rocket science. Most schools and workplaces have it as a matter of course. It was only because our president was a dinosaur that we didn't.

That was a requirement Melissa insisted on in return for dropping her case. She has transferred to Wellesley.

My fired colleagues who had not found jobs were hired back. There are four new regents. Three are women. One is Dean Whittier's oldest daughter.

There is a committee looking for a new president. Baker took an early retirement and is being paid to the end of his contract. That is nicer than I would have been, but at least he's out of power.

Henry Sumner is job hunting.

Dateline did an update at the end of their show before Christmas, right before they read the letters viewers send in. I wonder if Jane Pauley remembers using my toilet and eating brique.

Mother called to congratulate me. She couldn't talk long. She was late for her square dancing class. When she and Auntie Anne spent Thanksgiving with us, she had cut her hair and although her arthritis still bothers her, the warmer climate has helped a little. I can't say exactly why things are different between us, but they are and it is good. I felt sad when I waved good-bye at Logan and they disappeared down to their gate.

Jill and the girls have moved in with Ben. They just showed up on his doorstep two days before Christmas. She is working on a business degree at UMass. Boston. Harry didn't leave her. She left him. Right on, Sis.

My divorce is still pending, but David is no longer harassing me. I've heard from a mutual acquaintance that he is involved with a lawyer from his office. I don't know if she is the owner of the lace nightie or not.

They are probably much better matched than we were.

I'd be too goody-goody to wish that he was deliriously happy. However, I do wish him contentment, especially if it keeps him away from me. And to a lesser degree, I would like him to be happy for himself. He's not a bad man. In the language of political correctness that I still dislike, he's value-challenged, probably handicapped by being raised in a dysfunctional family.

Mohammed is back. Peter has two other employees who are working out and has thought about opening a second stand with Mohammed as manager. Then he realized the extra work would cut into our family life. He's given Mohammed a big raise and works less himself. Peter takes care of Chloe while I work. Maybe later he will expand, then again maybe not. Our measure of success is if we are good to each other.

As I push Chloe's carriage to the stand, I feel the cold. It was only a little over a year ago that I moved in with Peter. So much has changed. I'm so different, and I know no matter what happens I will never again pretend to be someone I'm not for anyone's approval.

When I was little, Mother used to tell me to eat my vegetables, because they were good for me. Little did she think one day I might marry one. Mother was right. Vegetables are good for me.

About the Author

D-L Nelson is an American writer, originally from Boston, MA, who now divides her time between her homes in Geneva, Switzerland and Argeles-sur-Mer, France. Her short stories and poetry have been published in six countries. This book won first prize in the 1995 Florida Literary Festival.